KNIGHT OF THE
CRESCENT MOON

Book One of the Crescent Moon Chronicles

L. E. Towne

Literary Wanderlust | Denver, Colorado

Knight of the Crescent Moon is a work of fiction. Names, characters, places, and incidents are the products of the author's imagination and have been used fictitiously. Any resemblance to actual events, locales, or persons, living or dead, is entirely coincidental.

Published in the United States by Literary Wanderlust LLC, Denver, Colorado. www.LiteraryWanderlust.com

ISBN: 978-1-942856-42-9

Cover design: Pozu Mitsuma

Printed in the United States

KNIGHT OF THE
CRESCENT MOON

1

In the distance, I heard the rumblings of others headed toward me—the rest of the pack was coming. The ghoul's claws lashed out again, digging deep into my forearm, the searing pain skittering all other thoughts from my brain, as my only weapon skidded across the well-trimmed lawn.

I swore and scrambled on the ground, groping for the knife in the dark. Hearing my own shallow breath, I felt my heart pumping blood steadily from the open wound in my arm.

The smell of the beast was overwhelming, mixing with freshly-mown grass and blood. He growled and lunged toward me again. Trapped against a headstone, with other hostiles on the way, I was sure this would be it. My unremarkable life would end on a random Tuesday night. And in a damn graveyard. H.P. Lovecraft would be rolling over with the irony. Or was it symmetry? I always get those two mixed up.

Four perfectly curved three-inch claws, red with

my blood, moved in for another swipe. I cringed back against the angled marble, arms up to guard my throat, my eyes slammed shut for half a second.

I heard a strange swish, a *thwap* of metal on flesh and I watched as the ghoul's head did a perfect somersault in the air, his eyes still open in surprise. His body slumped, and twitched on the ground, while his blood, black in the dim moonlight, spurted from the headless neck. I blinked, not quite believing what I was seeing.

Standing over the body, between me and the head, was a man dressed in something ridiculously frilly, with a long cape over his shoulders. I caught the glint of a sword to the side of him as his free hand reached down to me.

"Come with me if you wish to survive."

Seriously, who says that? I scrabbled away from him, hitting the granite wall of a mausoleum behind me. "Who the hell are you?" My voice croaked under the stress.

The low guttural noise of the pack sounded closer now. They could probably smell the blood of their pack mate oozing onto the grass, not to mention mine. I rubbed my blood-slick hand along my pant leg to clean it.

The dark figure standing over me had a calm baritone voice, not at all unpleasant.

"Good sir, I prithee, we hath little time for a proper introduction. Please heed my request and come at once. There be far too many for two defenders, especially with thy wound. We must hasten."

He reached down again and this time I grabbed his hand. Rising, I saw three or four gray shapes racing between the headstones. Renaissance Fair may be dressed funny, but at least he was human. We ran in the opposite direction of the approaching pack. For creatures that are mostly-dead, ghouls are surprisingly fast.

Across the cemetery and two blocks down, I couldn't go any farther. My car, along with my go-bag and first aid kit sat half a mile away while blood was pumping out of the gash in my arm with each step. My vision blurred and the only thing I could see was my rescuer—a guy in funny clothes, with long hair and a beard, looking at me with great concern.

"My God. You're a woman." Apparently, he finally saw me too.

"No shit, Sherlock."

The streetlight dimmed, and the figure in front of me swam and blurred until darkness descended and I lost consciousness. I had a vague sense of strong arms catching me as I collapsed like some friggin' damsel in distress.

I woke up in the emergency room.

An ER nurse, eyes harder than obsidian, glanced at my face as she took my pulse. "Good. You're awake. How do you feel?"

"Just peachy," I blinked against the brightness of the room.

"Well, Peaches, your vitals look good. You've lost a fair amount of blood, but there's no major arterial damage. The doc may want to keep you though. I'll send your boyfriend in. He's in the waiting room."

"I don't have a boyfriend," I murmured, wondering who she could be talking about.

"Too bad, because he's kind of cute. If you like that sort of thing."

I was too disoriented to try and understand her meaning so I ignored her and sat up, wincing at the pain in my arm. Not the one covered in gauze but the other one that had the IV needle inserted.

"Savages," I said lightly, the room spinning a second or two before coming into focus. The last thing I remembered was some guy pulling me along the street, calling me Good Sir. He must have brought me here.

I huffed out a breath. Just another Tuesday night in the life of Tam Paradiso.

I'd taken the long way home from X and Connie's. My usual path from my partner's house was a straight shot down Roosevelt, but tonight, I'd taken the scenic route and while waiting at the light, I'd caught a glimpse of movement out my side window—lurch, stop, stumble, stop—a shambling gait, fast and yet awkward. The walk belonged to a large guy, who judging from clothes alone, could be mistaken for a homeless person. But our eyes connected, and I recognized the hostile for what he was—a ghoul.

To my partner, Xavier Hernandez, (X for short) and everybody else, hostiles looked like regular people. But I'd been seeing them for what they really were for years now. I'd seen my first monster in high school—a vampire disguised as a librarian. Or maybe a librarian disguised as a vampire, either way, not a pleasant experience. High school, fortunately, was over. Not so with the monsters. It's years later and they were still very much a part of my life.

I became a cop like my dad, but I was the only one

who hunted monsters, demons, and vampires on the side. At least, the only one I knew of until tonight.

"I am joyous to heareth thou art well." My overly polite rescuer stood inside the curtained room—his dress and mannerism even more exaggerated in the harsh fluorescent light. The dark cloak over his shoulders almost skimmed the floor and he'd thrown it back, musketeer-style. And that was the most normal thing about him.

The rest of his attire came straight out of a Shakespearian play or maybe a "Purple Rain" era Prince look-alike contest. His outfit was mostly black, or, no, it was purple as I looked closer, a deep purple velvet vest with silver buttons and a belt. He wore a jacket and pants of the same material, the pants billowing around his hips and thighs and tucking into black knee-length boots. At his neck rested white fluff—a scarf or blouse, and I swear to God, I'd seen pictures of my Aunt Diana wearing the exact same thing in the eighties.

"Man, they have really good drugs in this place," I mumbled, trying to readjust myself against my pillows.

He approached the narrow bed. "I fear your manner of speaking confounds me." His accent sounded not quite British, but he definitely was not from Philly either. He stepped back into the most elegant bow I'd ever seen. Not that I'd seen men bow a lot—okay, never—but this guy knew how it was done. "May I present myself? I am Marlowe, defender of the realm, warrior against the dark and Her Majesty the Queen's humble servant; and, in this day and time, I am at your service." Beneath the beard, his lips quirked into a fleeting smile that could have been infectious if it lasted longer. The curve of his lips disappeared as he studied my reaction.

"Okay, Braveheart, I understand you cosplayers take your role-playing seriously, but could you nix the Queen's English and be normal for a second? I need to get out of here. The docs here are great and all, but they don't understand what just happened to us, and—"

I stopped, thinking about the headless body we'd left in the cemetery. The one made headless by the guy in front of me. With a broad sword. "What did you tell them? About what happened? For that matter, what do you know about what happened?"

"Stay thy fears. I am quite adept at subterfuge. I have told them nothing."

We were interrupted by the doctor breezing in and ignoring us completely as he peered at the electronic monitor for my vitals. "Ms. Paradiso, am I saying that right?"

Young and bespectacled, he didn't look up, but at least he pronounced my name correctly.

"Yes," I said, trying not to sound as impatient as he looked.

"You were injured on the job?" He looked surprised for a moment. "You're not in uniform. You're a cop, right?"

I had no idea why people were surprised when they learned of my occupation. It's not like all cops should have a certain look anymore, this wasn't the sixties. But I supposed I more resembled a college student than homicide detective. Not the co-ed sorority girl, but the punk rebel protester type. With my father's coloring, dark eyes and hair, and my own penchant for solid eighties rock music—I envisioned myself as more Pat

Benatar than Madonna.

I sighed. "I'm a detective, so no uniform. And I'm off-duty. It was a simple fall. I was walking to my car, tripped in the dark and must have caught a rough edge of something." I glanced at my rescuer. He'd leaned forward as though to catch all my words. After a moment, he straightened and looked directly at the doc. "Yea, er, yes, that is so. I came upon this lady—" he looked at me as if he wasn't quite sure I was one. "Seeing she needed assistance, I brought her here."

The young doctor peered over his glasses at Good Sir guy. I rushed to assure the doc that I could rest fine at home and would see my regular physician the next day.

"Fine," he said. "I'll sign your release." He ripped the curtain aside and was gone.

After convincing the nurse to leave us outside the emergency room doors, I turned to my stalwart companion. "Thanks for backing me up in there."

I was thinking of what to do next. My arm had started to ache, and my head was pounding. A slight breeze had picked up and threatened a cold front. I pulled my jacket over the sling on my arm. Apparently, my shoulder had been dislocated in the scuffle and restored while I was unconscious.

"We should go back to the cemetery. I need to get rid of the body."

The man beside me shook his head. "Nay, the beasts will have taken care of it. And thou art in need of rest. Do you have a method of conveyance? A motor vehicle perhaps? That we may travel to thine abode?" he asked in his odd formality.

"I am not taking you home with me." I scoffed at the

idea.

The guy gaped at me, his jaw slacked as though this was the rudest, most far-fetched statement he'd heard all night.

"Is it not customary to offer shelter to a traveler, especially one who has traveled far and has proven himself to be trustworthy and honorable? Surely, thy husband hath no objections."

"I'm not married, and please quit with the *thees* and *thous*. Nobody talks like that."

"Not at this time, I fear." He looked rather forlorn and sad at the loss of formal language. I paused for a moment, studying him. He seemed harmless enough, though I hadn't forgotten what he could do with that sword. But he did save my life, twice—killing the ghoul and carrying me to the hospital before I bled out on the sidewalk. I supposed I owed him one.

"You have no place to go? Where are you from?"

"England. Canterbury to be exact. And no, as thou art the first person I've met here. I have no place to go, as thou speaketh—" He looked impatient and backtracked, "or as you say."

We walked to the corner so I could hail a cab. In normal circumstances, I'd call someone to come pick me up, but I had no idea how I'd explain the presence of my Elizabethan companion. My exhaustion and aching arm wore me down as much as his stubbornness.

"If you can explain who you are and how you know about ghouls, I guess you can sleep on my couch. It's the least I can do."

"The least you can do. By all means, do the least possible." He smiled as though making a joke.

It took only a few minutes for the cab to show. The pain-killer wore off faster than I'd expected, and my arm hurt like hell. I was played out, done for the night. My instinct told me the guy was trustworthy, which was good since I hadn't the strength for more than conversation. I got into the cab and gave the cabbie the address where I'd left my car.

We both waited as Sir Galahad fussed with his enormous cloak, peeling off a backpack type harness for his sword, stowing the sword and harness on the floorboard of the cab, and stepping in head-first, backing out and contemplating the whole contraption before attempting to enter again. Finally, he backed in, his boot catching the bottom lip of the vehicle and falling the rest of the way, tucking his long legs against the seat in front of him. He looked at me with a pained expression. "Horseback is much easier when traveling with a saber," he whispered, reaching back to readjust his cape once again. In the glow of the overhead light, I looked at the weapon, beautiful in its simplicity. The blade and the hilt one solid piece—no forge marks visible. Almost of its own volition, my good hand reached out for it. His hand closed over mine.

"Have a care," he said, his voice serious. I felt compelled to tell him I'm no novice when it comes to weaponry, but at a glance at his face, I withdrew. I noticed two things I'd missed at our first meeting. His expression was not one of concern for my safety, but of possessiveness. I've seen it with my brothers in blue and their guns. Weapons are merely tools for me. I'll use whatever's handy to get the job done, but guys seem to have an affinity, an honest to God relationship with the weapon of their choice. This sword was Marlowe's weapon of choice.

The second thing I noticed was his attractiveness—despite his rather effeminate dress. There was a raw-boned power about him, an assuredness. His hair shone a few shades lighter than my own, a dark brown or auburn even, and worn long and unruly around his ears. A firm chin was visible under a goatee of the same color. Young in appearance, maybe early twenties, he possessed an agelessness about him. A strong, straight nose and jaw presented when he faced forward to peer at the digital meter on the dashboard. He still held my hand and I reluctantly pulled away from its warmth.

We got to my car without much conversation. As he slid into the passenger side, I apologized for the food smells and tried to clean up what would have been my lunch the next day. Connie always made extra food for me to take home after our Tuesday night dinners. I don't keep much in my fridge except the occasional six-pack of Molson and leftover takeout. It's not that I don't cook—I have an aversion to grocery stores.

Opening the door to my basement apartment, I realized that I hadn't cleared up the living room either. Empty beer bottles littered the coffee table, shoes did the same for the floor, and a stack of junk mail and bills were piled on the counter. Marlowe stood silently in the middle of the room, one hand on the hilt of his sword as he took everything in.

"It's perfectly safe here," I told him. But I watched him carefully as I kicked the shoes under the couch and policed up the bottles. I emptied the ashtray from Rick's cigar butts. "Bathroom's in there if you need it."

I paused, looking at him. "Which I will want to shower soon, so if you need to—"

He looked at me, confusion and doubt flashing across his features. I may not speak the Queen's English, but I thought it was at least close enough to get the gist of things. He finally pulled his gaze from me to look toward the bathroom.

"I see. Ah, no. Please go about your toilette. I'll—" he looked around, "wait here."

"You can't just stand there. You're making me nervous. There's a rack for your coat, or cloak or whatever. Food's in the fridge. I might have some beer left. If you need something stronger—" I pulled out a bottle of Maker's Mark and two glasses, poured two fingers into each glass, and handed him one. He seemed to relax, taking his hand off the hilt of his sword to drink. Clearing his throat, he looked appreciatively at the bottle.

Watching him pour another, I took my own glass into the bathroom with me, but not before pulling my sidearm from its customary place in the cabinet.

2

I felt much better after a hot shower. Marlowe had ditched the sword and hung up his cloak. After unwrapping my bandaged arm from the plastic bag I'd used to keep it dry, I looked in the fridge and found some leftover Chinese food.

"You hungry?"

He answered in the affirmative as he wandered around my tiny living room, touching everything. He peered at photos, picked up books, sniffed candles, he seemed particularly fascinated with the silk flower thingy on my wall.

"I told you food was in the fridge. You should help yourself."

He touched the silk arrangement tentatively, stepping back in apparent shock at the fake flowers. "I couldn't find the 'fridge,' as you call it."

Ignoring his comment, I pulled out the cartons of Mu Shu pork, zapped them in the microwave and handed him one. "Careful, it's hot."

He stared at me incredulously before sniffing at the food.

"It's not poisonous, and it's only from last night."

He stuffed a forkful of pork into his mouth and chewed thoughtfully, his eyes lighting up as he did. He swallowed and again, that disarming smile. "Mistress Paradiso, I—"

"How did you know my name?"

"The physician called you by name. I pay attention." He bowed again, as though we'd just been introduced.

Oh yeah. Apparently, he paid better attention than I did. Reassured, I put out my good hand in response. "Tamberlyn Paradiso, detective, Philadelphia PD."

"I surmised you were a constable. Is that a common occupation for a female?"

"No, not common, but there are a few of us. What's with the Renaissance schtick?"

"Stick?

"Schtick. It's like a routine, you know, comedy."

"I assure you Mistress Paradiso—"

"Tam. Please call me Tam."

He blinked. "I don't believe we are acquainted enough to address one another by our Christian names, though I do like Tamberlyn very much. It's a beautiful name."

"Thanks." I put down the carton of Chinese. "I take it that Marlowe is a last name?"

"My given name is Christopher. My friends call me Kit."

"Christopher Marlowe? Like the playwright?"

He beamed, his face lighting up like he'd found the Holy Grail. "Yes! Thou art familiar?" He slipped back into his old dialect.

"Sure, I'll play along. You're kind of famous. Not as much as Shakespeare, but—"

Frowning, he interrupted me. "Do not speak to me of that knave. He hath no original ideas of his own, no conscience, no—"

I stopped him with an upraised hand. Jeez, this guy had more mood swings than a hormonal teen girl. "Okay, okay. Let's not get too carried away here. You realize he's been dead for like hundreds of years, right?"

Marlowe sighed. "I am aware." He paced, glancing at me as he pulled at the ruffly thing at his neck. I told him to get rid of the distracting fluff. "Apologies for my attire. I attempt to travel in much more suitable clothing. Alas, there was little fore notice of this venture." He pulled at the collar-scarf thingy and laid it aside, then took off the velvet jacket and the vest. Underneath he wore a simple cotton shirt, long-sleeved, no buttons. He was much easier to look at without all that purple.

"Mayhap we should start from the beginning." He indicated that I should sit. I curled up in my comfy rocker while he settled on my secondhand couch. "I am Christopher Marlowe, Her Majesty the Queen's Humble Servant, and play-maker. I hail from Canterbury, England in the year of our Lord, 1587. In another capacity, I am a warrior against the darkness that surrounds us—the darkness that you, Mistress Paradiso, also fight against." He stopped to let me soak up his words. I resisted the urge to laugh in his face because he was quite serious.

"Wait. Just, wait. You see monsters? Hunt monsters?"

He nodded. "Did you think you were the only one?"

"Yes, quite frankly. I did." My phone beeped from

the counter. His eyes widened at the noise, and then he glanced toward his discarded sword beside my door. I grabbed the phone before it got the same treatment as the ghoul. I knew who the text was from—Rick, looking for his usual late-night booty call. "It's my phone," I reassured my guest as I thumbed an answer into the phone.

"Not tonight. really tired. talk tomorrow," I texted.

Marlowe watched me curiously.

"No phones where you're from?" I tested. "For someone from the fifteenth, or sixteenth, whatever—a long-ass time ago, you seem pretty acclimated to being here. I mean, if you are who you say you are, there are no phones, electricity, indoor plumbing, or cars, yet you asked about cars when we left the hospital. You're pulling my chain, right?"

He tilted his head a fraction as if the movement would increase his understanding. His hand brushed over his creased brow before his answer came. I hadn't noticed his weariness earlier, being pretty damned tired myself.

"You're observant. That will serve us well in the coming days. But your customary speech is difficult to decipher. Pray tell, what is the chain of which you speak?" I started to explain, and he stopped me. "To answer what I perceive as your query, I have traveled forward a great deal; therefore, I've had to avail myself of knowledge about whatever culture in which I find myself. I have some skill in acclimation. Most people fear what they do not understand, so to prevent being labeled a witch and being burned at the stake, I must not draw attention to myself. This includes the language and dialect and the learning of current customs and styles."

"Not many men dress in purple velvet nowadays. But not to worry, we outlawed burning at the stake like a couple of centuries ago."

He looked down at himself. "My attire is not of the royal color, I assure you."

"I hate to disagree, but it is." I sipped the rest of my bourbon, propping my bare foot on the leg of the end table so I could rock the chair back and forth. The Queen's Humble Servant noticed. And I noticed that he noticed. Modestly dressed in yoga pants and a tank top, an old sweater pulled on over the thick bandage on my arm, I should have felt at ease. But at his glance, I felt considerably less dressed. Not a terrible feeling, I thought. His eyes missed nothing as they roamed over me. I smiled, more to myself than to him. Even guys pretending to be from another century were still guys. "It's about the crappiest shade of purple I've seen, but..."

He sighed, smiling ruefully. "Her Majesty has outlawed the wearing of purple by commoners. This—" he indicated his outfit, "was a dark blue. Blood stains do not bode well in public, even in my timeline. My attempt to cover the stains led to this...shade."

"I got to say, you've researched this well. Do you know what year this is?" I played along, still not quite believing his story. Monsters I believed, I'd seen them with my own eyes, but time-travel stuff was a little too Syfy channel for me.

He didn't look away, and our eyes locked long enough to make my breath catch. "There was a pamphlet in the room where I waited for you. I am an educated man and can read." He told me the year and he was right. "We are in the new world," he paused only briefly, "—a place your citizens call the United States, in the city of Philadelphia, one of the older cities in this land. Currently, uniformed players of some sort have won a battle against another garrison. I believe you call them the Eagles. I'm assuming that's merely a pseudonym, and they are men, not fowl." I nodded for him to go on. The guy could spin a tale, that's for sure.

"I have been here twice before. During a war and once again 1951, a much more peaceful time where I had the pleasure of traveling in a motor car for the first time and on a train. Tell me, do you still have trains?" His eyes gleamed like a child's.

I almost laughed at his expression. He could be endearing when he wanted. "Yes, there are trains and even planes now. People fly through the air in vehicles with big engines." I shrugged.

His eyes widened in disbelief.

"It's perfectly safe. People do it all the time, now." Never having to explain the concept of flight to someone, I had no idea how to go about it. "But no one travels through time. I mean, it only exists in science fiction books and movies."

"Flying. I should like to try that." He sat back and crossed one booted foot over the other. The earlier heat I'd felt was gone, replaced by a long sigh as he seemed to relax for the first time since we'd met.

"I'd like to try the time machine myself," I said.

"Machine? There is no machine. It is simply my destiny. The ability to travel over centuries is fairly complicated, and while I'd like to continue this discourse, I..." His words faded and I realized again that he was exhausted. "It is quite a severe punishment on one's person."

He gave enormous yawn. I followed suit. The effects of the hot shower and bourbon ganged up on me and I stood, preparing to go to bed. Seeing this, he pulled himself up from the couch to incline his head and shoulders in another bow. "Look, you've got to quit doing that...bowing thing. It's gone out of fashion these days."

"Another sad fact of this time." Underneath the fatigue in his expression, there was a wistful dreaminess, as though he were not only tired but homesick. I grabbed a blanket and pillow from the closet and handed it to him. "It's not much, but it's not too bad." I indicated the couch and squinted at him. "And I'm armed, just to let you know."

He looked surprised for a moment and then a sardonic eyebrow lifted, and he nodded. "I assure you, I mean you no harm."

"We can talk more in the morning if you haven't zinged back through time or anything."

"Zing?" He frowned. I shook my head, indicating he should ignore half of what I say. Strangely enough, this non-verbal communication seemed to work better than words. "Since my reason for being here is not yet resolved, I shall be here come morning."

This put all kinds of questions in my head, but at another unconcealed yawn from him, I ignored my curiosity. "Sleep well."

He gave a short bow. "Good night, Miss—Tamberlyn."

The use of the full version of my name usually made me uncomfortable. I preferred Tam. But when said in a husky British accent, it didn't sound half bad.

That Tuesday had started out pretty much like all my Tuesdays. It had been a bright crisp fall day. The kind of day where you want to be throwing a Frisbee in the park instead of sitting in a cramped car with a hefty and bored police partner as the two of you watch an empty night club. X and I had been on the last shift of our stakeout of Balfour's digs, and Tuesday was the last day of our work week. Having nothing to show for our hours in the car but sore asses and short tempers, we'd headed to the office to fill out reports.

Both of us thought Gianni Balfour, the local crime boss, was prime for the murder of his girlfriend, Cynthia Wu. Unfortunately, we had no proof. To further complicate things, we were assigned to work with the Organized Crime Unit—OCU—and everything we did was scrutinized by Jason Munson, the lead on the case.

I had finished up my report when Parker stopped by my desk. A recent addition to the department, he was anxious to garner a big case, and for some inexplicable reason, he thought I'd be helpful. Over the last month or so, he'd been hovering around me like a carpenter bee on my grandmother's porch.

"Ah, you wanna grab a coffee after shift? You can impress me with your stories of how tough you are," he asked, his soft voice a little wobbly.

In the background, I'd heard X chortle, not quite covering the sound with a cough.

"Thanks." I threw my partner a warning glance and turned back to see Parker nervously fingering my nameplate. "Maybe another time, I have a thing on Tuesdays." Tuesday night dinners at X's were a staple on my social calendar. An arched eyebrow encouraged Officer Parker to leave my damn nameplate alone and walk away. "What are you snorting about?" I hissed at X across the desks.

"That guy so has the hots for you." X threw me his substantial smile. "I'm sure it's your skill in having perps jump eight-foot fences to get away. Maybe you can give him some pointers on a takedown." His eyebrows waggled up and down.

"Shut up." But I smiled. X and I had been partners for two years. A few years older, he was in his early thirties and was a five-year veteran in the homicide division. An imposing figure—former defensive end for a college team I couldn't remember—he wasn't fast enough for the pros or chasing bad guys down alleys. But he wasn't bad in a fight and seeing his bulk discouraged most from trying anything, and I was very glad he was on my side, snarky comments and all.

He had no idea about my sideline in the occult. It's not that I didn't trust X, but I'd found that the fewer people who knew what I did in my off-hours, the better it was for them. Because of my unusual sideline, I trained harder than most—combat warfare, martial arts, weapon handling, not to mention urban legends. Lots of research goes into how to kill monsters because very often, bullets from a police-issued Glock are useless. The hardest part was keeping things under wraps and figuring out a cover story for headless bodies and such.

Because most people don't want to know that stuff. They want to believe that their little mundane world is still within their realm of understanding—that the most dangerous things around are viruses and politicians. It's not that I'm not wary of right-wing extremists, or leftists for that matter, or pesky African viruses, but my realm is a tad larger than most.

"You're coming for dinner tonight, right?" X had asked. The answer had been a given. His wife Connie made the best carne asada this side of the Mississippi, and my food budget was nil. Most of my detective salary went toward weapons and old books on demon lore, not to mention huge sums to the dry cleaners on Fifth and Bradshaw. They can get monster blood out of a silk blouse like nobody's business. It had been on my way home that I'd encountered ghouls and my mysterious visitor, so not a normal Tuesday after all.

3

The morning after my run-in with ghouls and the crazy man with the sword, I left my mysterious rescuer sleeping on the couch and headed to pick up X for court. I figured I'd stop by the discount store for some jeans and T-shirts because his purple prose outfit smelled like it was from the sixteenth century. Maybe Goodwill had a pair of velveteen pants from the sixties he'd feel comfortable in. I considered letting crazy pants wear his purple duds out and about, that way he'd be picked up by men in white coats and solve all my problems. But on the off, very slim, next to nil chance he was telling the truth, I figured I'd cut him a break. We may not burn them at the stake anymore, but we sure do lock them up and stuff them with Thorazine.

Early November had the sun barely creeping over the city as I dressed. A white shirt, blue blazer and matching skirt, I nixed the pantyhose and jammed my feet into low-heeled pumps. I'm a sensible shoe girl, and even though I could use a little added height, I've never opted for platform stilts.

X was in his usual courtroom attire—black suit, white shirt—this time with a tie I hadn't seen before. I pulled up the to the curb of his red-brick row house, noting a sagging jack-o'-lantern that waited for the trash man to come and put him out of his misery.

Clambering into the passenger side, X commented on my outfit as he banged his knee on the dashboard. "Rick the Dick will enjoy that skirt."

"That's a really nice tie. I'd hate to have to strangle you with it." I gunned the engine through a yellow light. In five minutes, the fair commuters of Philadelphia would be streaming their way into the city, and if we were late for court, Rick would be pissed.

"You're late," X said, ignoring my empty threat of strangulation.

"Had to make a stop. I'll get us there, don't worry." I honked the horn at a Volvo that pulled out in front of me.

"Christmas shopping early?" He indicated the large bag in the backseat.

"You wish. No, my...ah, cousin showed up late last night. He's on my couch for a couple of days." Just in case X showed up at my place and I hadn't gotten rid of Marlowe yet, I'd better have a cover story. Sometimes, I think my entire life is all cover story.

"I've never heard you mention a cousin."

"Well, we're not close." Isn't that the truth? "But he had nowhere else to hang." Truth again, as far as I knew.

"And no clothes either?" He looked puzzled.

"His girlfriend kicked him out. I picked up some stuff for him."

"Really?"

I looked over. "What? Are you saying I wouldn't help the guy out?"

"That's exactly what I'm saying. Remember last year? Big storm, when the power was out in half the precinct. Everyone was taking people in. Hell, Connie and I had two guys sleeping on our floor. But not Casa Paradiso."

"In my defense, the guy who wanted to stay with me was Lipnitz. If he'd stayed at my place, I'd have shot him for jiggling the lock on my bedroom door. He was much safer sleeping on your floor."

It's not that I consider myself irresistible or anything. Lipnitz would screw anything with a pulse. It's that I'd worked too hard to earn their respect as a fellow officer to jeopardize it by sleeping with any of them. Very few of my co-workers even knew about my non-relationship with Rick.

Strangely enough, while I was decidedly uncomfortable with a guy like Lipnitz in my house, I hadn't the slightest worry that Marlowe would try anything. Whether he was truly from the 1500s or not, I think he took his chivalry seriously.

"You have serious trust issues, you know that?" X's big hand rested on the dashboard. He wasn't quite white-knuckling it, but almost. He hated my driving. And he had the gall to talk about my trust issues.

I nudged my car into the left-hand lane for a turn. "That's not true. I'm very particular. I trust you, don't I?"

He chuckled, but the sound faded quickly. I glanced over at him. His wide forehead crinkled, giving him the dreaded pensive look.

"Not everyone is out to get you, *hermanita*. Most

people in this world are trying to get through it without receiving too much damage."

"No one gets through life unscathed." I forced myself into a reassuring smile. "You are so friggin' optimistic. How do you keep this skewed view of humanity after what we see every day? People like the home invasion guys we're testifying against. People like Balfour, who leaves his dead girlfriend in a dumpster. "

"Granted, we see a lot of the dark side. But not everyone is like that. Take your cousin for example. His girlfriend threw him out, did he react with violence? No, he showed up on your doorstep, hoping to sleep on your lumpy couch."

"Cousin?" Then I remembered the man I'd left sleeping on my lumpy couch. The crazy one who'd looked far too innocent and young to be four hundred years old. "Oh yeah. And my couch is not lumpy."

We arrived at 8:00 a.m. and the courtroom was sleepy. An odd hush surrounded everyone sipping their coffee and checking their phones. Everyone that is, except the prosecutor. He was sharply dressed, very alert, and almost vibrating with anticipation.

Richard Davenport was an associate in the District Attorney's office known for his witness prep and case wins. He was also known in a very small circle of my associates as *Rick the Dick*. An over-worked, over-confident assistant district attorney, he was perfect for my current needs. Someone who asked no questions, got to the point, and left me alone when I wanted it. Rick was a ruthless prosecutor and too wildly ambitious to entertain a relationship. Since I've never been good at relationships that suited me fine.

X and I settled two rows back from the prosecutor's table. Just before I was called, Munson slid into the seat behind us. His cologne had the scent of old car fresheners and I stifled a sneeze. Jason Munson and I had graduated the academy together and had a not-so-friendly competitive relationship.

"Detectives," he groused behind us. X looked back and gave him a nod. I did nothing and focused on what I would say on the stand. "Don't screw it up, Paradiso," Munson chided softly as I rose to take the stand. *Asshole. What the hell was that about?* Munson wasn't even on the home burglary case.

I swore my oath to tell the truth and sat in the witness box. Davenport and I had been over my testimony at least twice ahead of time, so it went smoothly. The only reason homicide had been called was the thugs had misjudged their target and broke in while people were home. But their actions had resulted in the death of an elderly aunt staying with the family. They got manslaughter two. We had been after the ring leader, the one behind the series of recent high-end thefts.

My testimony against the two suspects was short and to the point. After me, X had his turn, reiterating most of what I'd said, and we were done. Whatever Rick's shortcomings, he was an excellent DA.

After his turn in the witness box, X insisted we stop at our favorite diner for an after-court breakfast. Over hash browns that were not on his diet, X reviewed our testimony.

"You know that neither of those defendants had the brain power to pull off a string of thefts. The previous jobs were perfectly executed. They knew what to hit and when. These guys were either copycats or decided to try a job on their own." X opened four jelly packets in a row before methodically spreading the sweet stuff on his toast.

"The Tanner's was a fluke. No one was supposed to be home and the old lady with a weak heart was visiting."

"Exactly. The guy with all the details wasn't in on this job. We've got these guys on manslaughter and home invasion, but the mastermind is still out there."

"What's our connection?" I asked, testing the steaming mug of coffee for heat before taking a sip.

"I don't know yet. Working on it. Hey, any idea why Munson was there today?"

I shrugged, "Maybe there's a connection to Balfour." It would be the only reason for Munson to be in court for an unrelated case.

"Balfour's into a lot of things, but home invasion's not really his style," he said. "Speaking of, maybe we should re-check our evidence on the Wu case. There might be more to it than we realize."

I pushed my plate away. "I think it's simple. Balfour got angry, killed her, and had his guys clean up the mess. We have no proof."

"Maybe there is a connection here. I'll check with the burglary division, see if any of the stuff has been recovered. Look for a connection to organized crime."

"Find the stuff, find the head guy. Any ideas on how to do that?" I asked.

"Again, I'm working on it."

"Actually, it looks like you're working on that five-egg omelet. Does Connie know about these breakfasts?" I grinned at him as he finished off his plate.

"What she doesn't know won't hurt her, so don't poke the bear." He glanced at me in warning. "Come on." He fished money out for the check. "I better get you home to your houseguest. Poor guy's probably sitting around naked and starving."

4

I carried a Styrofoam box full of the breakfast special into the living room and set it down. I'd been gone almost three hours and my visitor was nowhere to be seen.

"Marlowe?" I called out, acutely aware of how proficient my houseguest was with a sword. I did not want to lose my head by startling him.

X's comment about him being naked hadn't been too far off. The bathroom door opened revealing a man in a towel—a rather well-built man in a towel. I tried not to stare. His shoulders were broad, his waist appealingly narrow and the abs—the abs should have had their own Facebook following. His long hair was slicked back, and he held my kitchen shears. What was it with this guy and weapons?

"I have missed indoor privies. And hot water at the beckoning." He beamed at me.

"What are you doing?" I glanced at the scissors in his hand.

"Chancing upon my countenance in your looking

glass, I decided I needed a trim. It's been awhile." He fondled his now-neatly trimmed beard with his free hand. "Would you mind?" He handed the scissors to me. "I can't quite reach the back and my hair is getting quite long."

I should have minded. Quite a bit. But I made him sit on the couch and grabbed another towel from the bathroom to drape over his shoulders. As I did so, I couldn't help but see a vicious four-inch scar under the scapula. I poked it, gently. "That looks fierce."

"Yes, that was a barbed tail of a Reisen beast. It wasn't deep, but the poison was almost my undoing. Now, not too much. I can't go back looking like some of your celebrity...what do you call your actors? Stars. I know some players who would love the comparison."

I held the scissors out and peered at his expression. He smiled.

"I've used the time to do some research. You have a few pamphlets, mostly filled with advertisements to buy creams and such to make one's face ever youthful."

"Wait till I show you how to Google." I made a few careful snips at his hair. It was smooth and damp and I could feel the warmth of his neck against the backs of my fingertips.

"What?"

"Never mind." I lifted the towel from his shoulders, trapping the barest amount of chestnut brown hair inside. I indicated the stuff I'd brought home—breakfast and clothes.

He ignored the clothes in favor of the Styrofoam box, frowning at the plastic fork inside. "This time is full of major innovation, but this eating utensil is far from well made."

I grabbed a real fork from the kitchen drawer. "Here use this. I hate plastic too. I see you managed the coffee."

I'd left a sticky note with instructions. Push button. When light is green, pour coffee into cup. Drink. Same with the shower faucet, which he'd also figured out.

He seemed to notice my court outfit for the first time. "Your attire is much different."

I stopped and looked down at my skirt and blazer, an empty coffee pot in my hand. "This is my usual for court."

His eyebrows raised and I gave a brief civics class on our justice system. I turned on the TV, showing him how the remote worked. He started clicking through the channels and landed on a channel with women in spandex.

"Are you sure you're from the sixteenth century?" I tossed the shopping bag of clothes to him. Not that I minded him sitting around all day in a towel, but it was distracting, and I had work to do.

By the time I changed into jeans and emerged from my room, he was dressed in the clothes I bought him and engrossed in *General Hospital*.

"This woman, Natalie. She loves Trevor, yet she does not tell him. Instead, she's frolicking about with his brother, who is a cad to all who meet him. What manner of play is this?"

"It's called a soap opera. Back in the day, they used to sell soap to bored housewives. It's a dying art form these days."

"I can see why. There is nothing operatic about this." He clicked the remote and the TV screen went black. "This tiny box to control the big one, however, is wonderful." He tapped the remote again, the TV going on and off. I gently pulled the remote from his hand and set it on the table.

"Yes, it's wonderful. I have some research to do...is there someplace for you to be?" I dragged my laptop from my desk and sat next to him on the couch, checking the police database for any activity from our not-so-friendly ghouls. He watched everything I did but made no move to leave. "Why are you here, Mr. Marlowe? I mean, not that it's not fascinating to meet you and all, but—"

"I am a defender of—"

I stopped him with my hand. "Look, I don't need the whole spiel again. Could you be a little more specific?"

"I was chasing a demon, an evil that wreaked havoc on my city. The blue lightning caught him up along with me, I fear. Tis my fault he is in your fair city. My task is to find the creature and defeat it. Before I'm dispatched again."

"Blue lightning—I'm guessing that's your time machine?"

"There is no machine. The lightning just appears. I get a pain in my head, my skin tingles, and soon after I'm taken into the ribbons and land wherever, or moreover, whenever."

"You can't control it. You kind of go with it? Man, that's got to suck."

"It does. Sucks me in like the deepest mud hole, and like the vastness of the sea, I'm swallowed until it releases me."

"No. I meant, it sucks. Like...never mind. So, how long do you have here in tomorrow land, before you're sucked away by blue lightning?" I figured I'd play along with this acid trip, see where it went.

He shrugged. "My longest journey has been one hundred hours, the shortest—a winter's day. Not much time to learn. And there is so much to learn." He indicated the computer. I explained a tiny bit about the internet. Figure it couldn't be any weirder than blue lighting and time ribbons.

We spoke rather generally about monster hunting, and I showed him a picture of the ghouls and the info on the net about killing them. Most of it was fantasy, but there's a surprising amount they get right. For instance, ghouls are like vampires as they are technically dead but animated beings.

"This device gives you information on how to kill ghouls?"

"Yes, it says a silver knife to the heart will do it. And beheading of course."

He smiled. "Beheading works for most things I've found."

"Yes. Would you like more coffee to go with that sugar and cream you're drinking?"

He missed the joke. Or maybe he chose to ignore it. He held out his cup. "Yes, please. I very much like this hot elixir you've concocted."

Wrapped up in the conversation, I'd no idea how long we sat there, but I was less and less interested in shooing him out the door. I was becoming used to his weird way of speaking, plus the more we spoke, the more he adjusted his wording to match mine. His stories were littered with words I'd never heard before, as well as odd, out of place ones. He actually called my coffee pot a *spiffy* device, beaming at me like he'd nailed the latest pop-culture quote. I was enjoying myself.

Normally, my days off were quiet. I spent them mostly alone, doing laundry, catching up on my favorite shows, buying beer and frozen burritos from the convenience store on the corner. When you spend most of your time in a crowded office, or a cramped car with surly people, not to mention the criminals, one's solitude becomes precious. Yet, Marlowe's presence didn't feel intrusive. I wasn't uncomfortable like I usually am with strangers. That and now that he'd showered and changed into fresh clothes, he smelled really good.

"When did you first know that you were called?" he asked.

"Called? You mean the whole—I can see dead things—thing?"

He smirked but nodded.

"I was in high school. Sixteen." I added, in case he hadn't heard of high school.

Which he hadn't. "Please," he said, waving my explanation away. "If you pause to explain everything you think I don't understand we will never progress. I will query you if there is a need."

I shrugged and went on. "I was a sophomore at Benjamin Franklin High School, and I didn't frequent the library much, but I knew no one liked Mrs. Hatcher, the librarian. I'd never really seen her before that day. Not the real her, anyway. I was there to check out *Les Misérables*. It was for class, not like I would read it for fun."

I took a breath remembering that time. I was dateless for the upcoming homecoming dance, which wasn't unusual. High school had been miserable, and lonely, and was about to get more so. "I accidentally touched Mrs. Hatcher's hand as she passed the book over the counter. It was like some sort of science fiction time warp. Everything got quiet—well, we were in the library, but still—and no one moved. Hatcher's face had these weird eye bag things that folded over on themselves, but they drooped even farther, and I could see the red rims of her eyelids as they hung down. She smiled, her bicuspids lengthening into wicked points that touched her bottom lip. I backed up, but strangely enough. I didn't scream. I wasn't sure what I was seeing, but I wanted to get out of there fast."

As I told Marlowe the story, I curled my legs under me on the couch, turning more to face him. He mirrored my action, facing me, crossing his legs in front of him. He frowned slightly during this and made some comment about the discomfiture of tight jeans. I laughed. His returned smile was shy and deliberately neutral as if he were holding back. I stared at him for a moment. He'd taken my well-ordered hormones and put them to a slow stir. I noticed his intake of breath, deeper than normal, mouth slightly open, pupils dilating. Signs of either imminent danger or a sexual encounter. I blinked. Marlowe leaned in close to me.

"Please continue your refrain." He swallowed and I watched the movement of his throat.

"Oh yeah. Um, at the library, I wanted to get out of there fast. So, I grabbed the book and headed toward the door." My voice lowered—barely a whisper as I dove into the story. Suddenly, I am back there in that library, smelling the old books and the floor polish, and seeing old lady Hatcher's Aqua Net hairspray as it glistened on her steel gray hair. "She tells me to wait. I don't wait, but it doesn't matter, because she's there, faster than anything I'd ever seen. And growly—she literally growls at me.

"The horn-rimmed glasses she normally wears have fallen, and her irises are blood red. I must have made this little squeak because she pulls me behind the bookcase. She's so strong and dragging me along the rows to the back of the room. Nobody notices. I think I'm dreaming. I feel...powerless. Like I was hypnotized."

Marlowe had leaned in as I spoke, his hand coming to rest on my foot. The touch brought me back to myself. I drank my coffee and adjusted my position on the couch. He pulled his hand back abruptly, both of us noticing, and yet, neither said a word. He nodded at me to go on.

"She had me backed up against a wall of books, and all I could see was her mouth opening into this enormous gaping hole coming toward me. The only weapon at hand was Mr. Hugo's novel, so I shoved it into her mouth as hard as I could. Her teeth clamped down and stuck." I set the coffee cup on the table in front of us. I tended to talk with my hands and the coffee had grown cold anyway. "So, there we are, locked in this death struggle with a six-hundred-page book crammed in Hatcher's teeth. Her nails turned into huge claws, I mean scary, talon looking nails." My hand formed into a claw to demonstrate. "I remember the bell ringing and bringing me back to my senses. I could react all of the sudden, and I pushed her away. Still, there were the claws."

"We crashed into a wooden step stool and she's whipping her head side to side trying to dislodge the book. Somehow, I know that if that book comes loose, I'm dead. I grab a stool leg and use all my weight to cram it into her chest. She makes this horrible grunting sound. Then it's quiet. Before I can sit up and even panic about killing the woman, she dries up into little piles of dust and lint."

I smiled at Marlowe and managed a nonchalant shrug. It's always a good story when you come out ahead in a vampire encounter. Of course, there's no story if you don't, because you're dead.

"The hardest part, looking back, is that no one saw anything. It was a mystery. All they saw was some clumsy sophomore girl with a weird love for French novels. When I asked them if they'd seen the librarian, they looked at me like I was crazy."

"A siren vampire. I've seen one or two." Marlowe affirmed. "A type of vampire who stuns their prey with their voice prior to killing them."

There are many types of vampires, and unlike the popular type depicted in media, very few of them take human form. Think about it. If vampires existed like they do in books and movies, the world would soon be overrun by wildly attractive people who avoid sunlight and drive over-priced cars. Okay, maybe Hollywood is full of vampires. I never did like that town.

Vampires are monsters and they look like it. Scaly skin, black eyes, large bat-like ears, tails, the whole bit. Most haven't needed to transform between humanoid and monster form in so long that they have forgotten how. They live in darkness—perfect bloodsucking hunters. The ones who can appear in human form were turned by these creatures. But unlike in romance novels, it's a rare occurrence, because, hello—they *eat* people. They are not the lonely solitary figure brooding in corners over lost loves who just happened to be human cheerleaders. They think of us as cheeseburgers. Out of a thousand cheeseburgers they may come across, there's one with pickles and after taking a bite, they fall in love with pickles. The rest of us are a food source. After seeing what Hatcher really looked like, I have never again thought of them as romantic figures.

Marlowe nodded at me with a new measure of respect. "You did well to silence the monster before vanquishing it. 'Twas the only way." He paused. "Relieving one of its head would work as well." He said this with such matter-of-factness that I laughed, realizing it had been quite a long time since I talked about this part of my life.

After the vampire killing in the library, I'd tried to tell my best friend, but she never believed me. Not really, anyway. When I insisted, she got into it for about five minutes, in that teenage occult worship kind of way. Later, she told people that her parents caught us doing witchcraft and they freaked and made her quit hanging out with me. I guess my constant reading of demon lore and ancient legends labeled me as a bad influence.

"Tell me about your first time. Monster hunting, I mean." I felt myself blushing, which was so weird.

Marlowe didn't seem to pick up on it, though. "It was similar to yours. I was seventeen, about to enter Corpus Christi when a young scholar was killed by what we thought was a wild animal. Not unheard of in the country, but this was in London. A group of us decided to hunt the nearby woods for the culprit, but we found nothing."

"Werewolf?"

He nodded. "'Twould seem so. I went out alone, by the light of the full moon, on a notion. The beast was huge and fierce, and I was lucky to survive. I'd had lots of fencing training, but a rapier is no match for a wolf, and I'd not acquired my broad sword yet. Still, I managed to vanquish it." He paused for a moment, watching me. I responded by touch. Putting my hand on his knee, encouraging him to go on. "At first, I'd thought it was simply a lone wolf, a rogue animal. But after death, it reverted to its human form, another scholar from my class. I was horrified, thinking I'd been dreaming, or had visions which caused me to murder another human. I spent the following month reliving the incident with nightmares and daymares. I thought I was losing my mind and was going to turn myself over to the magistrate and confess."

"But you didn't?" I thought of the consequences of Marlowe's actions. Telling my story in high school got me ostracized by the students. Marlowe telling his would have gotten him jailed or tortured or even burned at the stake.

He shook his head. "No. Before I did, I saw another entity. A demon spirit, one that preyed upon children, and again I felt the compulsion to hunt it down and kill it. When I did, I realized this was my calling, my duty in the world. 'Twas only then that I realized the killing in the woods for what it truly was—the vanquishing of a werewolf."

I believed him. His story mirrored mine. Different time, different hostile, but the same feeling. The guilt he'd felt, the confusion and horror. The terrifying thought of going crazy. I'd felt these very same things at sixteen and it took me years to reconcile that this was my life now.

Marlowe wasn't half bad at this so-called profession. I pulled the laptop over to me and started to type his name into a search engine.

"What are you doing?"

"Reading up on you. I mean, I've heard of you sure, but history's not my strong suit."

"No! Stop. You must cease this instant." His hand closed over mine. He sounded a bit frayed.

"I believe you. You are Christopher Marlowe, and I want to learn—"

"You cannot tell me. I must not know my fate."

I searched my memory for random facts learned in English Lit. Marlowe was famous as a predecessor to Shakespeare. He had a few plays produced, wrote poetry, but was as famous for being killed during a fight.

"Okay. I won't." I lifted my hands away from the keyboard. "Don't worry."

"My apologies." His voice was gentle again. "I meant no harm. It is best not to know one's future. It is the one instance where too much knowledge is not a benefit."

"Because your choices are affected by that knowledge." I nodded in understanding and wondered what it would be like to know one's fate. Especially if said fate was to die violently before your thirtieth birthday. It would be only human to avoid that path and to try and stay alive. "How old are you?"

"Three and twenty. Why do you inquire?"

"No reason," I said hurriedly. "You seem much older."

He chuckled.

"I was born four hundred and sixty years ago, maybe that's why." He turned serious. "My fate is already set. If I know the particulars, I may be tempted to change it, and in so doing, change the course of history around me."

"The butterfly effect."

"Butterflies have nothing to do with it," he said.

"No, that's what it's called. The idea that when a butterfly flaps its wings across the world, the effect ripples to create hurricanes."

Marlowe laughed. "Your timeline has such odd beliefs."

"It's kind of a metaphor. Like the slightest decision can have enormous consequences."

He stood, pacing back and forth in front of me. "This is true. Though to be fair, I have not seen such things. During one of my voyages, this," He waved his hand in the air, "metaphor was explained by a scientist—a friend. He gave me hope that I could survive this phenomenon that is time walking. Prior to meeting him, I felt powerless against the forces that take me."

"How long after seeing your first hostile did this traveling start?" The answer was another twitch of his shoulders and a vague pursing of his lips. I let it go. "So, you have no choice when you travel, where, or when?"

"Always when the moon is waxing crescent. Otherwise, my destiny is determined by God, hopefully." His smile was sad, and suddenly I felt for the guy. I was a believer then—a full-on, no-holds-barred believer. No one could keep the act up for that long. I tried not to think too much on it. Because if I thought about the fact that I was sitting with the flesh and blood man that was *the* Christopher Marlowe, English bard, forbearer of the literary renaissance and a friend or adversary of Shakespeare, I got kind of wiggy about things. Like I wanted to ask—so, what is it about that Hamlet guy? Was he crazy or what? And what was Elizabeth I really like? Did she have that ethereal quality like the actresses who've played her in films, or was she bald with bad teeth?

"Does thy device conjure spells?" His voice shook me out of my Renaissance reverie. He continued walking casually around my living room, as if too restless to sit any longer.

"What?"

"Can you ask your device how to defeat a strigoi?"

"A what?"

I asked how to spell *strigoi*.

He obliged and I typed the word into the computer. The picture flashed across my screen of a pale creature with horns instead of ears. I flipped the laptop around so he could see it. He peered at the screen, getting closer until he finally touched it like he couldn't quite tell that it was real.

"Where did this likeness come from?"

I shrugged. "I don't know. Someone found it, or drew it, and posted it online."

"Master Gomfrey," he said. He sat back down beside me. "I've seen this drawing before. In fact, I watched it being drawn. In my time, there is an apothecary, a person of..." he searched for a word.

"I know what an apothecary is."

"Excellent. Well, Master Gomfrey is also an ally. He is

a conjurer—a fortuner. When I described my encounter with the creature, he knew of it, and drew this image."

"This picture is over four hundred years old?"

"For you, yes. For me, it is but a day."

"This is so weird."

Hours later, we were neck deep in research. Marlowe was pacing my living room again and reciting from memory what he knew about the monsters he'd followed through time. From my place on the couch, I listened while eating the last slice of a frozen pizza—the only thing I'd found in my freezer. There were two beers on the coffee table, his and mine, as well as a few books on the supernatural. I flicked a page of one with my toe to see the picture displayed. It was the same fifteenth century drawing we'd found on the internet. The artist, Marlowe's friend and consultant, had an attention to detail that served him well. The strigoi was depicted in a hunch, walking upright, and nearly hairless with an overly large head and huge catlike eyes.

"Art thou hearing me?" Marlowe drew my attention toward him yet again.

"I'm with ya."

"I know thou art with me. Speak not in metaphors, I beg of you."

"I mean, yes, I am listening. You said something about cats."

"A cat's howl. A strigoi's scream sounds like a cat in throes of lust, verily loud, and desperate."

"Okay, wait, that's something." I pulled the computer over. "I remember seeing something on the blogs about cats in the sewer."

"Underground? That is possible. Strigoi avoid

sunlight."

"Here. Reports of cats lost in the sewers in the mission district, near Platte and Rengold."

"Wouldst thou be amenable to hunting in this place?"

"I wouldst." The guy's language was getting to me. "I mean, yes, let's go have a look." I rummaged around in my closet for some old lace-up hunting boots, shoes worthy of walking through sewers. Holstering my gun, I looked at Marlowe, who was fully caped and sworded up.

"You can't go like that."

"Is this not the clothing you procured for me?" He turned, examining himself in a black T-shirt and faded jeans. I had to congratulate myself on getting the correct size—they fit perfectly, almost too good in fact.

"I mean the cape." I didn't mention the sword. I liked the sword. The sword looked good on him. "You look like Zorro."

"I always travel with this garment. It protects me during the leap. It was specially made for me."

"Don't get your feelings hurt, it's a great cape, but... okay, okay, we can take it, but it stays in the car."

He nodded, pulling the cape off his shoulders and folding it in front of him. I opened the door to find Rick the Dick in my doorway, still in his suit and tie, a six-pack of beer in one hand.

"Hey Tam, we did great in court today. Thought I'd come over and celebrate with you."

5

"Rick. You should have called."

"I did call." He strode into my house like he was in front of a jury, with a little bit of a strut to his walk. I was rather pleased to see him stop short at the sight of the tall man armed for a hunting trip to the sewers, which of course, included a battle sword strapped to his side. Rick turned back to me after a long glance at Marlowe. "You never called me back. Or answered my texts for that matter." He set the beer on the coffee table. I glanced at the books we'd been going over, open to some pretty gruesome pictures. At my look, Marlowe surreptitiously closed them.

"I've been busy," I said.

"I see that."

"This is my cousin, Marlowe. He dropped in on me unexpectedly. Marlowe, this is my friend Rick."

Rick extended his hand and after a moment of hesitation, Marlowe took it.

"Nice to meet you," Rick said. He seemed rather

relieved at my explanation. Marlowe only nodded in return, choosing not to reveal his obvious accent or bizarre speech. "I've never met any of Tam's family."

"He's from England. We haven't seen each other in a long time," I said.

"Man, you've traveled far to drop in for a visit." Rick smiled at him but took a step back toward me. I found this rather possessive, which was strange coming from Rick.

Marlowe's face quirked in amusement. "Aye, far traveling, to be sure...man." The word was uttered with the perfect inflection of a disinterested teenager. Watching those soaps on TV had paid off.

Rick glanced at the sword by his side. "Nice piece. That looks very authentic. Are you some sort of Renaissance guy or something?"

"Something of that kin," Marlowe replied.

I interrupted before this got too far. "Yes, actually. Marlowe is here for a big fair upstate. He decided to make a stop here first." I indicated the door. "We were about to go out."

"Great," Rick said. "Let's hit Rigoberto's. It's two for one night." He turned back to Marlowe with his usual insensitive enthusiasm. "You like Italian, man?"

Marlowe glanced at me. I made an awkward eating motion behind Rick's back.

"A meal? Oh, yes." He beamed and there was genuine pleasure in his expression—not an unpleasant look on him. The guy did like his food. "However, first we must dispatch a nuisance. Perchance, may we join thee, er, you for repast another time?"

Rick laughed. "Dude, you've got this Renaissance gig

down."

"He's kidding you. That's my cousin. He's a big kidder. Look, can we meet you later? I'll run Marlowe on his errand, and we'll find you at the restaurant."

After a moment's hesitation, Rick nodded and strode back through the open door. Marlowe insisted that I go through before him. We managed a little series of stops and starts before I gave up and let him pull the door closed behind us.

I breathed a sigh of relief that Rick was both confident and easy-going. A man less sure of himself may have insisted on hanging around. Either that or I'm a really good liar. Or maybe he didn't care if there was something between Marlowe and me. There wasn't. I'm just saying if there was.

I threaded my way through traffic to an alley behind Platte Street. Marlowe was quiet in the front seat, focused on the impending task. I'd thought he'd be full of questions about Rick or even modern-day sewers, but he was silent. I returned the favor and pulled into the alley, parking my Corolla behind a tiny smart car. As discussed, Marlowe left his cape in the backseat, but the sword was close at hand.

"Try and keep that thing out of sight of the normals, okay?" I nodded at the weapon.

"The normals?"

"Non-monsters, non-hunters—regular folk."

He smiled and giving a short bow indicated a metal grate set into the sidewalk. We lifted the grate and descended into the darkness.

I stumbled slightly and put my hand against the wall, pulling it away with a shudder. My fingertips covered in a cold slime. I didn't want to see what it was. Soon, the tunnel we were in compressed to a smaller enclosure. We hunched over to fit through and kept walking. Every few hundred feet, we'd stop and listen.

After a mile it seemed, my back ached from the awkward bent position and my stomach was looking forward to linguini with clam sauce. The sewer system of Philadelphia was not my ideal place for a pre-dinner date. Even sitting in a booth fending off Rick's questions would have been preferable. Now, if we'd found something to kill, that would have been different, but so far, the big hunt was nothing but a miserable trek.

"Hear that?" Marlowe stopped my progress. I listened. It was faint, and noise echoed in the tunnel, but eventually, I heard a distinct cat yowl, only longer, almost a howl. I moved toward the sound, but he stopped me. "This way," he turned away. "The echo is misleading, Mistress Tamberlyn."

"It's just Tam," I said, but I followed him down an even narrower tunnel. We stopped speaking, our footsteps soundless on the concrete. Or at least his were soundless, I tried to emulate his movements without much success. The yowl gave me chills—annoying and nerve-racking at the same time, becoming unbearable until it suddenly stopped. Marlowe and I looked at each other and gradually stood upright. I noticed his stance as we waited in a junction of sorts, a room where the tunnels interconnect. He was on alert, his sword drawn, feet apart, and ready to move. I took a deep breath and almost choked at the smell. Whatever it was, it wasn't our surroundings—my nose was used to sewer smell by this time. The scent was old, not musty old, but primordial old.

Water flowed through the tunnels below the grates under our feet, the sound of it the only noise I could make out. I pulled my weapon from my shoulder holster as we waited, both our flashlights pointed at the ground. I'm used to working alone, in most cases, I prefer it. But in that tunnel, in the dark, dank and smelly place, I was infinitely grateful he was there.

The air grew thick and cold. In the dim light of the averted torch, I could see my breath. You know that feeling you get when it's dark, and you're walking alone at night, and you hear footsteps? This wasn't at all like that. We didn't hear it coming. I directed my light toward the ceiling at the last second.

This thing—that's the only way I can describe it, a thing—skittered along the walls with such speed it was barely a blur. I tracked the blur with my light, both Marlowe and I turning to keep it in sight. We failed. Milliseconds after we lost it, it landed on Marlowe's shoulders. He reacted instantly, railing back several steps, slamming himself and the creature against the wall. It was enough of a blow that the creature released its grip on him as he wrenched himself away. I whirled around, my light searching for the creature. Marlowe's flashlight rolled to a stop in the space between two grates.

My hands crossed in front of me, one holding the light, the other, my gun. I kept Marlowe in my peripheral vision as I scanned the walls and corners.

"There!" Marlowe said. I turned in the direction

he pointed and fired three rounds. Two hit the beast's chest. One pinged into the cement wall. The creature was no longer there. It clambered up the wall again and perched like a cockroach. It hissed and turned its head almost three quarters around in our direction.

Large pointed ears had long white hairs springing from the flap of skin where it joined its head. The head was large, too large for its small body, which was about the size of a Boxer dog. The glowing eyes faced forward and bulged in its head as the creature's mouth opened wide into a growl. My bullets had only served to piss it off. With incredible speed, it leaped from the wall, turning in mid-air, claws out toward me. Marlowe slashed at it, but it turned again, the blade missing its torso by inches. The deflection gave me time to scramble backward. The strigoi landed where I had been a moment before. Marlowe stepped forward and side-stepped, narrowly avoiding a swipe of claws. I swung my light and gun to get another shot in. The light shone in the beast's face and it howled, head turning away. On all fours, it blurred again and disappeared into the darkness.

Marlowe took off after it. I took off after Marlowe, my flashlight's beam bouncing ahead of me. My heart pounded as I followed, as much from the encounter as from the quickly diminishing space around me. I could reach out with either hand and touch the walls. If we'd have caught the thing in the cramped space, it would have had the advantage.

Focused on the ground in front of me, I nearly ran into the back of Marlowe in the narrowing tunnel. I bent over, panting.

"I fear we shall not find it again." He was hunched

over also, but more from the tiny space than to catch his breath. We'd lost all trace of the creature.

"Light seems to hurt it."

"Did I not say that?" he said, obviously frustrated at the missed opportunity.

"You said it avoids sunlight. Not the same thing." I snapped at him.

His voice softened as we headed back toward the large room. "You do heed my words."

"You seem surprised." I glanced at him in the darkness. Retrieving his flashlight from the floor, I handed it to him. "Let's get out of here. That is if we can find our way out." I realized as he took the light from me that he'd chased the creature into almost complete darkness, without heed to his own safety. "I'll keep an ear out for trouble on the scanner, just in case."

I turned and headed back the way we came.

"Tamberlyn, pray follow me. I shall lead." He indicated the opposite direction. After a moment, I followed. After all, he seemed to have far more sewer experience than I. As we continued our way through various tunnels, he talked, as if to keep my mind off the enclosed space, though I hadn't mentioned my discomfort.

"This is not dissimilar to the mazes at court."

"Queen Elizabeth? That court?" We were back to the hunched-over walk. Every surface was cold, and damp, and I didn't want to touch them. Now that the adrenaline had faded, my back started to ache again. I imagined the tunnels were more difficult for the taller man beside me.

"Not that I'm privy to Her Majesty's court, but in a rare instance, I will receive a summons. On such occasions, I might walk the grounds or linger in the main hall. After a meeting with Lord Walsingham, I had such opportunity. I met a young maid, who showed me a maze of hedges taller than a man's head by several lengths. The maze itself measured larger than my home town. For one such as I, who grew up in cramped quarters with a large family, it was almost as strange as the futures I've encountered. The maid was comely and led me on a merry chase through the narrow passages, offering me a reward if I could catch her."

"And dare I ask what that was?"

"Nothing sordid, mind you. A simple kiss. She was a virtuous maid of good birth." He stopped for a moment, the beam from his flashlight shone on one tunnel and then across to the other. "This way. This maze of tunnels is not nearly as elaborate as Her Majesty's mazes, and I assure you we will return to our beginnings in good time."

"Well, I can offer a meal as your reward," I said. This was a given. I was sure my traveling friend might have had some highly valuable gold coins on him, but nothing he could use in modern-day Philadelphia. He said nothing in return.

Soon enough we got to the grate where I'd left my car and he hoisted me up without preamble. After scrambling to the street level once again, I reached down to help him up through the narrow opening.

"You seem disappointed at my offering of a meal," I said.

"Not in the least." He replaced the grate. "Are you disappointed that I do not claim more as a reward?"

I laughed. The guy had game, I'd give him that. "Get

in the car. I need to go home and shower before dinner with Rick." I could feign indifference with the best of them.

6

Nervous about meeting Rick, I coached Marlowe on twenty-first century behavior as we drove to the restaurant. "Your language is getting better. Just follow my lead and say as little as possible."

"To what place do you lead?"

"No, I mean, when we're at dinner with Rick. He's going to ask questions. He's a lawyer, that's what he does." At Marlowe's look, I explained further. "Rick's a prosecutor with the district attorney's office. He puts the bad guys in jail."

"I thought you did that."

"I arrest them. He makes sure they get what they deserve."

"He is of similar circumstance to our own, then?"

"Only he deals in strictly human criminals. He has no idea about hostiles. To him, I'm just a cop."

"I believe there is more to this than what you speak."

"Not really."

"He brings gifts." Marlowe ticked off his fingers as he

spoke. I found it both a modern and antiquated gesture. "He arrives unannounced, and without invitation. He's attempting to persuade you into his bed."

I slammed on the horn as someone pulled in front of me. "Drive, you idiot!"

"Have I spoken unduly?" His tone indicated that he knew more than he was saying. He was being cagey, but the guy had super powers of observation.

"No."

A barely muffled snort told me he didn't believe me. I shouldn't have cared. It was no business of his. And yet, I felt compelled to explain. "Rick and I are complicated."

"You are betrothed? Promised?"

"We are friends. And on occasion, more than that."

"Is this common? For a woman of stature to be so blatant about losing her virtue?"

I gave a slight laugh at his phrasing, but it took me a moment to answer. My first sexual experience was a sore subject with me. It hadn't been unpleasant. It had been all too pleasant, otherworldly so, and so disastrous afterward that I'd buried it deep.

"Not to worry, my virtuous ship sailed long ago," I said.

He seemed to know it wasn't a topic I wanted to get into, and we rode the rest of the way to the restaurant in somewhat uncomfortable silence.

"I'll have the saltimbocca and your bottle of Chianti. The good kind." Rick smirked at me as he ordered. We'd eaten here the first night we got together half a year ago—finished a bottle of Chianti between us. What I can recall of it, it had been was a good night.

Tonight, however, things had changed. Rick was

posturing and I didn't like it. He wouldn't know a bottle of good Chianti if it hit him over the head. And I was inclined to do just that to keep him humble. For some reason, I wanted Marlowe to be impressed with him.

Though I'd showered and Marlowe proclaimed it was the cleanest sewer he'd ever been in, which is a weird statement in itself, I felt like the stench clung to my clothes.

Rick had been waiting for us and after a moment's hesitation, I chose to sit across from him and slid into the booth next to Marlowe. I told myself it was to help him through the conversation—particularly if Rick got too drunk to notice my whispering to him. But this wasn't all. I'd been up against some pretty scary things in my days as a hunter. Vamps, one giant-ass snake monster, a few demons, and some possessed humans—which are the hardest to deal with, by the way. Anytime the human element is involved, it gets tricky. In all those encounters, I'd never seen anything that could move like the strigoi and I was more than a little shaken.

After that night, having seen what we were up against, I felt strangely at ease with Marlowe's tall frame beside me. Rick was a sizable guy, about six feet and two hundred pounds. He was also a cutthroat lawyer and professional trash talker. But he couldn't fight his way through a line at Disneyland. The man beside me, however, wouldn't hesitate in lopping off the head of anything or anyone who was after us. I'd seen it firsthand.

I was halfway through my linguine and white clam sauce before Rick decided he needed to show off his cross-examination skills.

"So, Marlowe, what is it you do across the pond?

When you're not running around in tights and chasing dragons, that is." Rick pushed his plate away, only half finished. He was on a roll, I could tell, and didn't want to ruin a good buzz by eating too much. I had started to relax my guard on the conversation and almost missed Marlowe's obvious confusion at the question. Because for him, tights and dragons—at least mythical ones— were a reality, but I was pretty sure he'd never heard the Atlantic Ocean described as a pond.

"I'm a poet." He stopped there, as my foot landed gently across his under the table.

Rick laughed, as he was prone to do whenever he felt out of his depth.

"A poet? Can't be much money in that, is there? But hey, good for you, following your art and all that."

"Sadly, it's becoming apparent that it's not the most lucrative of professions." Marlowe looked at me. "Even now."

I shrugged and thought I should introduce Marlowe to the works of Jay-Z and 50 Cent. Some of our more lucrative modern-day poets.

Rick had to push things, though. "You must supplement your income, right?"

"Does it really matter?" I asked.

Rick, of course, ignored me. I saw the gleam in his eye, the one he got in court. I realized I'd made a mistake in choosing to sit on Marlowe's side of the table, allowing Rick to study us both. He may be a blowhard, but he wasn't stupid.

"Just making conversation, babe." I rankled at his use of the endearment. He said it often, but it had never bothered me until now. I sighed and let it go. Eyes on

Marlowe, he barely noticed my tension. "This is the first family of yours that I've met. I want to get to know him. What do you say, Marlowe? Tell me about yourself."

Marlowe hesitated only a few seconds. I figured he was probably thinking more of how to frame his statement rather than what to say.

"I am a simple man. Indeed, there is not much to tell. I grew up in Canterbury, my father, now passed, was a—" he hesitated, and my foot nudged his again, "craftsman. We were not wealthy. I had an inclination toward the written word, by which, got me into Corpus Christi."

"Texas?" Rick asked.

"Cambridge." His eyes flicked up at Rick, who sat back, finally having nothing to say. I hid a smile behind my glass of Chianti.

Marlowe turned to me for a second before continuing. "After I left school, I made my way in the world, writing, which as you've affirmed, does not afford me wealth. I take the occasional assignment."

"Mostly manual labor—odd jobs, that sort of thing," I supplied. Marlowe nodded in agreement.

"Odd indeed." He smiled at me. That same, slightly crooked smile he had when he introduced himself in the emergency room. I didn't realize I was staring at his mouth, admiring the fullness of his bottom lip until Rick cleared his throat. I looked from one man to the other, not caring in the slightest about Rick's obvious irritation.

The waitress came over to clear plates. Marlowe thanked her in his over-effluent way. The girl lit up like a Christmas tree from his attention, which left a dark place in my gut. Suddenly, I wanted to be away from this place, these people. I told myself it was because I didn't want a creature roaming my city. But there was more to it. I found I admired Marlowe's cool-headedness in a fight, his easiness in a social setting. I didn't want to waste time on the mundane. His longest time in the future was under four days, and we were a full day into that stint.

Rick insisted on paying. I let him. He made more money than I did, and it made him feel better. The waitress lingered at our table, the credit card receipt and tip in her hand.

"You guys have a good night. Come back soon, okay?" Her eyes grazed over Marlowe, who smiled at her appreciatively. "A bunch of us go over to Nero's after shift." She batted her eyes. "You should come. We have a blast."

I leaned over to look at her around Marlowe's shoulder.

"Thanks, but we have an early call in the morning." My voice sounded peeved. It shocked me a little.

"Sure." She sashayed away, both men watching the movement of her ass.

"You could so tap that, man," Rick said. "Do a little of that poet shit and you'd have them flocking to your door."

Marlowe seemed taken with the idea. The words may be strange to him, but the intent was clear.

"Your suggestion is—" He stopped as my elbow jostled his.

"Probably not a great idea," I interrupted. "We need to get back. And we still have to get that, you know, that thing." I watched him carefully. His hazel eyes flickered at me in sudden understanding.

"Thing. Yes, of course. We should do that." Marlowe stood up to let me out of the booth. He put out his hand to shake Rick's, and I felt a tingle of pride that he looked so normal, like he could fit in. The idea hit me that he could belong in this time. We could find him a job. I would help him acclimate; we'd kill the bad guys together. He could write poetry on the side. I caught myself in this fantasy, realizing that in a couple of days, he would disappear.

Every gesture, every courtly manner, the way he stood, even his speech pattern was a startling contrast to every man I'd ever met. But he had a comfortableness about him. He'd learned so much in a short time. His language had changed quickly, dropping the *thees* and *thous* like hot coals. He was smart, capable, and devious enough to blend into any surrounding. Suddenly, I wanted to work on the mechanism that brought him here. Fix it so that he wouldn't have to go back. But I was being selfish. He had an entire life back there, friends, family, maybe even a woman. I stopped myself from thinking on that further, realizing how my jaw tightened and my shoulders tensed. Distracted from the two men's conversation, I picked it up again when we were out on the street.

"Hey, say something poetic. I want to see if that shit really works." Rick's tone was only half-teasing.

"Rick, don't put the guy on the spot, come on." I started to pull Marlowe away. He came with me but stopped after a couple of steps and turned back to Rick. He paused only a few seconds, composing in his head.

"Dark vaults of filth and grime together pass

As I of long-forgotten tryst recall
Another maze, another time, a lass
Whose grateful kiss rewarded efforts all—
Not so this lass, who tried to pay the price
With hearty meal she thinks should well suffice
And yet such meat will not appease my greed—
Another kiss, another time. Another lass I need."

Rick stood open-mouthed and silent until we said our goodbyes. I linked my arm through Marlowe's as we headed toward my car. His poem did two things. It confused the hell out of Rick, blasting the superior smirk off his face, and it caused me to view Marlowe differently. I'd had these moments before—when I'd caught him looking at my legs during our little exchange at the sewer entrance. Moments where I felt like this could be something. Sure, the chemistry between us was pretty clear, but it was more than that. A flicker of feeling that made me happy walking arm in arm down the street. I should have let it be. Let it play out. But I have never been one to leave well enough alone.

"What was that all about?" I asked him as we got to my car. He shrugged as he opened my door.

"He sought to discredit me. To gain your favor, I suspect. I merely spoke my mind—a couplet, hastily composed." He frowned. "Was it poorly stated?"

I regarded him thoughtfully, not as a fellow hostile hunter, or crazy-assed time traveler, but as an artist, a sensitive poet. Every moment showed me a different side of this man.

"Not at all. It was beautiful."

As I pulled out into traffic, he spoke again. "Fortune favors thee in not being betrothed to that fellow. He has a manner which speaks of ill repute."

"Rick's alright," I said. "He's just—"

"A heathen? A braggart? A fool?" Marlowe asked.

"All of the above," I said. "Now where? Back to the maze of darkness?"

My fellow hunter nodded, his face set to the task ahead. Yeah, I could definitely handle having him around longer.

⚲

Four hours later, we arrived back at my apartment, dirty, exhausted, and frustrated. We hadn't seen the strigoi anywhere. After two hours of searching tunnels, we'd managed to assuage our pent-up aggression on a pack of giant rats. Common enough in sewers but these guys were particularly aggressive, not to mention the size of overfed cats, their little beady eyes glowing in the reflection of our flashlights. It was Marlowe who fashioned a torch from his new shirt, soaking it with bourbon from a flask I carried—for medicinal purposes—and wrapping it tightly around a piece of PVC he'd run across. Swiping the flames across the ground in front of us, he'd hacked our way to the surface while I covered our back with a few hastily-aimed bullets.

I shuddered as the rats' dying squeals echoed in my ears.

"Are you well?" He asked for the third time.

"I'm fine." I toed off my boots and padded to the cabinet to pull out the bourbon we'd shared the night before. At this rate, I'd have to make a trip to the liquor store to resupply. "To our successful extermination of the city's rodent problem." He was in my kitchen, cleaning his bloody sword on my newest kitchen towel. I didn't care. He paused to lift his glass to mine. Both our hands were still blood-spattered. In fact, the bottom half of him was covered in rat-guts, blood and sewer grime, but damn, that sword was clean.

"To a well-fought battle."

I shuddered again. "I hate rats."

He smiled.

"What?"

"I find it strange that you have no fear in confronting a demon, but a lowly vermin unnerves thee."

Truth was I'd been scared shitless in the sewer with that demon, but I didn't say that.

"There were lots of the lowly vermin."

He drank from the bourbon glass, his eyes on mine.

"Lots and lots of them," I said. I was tired, but I didn't want to sit on my couch in my filthy clothes. He removed his scabbard and sheathed his sword, hanging the whole works on my coat rack, and shook out his cloak to hang over it.

"Can I try it on?" I asked. After a moment he held it out. I turned away from him as he folded the cloak about me. The garment's hem touched the floor, reminding me again of Marlowe's height. I felt the warmth of his hands on my upper arms as he let go of me. I turned quickly like a little girl with a new dress, feeling the material swirl around me.

"It's lighter than I would have thought."

"It is of a rare material, woven by a master textile craftsman. My friend Albert had the idea of interweaving the conduit into the wool. If you look closely you can see it." He pulled me under the overhead light, holding a portion of cloth up to my face. "See the silver thread, here? This absorbs the blue lightning when I walk the ribbons. It keeps the fire from me—protects me."

His face was close to mine, so close I felt his breath on my cheek as I looked down. He held both my hand and the cloak, running a finger to align with the silver thread—so close I could have moved another inch and kissed that finger. We were caught in that moment, the magical cloak and all its properties forgotten. He crooked the finger under my chin, lifting my face to his. His eyes were gray in the light, intelligent and thoughtful as they studied me. My inner romantic kicked me in the gut and my eyes fluttered closed. I waited to be kissed. Cinderella at midnight—something I hadn't done since I was seventeen.

Nothing happened.

He stepped back, did a half turn and finished the glass of bourbon in one gulp. "For my sake, it was most fortunate that I encountered my knowledgeable friend in only my second or third venture. Prior to the cloak, I'd arrive with clothes in tatters, or burned off in the transition, my eyebrows and hair singed and skin as red as a branding iron."

"So, that's why you don't want to be without the cloak." I cleared my throat, recovering from my foolishness. I hung the long garment on my coat rack.

"Yes. It behooves me to keep close company."

"I'm going to grab a shower." I was thinking the colder the better. I needed to get my head straight. "And put your clothes in the washer. I don't want rat-blood all over my couch." My voice sounded harsh and I chided myself for being irritated. What did I expect? For him to sweep me off my feet to the bedroom? Prince Charming was never in the cards for me. I'd been giving very clear back-off signals since his arrival—given every indication that we were merely compatriots battling a common foe. Could I blame him for not trying for more?

He stood in my living room, a battle-weary warrior from another time with the smile of a twenty-first century playboy. Customs and language aside, he knew exactly what had happened, or rather what didn't happen between us.

When I returned, composed, refreshed, and much cleaner, he'd also cleaned up, probably at my kitchen sink. He'd changed from his torn shirt and bloody jeans to a new T-shirt and sweat pants from the discount store bag. His boots were set aside, and his bare feet were on my coffee table, crossed at the ankle. An open book lay across his lap. He was studying the pages with the intensity of a surgeon.

"I've brewed some tea." Without looking up, he indicated my grandmother's seldom used china teapot on the counter top.

"Find anything?" I asked, pouring myself a cup, lacing it with sugar and milk and trying to decide if I was disappointed or grateful that he was all business once again.

"Aye. There are two kinds of strigoi—a *strigoi mort*, or the undead, and *strigoi vii,* a living perversion of human. Here it says the *vii* are hewn from unhappiness, from the despair of humanity. The *mort* are summoned from the grave by incantation."

"Which one are we dealing with?" I curled myself onto the couch next to him, sipping at the tea—Earl

Grey, of course—hot, strong, and slightly bitter, much like my previous thoughts of him.

"I believe mort. Here." We exchanged book for tea cup, and he read over my shoulder. "From a Romanian folktale, witches were thought to summon the strigoi as weapons against humanity. A strigoi mort so summoned is under the witch's control until he completes his given task and can return to his place of rest. Strigoi mort are often pained by bright light and dwell in darkness, where they can see exceptionally well. They have an adapted sense of smell and can sense human blood from far distances. It is this blood scent that draws them, and they will kill anything in the way of their prey. The summoner puts them to action by scenting them with the intended victim's blood."

"Like a bloodhound. Or search dog," I said.

I was disconcerted by how much his voice affected me. The accent, the deep resonance of his baritone went through me like a November storm front. He read well, considering his ancient language was significantly different. He'd paused once to ask the pronunciation of a word, and explained that the letters I and J were interchangeable in his time, as were U and V. His question had given me time to get myself under some sort of control. Inside, I still felt like a teenage girl, all quivery and giddy.

Marlowe faced me, questioning and it took me a second to realize that he was asking about search dogs. He drank from my tea cup almost absentmindedly as I explained. When he was satisfied with the answer, I reached out to retrieve it, drinking after him. "Any lore on how to get rid of such a creature?"

"They are weakened by light and can be killed by beheading."

"Your specialty." I couldn't help but smile at him.

"But must be weakened first with a weapon drenched in the blood of the one who controls them."

"Great. So, we've not only got to find this bloodhound of death but also its master."

"Quite so." He looked to his own empty cup on the coffee table. I handed him my half-full one and he drank from it again. "It seems that you have a witch capable of summoning this demon from not only the grave but also from another time. Very powerful. Even in my time, the strigoi were thought to have died out. No one had heard of one for years. The last one sighted was in the Carpathian Mountains, in the province of Moldavia."

"Known as Romania today." I stood up, pacing. "Maybe that's our connection. The average Philadelphian wouldn't know a witch's incantation from a cocktail recipe, especially not an ancient Romanian one. But if there is a Romanian community or neighborhood here, that might be a place to start. Find the master, find the dog."

"I will make ready."

I put my hand out to stop him, lingering along his forearm. "Whoa, there. I think we've battled enough evil for tonight. I have a day job, remember? I have to get some sleep. I have work in the morning."

"I have little time here." He sounded frustrated but also as tired as I was.

"We will find him." I stifled a yawn. His hand closed over mine.

"Forgive me. You should rest. I will investigate

further." He turned to the book again.

"Here," I signed him into a search engine on my laptop. "This might be better. Type in the little box, whatever you want to know. Like—" I typed in history of Romanian people in Philadelphia. "See all these headings? Click on each one to read what they have, use your finger on the pad." I took his hand and isolated his forefinger, running it along the mouse pad. "It takes some practice, but I've no doubt you'll master it." I put the laptop on the coffee table. He stood up when I did and took my hand.

"You have my utmost gratitude for helping me with this quest."

"Monster hunting's what I do." I shrugged.

"Adieu, fair Tamberlyn. Sleep be gentle upon your brow this night." He bowed low over my outstretched hand. Just prior to his lips touching it, I withdrew.

"Okay then. Good night."

After leaving my noble knight with his hand out, I was extraordinarily pleased with myself for being oblivious to his charm. Let him toss and turn on my couch, it would take more than a trek through the sewers and a fancy poem to impress this girl.

Except, I was the one who tossed and turned. Replaying the battle with the strigoi, the dinner, Marlowe's eyes as they watched my verbal sparring with Rick. After a couple of hours, I gave up and got out of bed, thinking to help Marlowe with his internet search, or maybe turning on an old movie. I'd found him fast asleep, hunched over on my couch, the cast aside laptop glowing from the coffee table. After stealing a moment to watch him, I'd covered him up with my mother's knitted afghan and went back to bed.

My phone buzzed next to my head. I glanced at it to see a picture of X and his kids on the screen. "Mumpf," I answered.

"Get your ass up, we've got a body. Or three. I'm on my way. Be there in ten."

The phone clicked in my ear. I blinked at my clock—barely 7:00 a.m.

7

Rousing myself, I pulled on some black slacks and boots and a white shirt and walked into the living room. As I threaded my shoulder holster on, I noted the vacant couch. Marlowe was up, standing in my tiny hallway at the washer and dryer. He pulled on some clean jeans. Maybe he'd heard my phone. Hunched over his crotch, he was trying to negotiate that difficult device that we called a zipper. Thankfully, he didn't see me watching him.

"Morning," I said, trying my best not to look at his shirtless torso yet again. The man obviously had no shame being in various stages of undress around me, and for the life of me, I couldn't say this was a bad thing. I didn't bother starting a pot of coffee. X was used to me and would arrive with a to-go cup in hand, for his own self-preservation.

"This clothing seems to be ill-fitting today. How can that be?" He'd managed to zip his pants. However, he stood stiff and unmoving.

"They will stretch as you move. It shrinks a little in the dryer. Try some knee bends." I demonstrated. "My partner will be here soon. I'll be back as soon as I can, and we can—"

"I shall accompany you."

"You can't." Before Marlowe could protest, X had arrived. He had his usual knock, two short raps, a pause, and a third. I opened the door to his smiling face, and I smiled, seeing the coffee in his hand.

"We should never take a day off, Paradiso. As soon as we do, all hell breaks loose. Hello." He stopped at the sight of Marlowe, still shirtless and doing knee bends beside my couch. X turned and looked at me with a smile I could have smacked right off of his face.

"X, this is my cousin, Marlowe. He's visiting from England. Marlowe, this is my partner, Xavier Hernandez."

"Of Spanish descent. *El placer es todo mío conocerte.*" Marlowe rolled the "r's" perfectly off his tongue in a strangely accented Spanish. X looked mildly confused. I only had a vague idea of what Marlowe was saying. It must have been okay because X answered him in Spanish and moved forward to shake his hand.

"Can we let him ride along?" I glanced at Marlowe, who had finally decided he needed more clothes and was headed toward the dryer again. "He'll stay in the car."

X rolled his eyes at me, but Marlowe said something else to him in Spanish and he relented. As we headed to the car, I asked him what Marlowe said.

"He said he would learn a lot about my culture by observing me in my area of expertise. Though, he used the word vocation." X smiled as he said this. "This guy an anthropologist or something?"

"Something like that." I smiled back. "So, what do we have?"

"Three bodies, part of Balfour's gang. Looks like they got hit last night. According to the guys on scene, it's pretty gruesome."

"Where was Balfour?" Gianni Balfour's outfit had been in an ongoing territory war with the Russians for years. When Cynthia Wu's body showed up, Munson and the OCU listed the Russian mafia as prime suspects. It was only X and I who'd originally thought Balfour was responsible.

"According to the surveillance detail, he was home. Same place we've been watching him this whole time. Cruz left some time last night and hasn't been seen since."

"Maybe he's one of our victims." I closed the car door. In the back seat, Marlowe had stored his cloak and sword on the floorboard.

"We'll have to see." X glanced at Marlowe in the rearview. "I'm going to get this whole story later, right?" he asked me. I gave a sigh and sipped my coffee, my eyes on the road.

It took twenty-five minutes to get to the docks. The scene was already blocked off by patrol cars and X pulled out two pairs of latex gloves from his over-stuffed jacket pockets. Marlowe, of course, did not stay in the car. He followed behind us, but he was quiet. The forensics team was already on scene and uniforms were redirecting traffic. They probably assumed he was with us. I could tell he was curious and not squeamish at all, so I told him he could look but not touch. And not to start any unusual conversations. He nodded with a wry expression, his eyes intent on the scene.

X waited at the line until the photographer gave the okay and then he held the tape up for me and Marlowe. We approached the first body—one of Balfour's guys alright, inner circle even, but it wasn't Cruz, Balfour's second in command.

The guy still had his face, but that's about all I could say for him. His rib cage had been ripped open, bones sticking naked out of his flesh, a gaping hole where his heart should have been. Dried blood covered everything—the shredded remnants of his dress shirt, his jacket. He was formerly a well-dressed human. The photographer snapped away as I stood there, his digital camera whirring.

"Get the hands, okay George? I'm guessing there's defensive wounds under that blood."

George stooped to get closer and made a disgusted sound in his throat. "Poor bastards. They may be criminal scum, but this is definitely overkill," George said.

I moved on to the next body. He was on his stomach, one leg awkwardly under him. "You snap this one already?"

George looked over, giving a grunt of assent. Our dead body had been a stocky fellow, close-cropped hair framed a bald spot on the top of his head. He was well-dressed like his co-worker, dark suit and decent shoes. I asked the forensics guy to help me turn him over. We flipped him and saw his chest was also ripped open and the leg that sat so awkwardly under him was loose, detached from his torso, held in place only by his pants leg.

"They must have tortured them first," said the forensics specialist.

Marlowe cleared his throat from a short distance away. When I looked up, he jerked his head to indicate he wanted to speak out of earshot of the cops. We walked several feet away.

"This is not the work of a human," he said. "To disengage a limb from a body takes a huge amount of force. A device, or horses, a blade of some kind, but this was no weapon."

"A strigoi perhaps?" I said quietly. He nodded again, grimly this time.

"Here," I pulled another pair of gloves out of my pocket and we both approached the second victim again. We waited until another tech finished taking samples of blood-spattered gravel.

I nodded at the forensics guy, who was picking up the numbered placards that had identified which body parts went with which. It was a guessing game for the most part.

"Mind if my consultant and I have a closer look?" I asked.

He shrugged. "Coroner will be here in a bit. We'll get more samples during the auto. You know the drill."

I nodded at him and Marlowe and I bent toward the abused torso. The thing about seeing dead bodies on TV is that you don't get the smell. The stench of blood and guts and shit wafted up from this shell of a man. He was stiff from rigor and surprisingly light, having been relieved of one leg and most of his blood. I held my breath as I got closer. Marlowe seemed unaffected. I guess living in the Renaissance will do that for you.

He asked if he could remove some of the clothing. We peeled back what was left of the man's shirt. It was difficult to tell, but Marlowe pointed out the jagged edge of skin torn along the neck. Upon closer inspection, I saw teeth marks. Not the flat squared off indentations of a human bite, but pointed sharp indents, with tears and rips, indicating flesh had been clamped down upon and then torn away. I looked up at Marlowe. His expression was one of anger and some guilt. If we'd had gotten this thing in the sewers the day before, this wouldn't have happened. Or at least, it wouldn't have happened this way. Someone had it out for Balfour and his crew so these guys may have died anyway.

By the time we got to body number three, my friend Ziggy had arrived with the morgue transport. She was my ally in this monster hunting gig and she helped me give plausible explanations for implausible deaths from the supernatural. I introduced her to Marlowe and as he gawked at her nose ring and the streak of florescent green in her dark hair, I explained her job to him.

"Good," he said. "You are familiar with alchemy? Anatomy?"

"I'm familiar with whatever you want me to be familiar with," Ziggy answered his odd questions with a look at me.

"I'll explain later," I mumbled at her as X came up to us.

"None of these guys is Cruz," he said. "So, he either escaped or was on some other job at the time."

"We're thinking Russians for this right?" I asked him. Marlowe and Ziggy had gone off to examine the first two bodies. I'm sure Marlowe was showing her the teeth marks he found. I only hope he maintained those discretion skills he'd talked about. Ziggy may believe in monsters—she's seen enough of them, both the human and non-human variety, but a time-traveling poet was quite a different horse.

"Possibly. It's worth a trip to Krotsky's warehouse, anyway."

"Let me see if Zig can take Marlowe back to the lab with her. It'll be dicey enough with Krotsky."

X nodded and picked his way back to the car, edging his large feet around blood spatter and body parts.

Ziggy's fast, and she and her assistant were zipping up the first body as I got to her. "Zig, I need a favor."

"Don't you always? Does it have something to do with tall, dark, and musketeer over there?"

"Wrong country, but yeah. Can he hang out at the lab with you? I'll come by and get him later. I need to go see about a thing."

"Is he right? This was not some wacked out serial killer, was it?"

"Nope, and he's somewhat of an expert. He may be able to help, but it's on the down low. He's unusual."

I helped her roll the gurney into the large van.

"He's unusually good looking." She side-looked me. "But I'm sure you've noticed that." Ignoring her comment, I peered into the van. "Are you going to have enough room for all three bodies?"

"Sure." Ziggy chomped her way through a fresh stick of gum. I could smell its minty freshness from where I stood. It smelled better than death, I guess.

Marlowe and I transferred his stuff from X's car to Zig's van and I cautioned him against freaking Ziggy out by fully disclosing his identity. He threw me a knowing smile.

"Take care on your journey, Tamberlyn." He turned back toward the mayhem inside the police tape, not at all concerned about being on his own in the twenty-first century. I had a vague sense of worry as X and I drove away.

Gregor Krotsky was one of the less scary guys in the Russian mafia. He was about sixty years old, had lived in Philly for forty years, and reminded me of that koala bear the New Zealand airline used in their ads years ago. Maybe because he had such a cuddly demeanor, he kept some of the surliest looking guys as his assistants.

"Detectives Hernandez and Paradiso." I flashed a badge at two men, both bald with tattoos in Cyrillic swirling from their temples, around their ears, and down their fat necks. They looked unimpressed. X said nothing, but instead of looking grim or imposing, he smiled. His white teeth lit up his wide, brown face. "We'd like to speak with Gregor if we could."

"He's not here."

"Tell him Tam and X are here and need to talk to him."

One guy pulled out his phone. I figured we were getting somewhere. After speaking in Russian, he handed it to me. A slow, sleepy voice came on the line.

"Paradiso, it is pleasure speaking to you."

"Hello, Gregor, it's been a long time."

"Not so long. Why not you visit my place of business, eh? We got specials on granola, all natural."

"Thanks, Gregor, but I'm all good in breakfast foods." Krotsky started out as a sports book operator and loan shark. His business was fronted by a small chain of natural food stores. The business featured natural honeys and homemade muffins. I'd purchased some wares on occasion back when I worked in vice.

Back in the day, my police-detective father spent a considerable amount of time trying to incarcerate Krotsky, to no avail. Gregor was a shrewd koala bear and had expanded the chain stores to include underground dealings in guns and prostitution. These days, he tended to stay off the police radar. "Balfour's crew was hit last night, near the warehouse docks. You know anything about that?"

There was silence on the other end of the phone.

"Gregor?" I watched his guys as I waited for his answer. X moved closer to me, his hands on his ample waist, near his gun. The guys in front of us looked nervous—and nervous was not a good look for them. My injured arm started to throb. I switched the phone to my other hand.

"I'm sorry to hear this. You know me, Paradiso. I'm good guy, peaceful guy, good business man."

"So, you don't know anything about three guys, guts all over the place? All three were killed in the same way?"

"Was heart there?"

"What?" I couldn't believe Gregor had been in this country for forty years and still talked with an accent like a Russian winter. I figured he did it to irritate me.

"Was heart there? In the bodies, do they have hearts or no?"

"No. How did you know that?"

Another long pause. "You come see me. I tell you. 1127 Firth Street, downtown." The phone clicked off and

I handed it back to Gregor's man.

I filled in X on the way to Gregor's location.

"So, we were right. This is a territory war," he said as he drove.

"And Gregor was so anxious to own up to his part in three murders? I don't think so. He sounded scared, X. Something's going on." I had that feeling in the pit of my stomach that I get whenever I have to skirt around a monster sighting with X. I told myself I was trying to keep him safe. That the less he knew about this, the better for him. But I hated lying to him.

"Rick come by yesterday?" X asked. "He mentioned he would. He was excited over his big win."

"Yeah, he came by," I said.

"And?"

"And what? You want details? We had dinner. All of us, Marlowe, me, Rick—it was fine."

"He bought the cousin Marlowe story? I always knew he wasn't that bright." X chuckled. True, there was no love lost between my partner and my non-boyfriend. When Rick prosecuted our first big case, he spent a fair amount of time deposing me as a witness. At first, I thought it was because of the publicity the case had generated. Turned out it was a little more than that.

It was his competitive nature that first attracted me—that courtroom swagger. Rick Davenport was smart-alecky smart and had a way of looking at me that I hadn't experienced in a long time. While I'd never been the sort of girl who needed pretty words to make her feel desirable, they were nice to hear once in a while.

X, it seemed, had a sense of duty when it came to his partner/surrogate sister. Even though I'd stressed the fact that Rick and I were very casual, emphasis on *very*, X still thought I could do better and often said so.

"Even if he didn't buy it, it shouldn't matter," I continued. "It's not like we're serious or anything."

X ignored my comment. "Marlowe seems interesting."

"You don't know the half of it."

"You gonna tell me?"

"Sometime, maybe." I pulled out my phone and texted Ziggy, mostly to avoid talking to X any more. I loved the big guy, but when we got into my other life, I had to start censoring myself and he always seemed to know I was hedging. I asked Ziggy how Marlowe was doing and got a text back right away.

He's all suited up. This guy can handle a bone saw like nobody's business.

Okay, then. I thumbed my phone off and shoved it in my pocket.

X parked on the street and we walked down to number 1127. It was a dialysis center. Gregor was kicked back in a vinyl chair, blood pumping in and out of his arm through a shunt.

"How long has this been going on, Gregor?" I indicated the machine whirring away next to him.

"A few months. You want to donate kidney, detective?" He nodded at X, who stood some feet away looking horrified. The guy didn't take a second look at dead bodies, but apparently, dialysis freaked him out. I looked back at X.

"Why don't you get some air? You don't look so good." He started to protest, but then turned and headed toward the door. This was good. If this had something to do with the strigoi, I wanted to hear Gregor's story alone.

"What do you know, Gregor? About the hearts missing in my dead bodies."

"My cousin, Ilya. He went missing two nights ago. We found him last night."

"Rib cage busted open, heart missing?"

Gregor's eyes closed in pain. For a mob boss, he was a sensitive sort. Like I said, a koala bear.

"Yes. You know what animal does this to a man?"

I had a hunch but wasn't at liberty to say. "I'm not sure, but we'll find it. Why didn't you call us?"

"I thought it was internal problem. I fix."

"Internal problem? Like Balfour? And your guys didn't retaliate?"

"I swear. Was not me. Not my guys. Ilya was good guy, not too smart, but good. You find out who did this, you bring him to me."

"You've already cleaned up the crime scene, Gregor. Where's the body now?"

"We had funeral. Nice music, prayers. He's at peace now."

"This isn't the old country. When someone gets murdered, there's an investigation."

The old man shrugged. "Cops. Cops do nothing." He looked at me. "No offense, Paradiso."

"Tell me where you last saw Ilya alive, and then exactly where his body was found."

Gregor found some paper and drew me a crude map. Poor Ilya had been working near Platte Street—near our sewer hunting ground from the day before. The body count was climbing fast.

I folded the map into my jacket pocket. "Thanks, and I'm sorry about your cousin."

Gregor seemed morose. "He wasn't just cousin. He was going to donate his kidney. My kidney."

I murmured another condolence and got myself out of there. X met me at the door where we could both hear strains of Gregor's lament over and over again. *My kidney. My kidney.*

In the car, I relayed the story of the ill-fortuned Ilya, and we decided it was time to pay our surveillance target a visit. Gianni Balfour was the antithesis of Gregor. He was young and cocky, and when it came to criminals, I'd take old and experienced over young and cocky any day. My mother always said youth was wasted on the young. I tried not to make her right so much in my case, but she certainly was in Gianni's. A good-looking guy with slicked back hair, I was sure he envisioned himself as a character out of *West Side Story,* just a good guy from the wrong side of the tracks.

I'd much prefer sitting in the surveillance van, monitoring him from a safe distance, but sometimes a face-to-face was necessary. Three dead bodies, known to be employees of Balfour's, required a visit. His security guy was as big as my partner and they sized each other up like pit bulls. X's attitude with this guy was the complete opposite of what it was with Gregor's men.

"So, before the growling and circling begins, can you show us up to Balfour's office?" I craned my neck to look up at the guy. Turning to the corner of the foyer, I spied a tiny red light from a hidden security camera. "Tell him it's about three of his crew being dead."

"Yes," X boomed out from behind me. "We're here

to help."

The security guy led us to the elevator and pushing the correct button, he indicated we should enter without him. He watched us as the doors closed. I stared at our reflection in the steel doors.

"We're here to help? Seriously?" I asked him.

I felt X's shrug more than saw it. The doors opened and we were met by another pit bull, this one shorter and stockier with a hairstyle identical to Gianni's. He checked our IDs and badge numbers and led us to a plush furnished office. An empty office. I started to get nervous after five minutes of pacing, but finally, I heard a voice coming from another room, beyond a closed door. There was the sound of a toilet flushing and water running in the sink. X smirked at me. The door opened, and out walked Gianni Balfour, a cell phone tucked under his chin.

"I said Friday, not Thursday, not Monday. Friday. Don't make me say it again." And then, upon seeing us, he said it again. "Friday." He hung up and gave us a slimy smile. "If it isn't Philly's finest." Through the window, the sunlight reflected off large gold rings on his slim fingers.

Last time I saw Gianni Balfour this close was two years before, as he was holding court with three Asian girls in a corner booth of his nightclub. His hair was longer, a thin cigar dangling from his wide mouth.

My mind immediately flashed back to that time I worked in the vice unit, and my former partner, Ava Knox, had taken the lead on questioning Balfour. It gave me a chance to observe. You can learn a lot by paying attention.

As he had listened to my partner's spiel, Balfour's rings glittered with overstated opulence as he flicked his cigar ash into the salad plate of the girl next to him. She had taken a bite of the wilted, over-dressed Romaine and her eyes met mine as the ashes fell. She didn't protest but put the fork down and pushed the plate away. Prettiest of the three, her jet-black hair was cut on the bias and highlighted with fake red tips. She also seemed the soberest, and her look at me was one of wry amusement—as though the two of us were in the same boat, both women trying to survive in a male-dominated society. As far as gender bias goes, there's not much difference between cops and crime bosses. Years later, I'd made detective and some progress with my male counterparts. The girl had ended up on a slab in the morgue.

The rings on his fingers flashed again in front of me. "It's nice to see you again. Detective Paradiso, is it?" Balfour leaned his butt against the front of his desk, crossing his Armani-clad legs in front of him. I clenched my fists, the motion pulling at the stitches in my arm.

"Yes. Wish I could say the same. I'm assuming you're aware of the bodies we found by the warehouse docks? Your employees." I'm not tall and I felt petite next to Marlowe, and miniscule next to X, but I was almost eye to eye with this guy.

I straightened up, leaned in, and waited.

"Yes, we are very sad. My employees are like family," Balfour said. His eyes flickered into a squint.

"Any problems in the family that would cause something like this?"

He gave a sardonic laugh. "You're knocking on the

wrong door if you think this was internal. My guys may have minor squabbles, but I value loyalty most of all. I have many enemies, Detective. You should be looking at them."

"We're looking at all angles on this one," X said. "Where's Cruz? We haven't seen him in a while."

"Do you miss him?" Gianni showed a row of perfect, white teeth. The same smile he'd used in the nightclub. "He's on a job for me."

"We'd like to talk to him," I said. "You know, to cover the angles. Do you know where he was last night?"

"Do you?" Balfour asked. It was a nod to our known surveillance of his house and offices.

"No, actually. Our guys lost him around midnight." X changed tactics. Sometimes, blatant honesty worked.

Balfour laughed. "I like you guys, so I'll tell you. Enrique has a sick grandmother and was helping her last night, I believe. He's a dedicated family man." His grin smacked of spoiled over-confidence. "As I am."

"Speaking of that," I said. "Condolences on the passing of your lady friend."

"Sin," he said, and his eyes flickered again. My brain clocked the pattern, trying to discern his mood. If he felt guilty, I couldn't tell.

"Short for Cynthia?" I asked. My mind went to where I'd seen her last. On a table in Ziggy's lab.

Where my realm was full of nightmares, blood, gore, and evil—human and non-human alike—Ziggy's world was sterile. A clean room of sparkling white ceramic tile circling drains in strategic alignment, stainless steel counters, and white enameled equipment. Ziggy's realm held more than its share of blood and gore, but it was the blood of the vanquished and the gore of the victims.

I remembered Ziggy's call in the early morning hours after Cynthia Wu's body had been found. X and I had been at the diner, eating breakfast before our shift.

"I've been here since 4:00 a.m.," Ziggy said tiredly as she pulled back the sheet revealing the girl's body. "Anonymous tip called it in. A dumpster on the east side of town. They're still working the scene, but this was pretty cut and dry. Multiple contusions, some defensive wounds. Blunt force trauma's what killed her. A blow to the back of the head sometime late last night."

The girl's face was bruised, but I recognized the blood red tips of dark hair from the salad girl two years before.

I can still remember the sound of X's sigh when I told him that Cynthia Wu was our victim. It was the sound of someone well acquainted with death. X had probably seen more than his share, and though he never worried about himself, he worried about his kids, his wife, and of course, his partner.

X had come with me to her funeral. We'd stood in the bright sunshine along with her father, who spoke no English. Balfour hadn't shown. In fact, he'd seemed to have some emergency trip to the Cayman Islands that week. He'd left his second in command, Cruz, to pay his respects for him. Cruz had lurked in the background among the tall headstones and mausoleums and had the good manners to look mournful.

More mournful than her boyfriend who stood in front of me now, with his toothy smile and slick hair. Life without parole would be too good for this scumbag.

8

Our offices for District 27 were in the old courthouse building. From the outside, it was beautiful—gray marble façade, slightly dingy with city grime, the top of its three stories had decorative eaves like all those classic Jeffersonian buildings. Wide steps and a portico introduced the main entrance, but the majority of us came in from the underground parking lot, or the lot next door.

On the inside, it was drafty, the floors were uneven, so every desk was propped with wads of paper in one corner or another, and the windows leaked when it rained, as it was now.

X headed to the tiny alcove we called a breakroom, presumably to see if there were any doughnuts left. The homicide division was housed in one big room with low walled partitions surrounding each team's work space. At one end of the room, there was a conference room and the captain's office, which I tended to avoid.

Our cubicle was not too far from the breakroom and

I heard X talking to the other Balfour surveillance team, more or less giving them shit about what happened on their watch. After checking my email, I headed to the forensics lab, which appropriately, was in the basement. I walked through the double doors to a much brighter, cleaner space than my own.

I saw Ziggy right away, talking to one of her co-workers. Both were dressed in blue long-sleeved smocks and rubber gloves, their heads bent over a naked, mangled body. I recognized Ziggy because of her black velvet boots under the smock. My nose wrinkled at the antiseptic smell. No matter how many times I came down here, I couldn't get used to it.

"Hey Zig," I called out softly behind her, not wanting to startle anyone in case they're slicing and dicing. No one moved. Then I noticed the earbud cords, one ending in Ziggy's ear, the other in her assistant's. I hailed them again, a bit louder this time and they both turned.

I was surprised to see that Zig's assistant was Marlowe, wearing what resembled a clear welding mask over his face. He pulled the earbud from his ear, smiling at me. His hair was restrained from the strap holding the plastic shield over his face.

"Tamberlyn! This is most fascinating. Mistress Jane has been showing me the wonders of the human body."

"I bet she has." I put on a smile, mostly at his unintended entendre. Ziggy moved around to the counter and grabbed a metal dish. "Jane?" I looked at her. I'd known Zigfield for two years and had no idea what her first name was. Any question toward it was met with, "Call me Ziggy." Yet Marlowe, who'd been here all of four hours knew her as Mistress Jane. It wasn't like

I really needed to know, she called me by my last name half the time, but their familiarity bothered me.

"Marlowe's observing. But he has a great eye. Look what we've found."

She thrust the dish under my nose. Inside was a tiny white object, pointed at one end, a quarter of an inch in diameter. The blood and guts had been washed away. I hesitated to look closer. Ziggy has been known to show me everything from burst appendixes to stomach contents.

"It's a fang," Marlowe said.

"A fang," I repeated dumbly. Marlowe took the dish from me.

"Yes, and only the tip," Ziggy answered. "Apparently, our perp hit the pelvic bone during his meal and broke a tooth off. I'm sending shavings to an anthropologist at Carnegie Mellon to be analyzed."

"Did you really let him work the bone saw?" I asked her when Marlowe turned away. She smiled and shook her head.

"Not really, but with three bodies and the coroner in court, I'm backed up. I still document the evidence, but he's been a help." She seemed inordinately pleased. Zig had a medical degree, but no interest in the political post of county coroner. She liked the night shift in forensics and was good at it. Her usual manner was much more solid and even morose at times, punctuated with her macabre sense of dry humor. Today, she was animated and almost giddy. My eyes slid over to the reason for this sparkly demeanor. Marlowe had a magnifying glass and was peering at the fang in the petri dish.

"Oh," she spoke up again. "I found something

else. On the Wu case." She moved to fetch her tablet and brought up a file on the device. I looked over her shoulder at a series of pictures. Cynthia Wu had been a pretty girl before she was killed. "Right here," Ziggy pointed to a small bruise under a chin. "I thought it looked irregular, so I magnified it. The impression looks like a bird's wing."

"An imprint from a ring?"

She nodded, looking pleased. Putting the tablet aside, she turned back toward Marlowe. "He's really great," she said. Apparently, there was nothing better than having a mysterious new assistant and rocking out to the same music while cutting up dead bodies. I figured I should leave them to it. I should have turned around and gone back upstairs. But I had a job to do.

"Find any kidneys?" I asked, explaining to both about Gregor's story, as well as our visit to Balfour.

"Moldavian ancestors?" Marlowe asked. Ziggy watched him. He must have told her all about our search for a Romanian summoning-spell caster. I had an urge to kick him under the table. Had he told her everything? Did she know who he really was?

Zig launched into an explanation of their previous conversation. Marlowe filled in the gaps like he'd been born to it. My jaw was clenched so tightly it hurt.

"I have paperwork to do." I didn't realize how abrupt this sounded until they both stopped talking and looked at me. "Give me a buzz when you're finished." I turned away.

"Tamberlyn, is there something afoot?" Prior to this, his speech had been spot-on twenty-first century. I stopped to look at him. He'd removed the plastic shield helmet and his hair was wild around his head. My fingers itched to smooth it down for him. Tempted to apologize, I knew I was being silly and unprofessional. And then Ziggy reached her ungloved hand toward him, brushing away a lock that had fallen across his forehead.

"Nothing afoot. Nor an elbow or a knee, unless you count the four dead bodies this thing has racked up so far. But you go ahead, plug in your earbuds and continue on. I'm sure you'll solve the case from here." I stomped out the door before he could say anything.

"What's got you in a snit?" X asked as I slammed the phone down for the second time. Our scarred metal desks faced each other, our respective monitors on opposite sides, leaving a clear space in the middle for a shared inbox and conversation.

"Nothing."

"Come on, spill. It's got something to do with your houseguest, I bet."

"He can be kind of irritating, that's all. And we have a really big case here. I'm busy. I don't have time to drag him around all over town." I picked up the phone again.

We were running a list of addresses of people in the warehouse docks area, hoping someone had seen something. Hard to believe three men were killed that brutally without any witnesses. Most of my calls had been to small businesses, and it was rather pointless, especially since I knew what caused the men's deaths, but it was the job. And a certain amount of cover activity has to be done.

I was also working off another list—known associates and enemies of Gianni Balfour, cross-referencing them with any kind of Romanian-sounding name. Part of my other job, but today I was irritated that it wasn't my mission, not really. It was Marlowe's mission and he should be working it, damn it. I'd overreacted to the scene in the lab, and I knew it. Ziggy was Ziggy, she got so into her work, it was infectious, and logically, I could understand why a guy from the sixteenth century would be fascinated. And even if there was something brewing between them, why should I care? It's not like we were... anything really. I snatched up the phone up again and punched in the numbers.

X couldn't see my computer, but he could see my expression as I talked to yet another bored receptionist. When I hung up and crossed another business off the list, he tossed a chocolate kiss across the desks.

"You could use some sweetening up," he said.

I frowned at him but grabbed the candy. "I'm so fucking sweet, I melt in the rain." I popped the unwrapped kiss in my mouth.

"You're so sweet, people sprinkle you on cereal."

I shook my head at him, smiling now. "I'm so sweet, there's a Disney ride named after me."

"The Raging Paradiso," X replied. "So sweet, the sappy romance guy will write a book about your life."

"The Raging Paradiso. I like it." I smiled at my partner.

"Feel better?"

I nodded and ate another chocolate kiss.

"So, how long is he here for?" X asked.

"Who?"

X just looked at me. He knew me too well.

"Not sure, couple days, maybe. He has a job to finish before he can leave. Which I don't know how he's going to do, fooling around in Ziggy's lab all day."

"You're the one that sent him off with her."

"I know." I held my hand out for another piece of candy. X opened his bottom drawer and fished around, throwing a few pieces my way.

"Thought you were sweet enough," he said.

"Apparently not. Did Ziggy show you the picture of the bruise on Cynthia Wu? Looks like an imprint from a ring, a bird of some kind."

He nodded. "I've pulled up a database of school rings, but there's not much there to match it to."

"Detective?" I turned to see Jenny, our one civilian admin peek around the partition. Behind her was Marlowe, in his regular clothes, his cape-wrapped sword under one arm. "This gentleman is here to see you."

"Okay, thanks." I nodded at Jenny and squinted angrily at Marlowe. He ignored me for the moment and gave her a gentle tip of his head.

"Thank you, dear lady, for your most able assistance." Jenny, who was used to working with our crude bunch day after day, blushed as she walked away.

"Careful," I told Marlowe, "you'll be giving her the vapors."

X hauled a chair over and Marlowe thanked him as he sat down close to me.

"We must make a plan of action," Marlowe said quietly.

"That's what I'm trying to do." I showed him the list I've been working from. The list that so far, had produced very little. After a glance at us, X got back to his phone calls. I made a few more calls as Marlowe searched through a list of names.

"None of these surnames have—" he glanced at X, "the quality we're looking for."

"I know, but they could be related by a female, who wouldn't continue the name. Not usually anyway."

Marlowe frowned at me. "Not usually?"

I felt heat rise in my face. "My name, Paradiso, is from my grandmother. She was unmarried when she had Dad and so passed on her maiden name."

He nodded, pursing his lips. "It's known to happen in my...country, as well." He reached out and picked up one of the silver wrapped candies on my desk.

"Have a kiss," X said, and Marlowe dropped the candy, confusion flitting across his face.

I picked it up. "A chocolate kiss," I said, putting it in his hand. "Unwrap and eat." This last bit was said under my breath. Marlowe did as instructed, his face lighting up as he tasted the chocolate on his tongue.

"These are most delightful." He turned to X, thanking him in Spanish. At least, I think there was a "*gracias*" in the litany of words he rattled off.

"Where did you learn your Spanish? Your dialect is really unusual," X asked.

"I have a friend from Spain, Lord Luis Cristobal de Castille. We've traveled much together; his English is poor and so we converse in his language. He is a descendant of Katherine of Aragon. You've heard of this queen?"

X nodded. "Sure, I've watched *The Tudors*."

Marlowe smiled at this. "As well do I, but mostly from afar. I find it much safer that way. Could I beg of you for another kiss?" he asked. He'd asked this of X, but his eyes shifted to mine at the last second. X chuckled and plopped a handful onto my desk. Marlowe unwrapped one and beamed at me like a child. He chewed thoughtfully. "Another kiss, another time. Another sweet indeed." His eyebrows raised.

I closed my computer screen trying to ignore him. The word "incorrigible" came to mind as I felt a smile twitching at my lips.

I glanced over to see X watching both of us. "Are we on tonight?" I asked him. "I might have a unit run Marlowe and I home for a bit. Then meet you."

X leaned back in his chair, scratching his belly.

"The other team has it till eight. I'll see you after that."

Marlowe and X conversed a bit more in Spanish as I headed into the hallway. Ziggy, changed from her blue smock into street clothes, hailed me from the stairwell. She ran to catch up with me.

"Hey, I've found some stuff for you." She thrust a sticky note into my hand. "I've called these guys. They have two floodlights and a smaller spot, all battery operated."

I blinked at her.

"Didn't he tell you? We had an idea of how to catch this thing."

Marlowe strode through the double doors to greet her. "Miss Jane." He smiled so brightly it set my teeth on edge.

"I'm headed out. Got a body on Belmont." Ziggy said. At my raised eyebrows, she clarified. "They're listing it as suicide, so rest easy."

"Can you drop us at my place?"

As Ziggy drove us in the morgue van to my apartment,

she shared their grand plan of action. It wasn't bad, I had to admit. I wasn't sure how I felt about leaving Marlowe alone in the tunnels waiting on a super vampire while I went on my surveillance of Balfour, but I wasn't about to let Ziggy go with him. The van pulled up in front of my place.

"You kids be careful, you hear?" she said. Marlowe reached up front between the seats and brought her hand to his lips.

"It was a pleasure making your acquaintance, Mistress Jane. Thank you for allowing me to witness your brilliant techniques."

"Thanks for the ride, Zig," I said a bit too brusquely. I shook my head as I got out of the van. What was wrong with me?

"Tamberlyn? Are you vexed with me?"

Ignoring Marlowe's words behind me, I headed into the dark apartment. My arm needed to be rewrapped. I'd neglected it that morning in my hurry to leave, and the pain was ramping up. I told myself it was the pain that was making me grumpy.

At Marlowe's innocent look, I snapped. "Really? 'Mistress Jane?' You move pretty fast for an old-fashioned guy. Did you tell her the whole story? Of your blue lightning? I'm surprised the two of you aren't stalking dead bodies and sewers together." As soon as I'd said it, I realized it sounded silly, but it was out there, and I couldn't take it back. Marlowe's face changed from innocence to mirth.

"Art thou jealous?" He smiled.

"Don't even." I held up my hand to stop him from laughing at me, which he looked clearly about to do.

I stomped into the bedroom and changed into jeans and the old boots I'd worn in the sewers. I grabbed the gauze and tape and headed to the kitchen, where I found Marlowe opening and closing the refrigerator door.

"Are you hungry?" I asked. My voice had found its normal cadence and calm. Neither of us spoke of my previous outburst.

"Does this light stay on when you close the door?" He inched it closed while trying to peer into the cold space. I laughed.

"It's an age-old question, my friend, kind of like the tree falling in the forest."

He turned to me with a slight frown.

"You jest."

I handed him the roll of gauze.

"A little bit, yeah. Do you mind? My arm hurts. Remind me to take an ibuprofen before we leave."

He pulled me to the counter where the light was better. When he unwrapped the wound, he hissed slightly, and his normally gentle touch sent hot iron pains through my arm.

"'Tis pustulant. We must remedy this and quickly."

"No wonder it hurts." I turned my arm to look at the long gash, neatly sewn with stitches along the backside of the forearm. The upper half was good, healing well, but toward the elbow, where the wound deepened, the skin was pink and puffy, hot to the touch.

Marlowe went to his cape and sifted through the folds. He came back with a tiny round pouch tied with a drawstring and a long leather kit about the size of a glasses case.

"I need light and you should sit." He pulled me over

to the couch and adjusted the reading lamp over my arm. "Do not fret. I have seen this before."

"Me too. It's infected. I should go to the hospital. They obviously missed some ghoul grime."

"I watched the healer sew the wound. He was very thorough. But ghouls are filthy creatures."

"Yeah, almost as bad as rats." I smiled at him. He smiled back, but only a little. He was clearly worried about me. He'd left me to put a tea kettle on the stove, turning the gas on and jumping slightly when the flame came up.

"Wondrous device," he muttered.

I tried to reassure him. "Look, we can stop by the emergency room. They'll give me a shot of penicillin— knock this stuff right out." His look was incredulous. I supposed when you're from a world where an infection from a tiny cut could kill a person, a wound like mine would be considered deadly. We really take the progress of the modern world for granted.

He'd been working while we talked and came back to the couch with a towel, a cup of boiling water, and my bottle of Maker's Mark. He poured me a glass.

"Drink this, it will help." His hands were freshly scrubbed and looked cleaner than I'd ever seen them.

I drank. "You're really starting to scare me now."

He sat on the coffee table in front of me and unrolled his kit. Nestled inside the leather, were glinting silver instruments. They resembled a tiny set of silverware— two knives, blades as thin as scalpels, a three-tined fork and a spoon the size of a pea. He put the cutlery into the glass of bourbon next to him.

"Ready?" he asked gripping my injured arm in one

hand and holding the tiny knife in the other.

"No," I said. He stopped.

"Dost thou trust me?"

I nodded and he placed the blade against the lower half of my stitches. With one decisive cut, he sliced through the stitches and the skin parted. Blood and pus ran from the wound. I tried not to cry out and failed. The pain seared up my arm and straight into my eyes, filling them with tears. I squeezed them shut. Marlowe's voice was low and soothing as he worked.

"This is not so bad. I've seen much worse."

He worked quickly, but I couldn't look at what he was doing. I could barely keep my eyes open through the pain.

"Tell me," I said through gritted teeth, hoping to get my mind off the procedure. "About the worse thing you've seen."

He thought for a moment. "My second time to this fair city. A great battle between your people had been won by the North near a town called Gettysburg. I was here to extinguish a demon who preyed upon hatred and fear. War was his perfect hunting ground—a war between brothers even more so.

"With the battle won, there were still many wounded, and some of them had come home. They were housed in a great hospital some distance from the city. I tracked the demon from the battlefield to this place and when I arrived, I was befriended by a healer, Elliot Beard, and his sister, Mary. Mary Beard was one of the few laypersons who helped nurse the wounded. Most of the nurses were nuns—Daughters of Charity.

"The demon had followed many of the wounded men

to Philadelphia, where he could feed on the pain and despair. Men had lost limbs in horrific ways, and eyes, ears, one a nose, sliced completely off with a bayonet—some of those we could save, if the green vile didn't set in. The physicians and nurses worked tirelessly to aid the sick and wounded and I, as an able-bodied man, was put to work transporting the wounded to and from the surgery. It was a time of violence and desperation that mirrored some of my own timeline."

He paused and I watched his face. His broad forehead was crinkled in concentration as he cleaned my wound. His dark brows were slightly too thick to be perfect, yet they accented his eyes beautifully. Eyes that I finally decided were hazel. I watched his tongue touch his bottom lip as he remembered his story.

"By the second day of my time here, I had defeated the demon. A Latin spell and some blood work vanquished him back to hell. But I stayed in this timeline through some miracle and learned much working alongside Elliot and Mary to help the wounded. Elliot was very skilled, but his demeanor was stern and unfeeling. Mary was his perfect foil, kind and gentle. She soothed the psyche as much as the man."

I watched his face as he told the story. He was intent on his hands, but at the mention of Mary, his forehead smoothed out and there were tiny lines around his eyes as he smiled at the memory. I remembered then, how young he was, four years my junior. His manner and experience made him seem older, and perhaps, in his time, a man of twenty-three was practically middle-aged.

"Her eyes were lovely and dark like yours." He

glanced at my face for a moment. "But she was fairer, her hair a russet color, like autumn."

"My mom was a redhead," I said. "I get my coloring from Dad." I don't know why I said that. I must have been delirious. "You were in love with her—Mary."

He nodded once, and his lips pressed into a line. He reached back for more gauze, soaked in the boiling water. I had a vague impression of heat against my arm. It felt better.

"You might think me frivolous, finding love in the darkness of war and savagery, but Mary was an extraordinary woman. We worked long days, and at night, we'd retire to the house she shared with her brother. They'd taken me in, much as you have. As skilled a physician as Elliot was, he was just as unskilled at cards. Nevertheless, he loved a game and would often leave after sup, playing well into the night. Mary and I became—"

"Lovers?"

He nodded once again, sharply this time. "There was no hope for it. I should have kenned this well. I'd been traveling for some time and knew that I would not stay, even as I prayed I would. I could have lived out my life there, with her." I felt his fingers pinch the flesh together on my arm, the pierce and tug of stitches being sewn. It should have been more painful than it was. "Alas, that is not my providence."

"How long were you there?"

He shrugged. "Not long. Heretofore, that was my longest journey, almost five days. On the last day, when I could feel the pain in my head and eyes, I knew that staying was futile, our time together short. I attempted to explain to my love why I could not stay." He sat back, adjusting the light, looking at his work. His eyes were sad and beautiful. "While she was worldly in the ways of war and politics, she was naïve about love. She did not have your modern open-mindedness. At first, she thought me irrational, full of hysteria, perhaps brought on by the horrors of what we had seen. Later, she thought I was merely making excuses to leave her and not wishing to marry. I heard her voice these concerns to Elliot, but he had come from gaming and was far more distraught by his losses than anything his sister told him. It was during this overheard conversation that I felt the pains of my impending travel and knew I had only a few moments. I penned Mary a letter, in which I professed my love and sorrow and that I must return home before I caused even more pain. I apologized for my earlier hysteria, and prayed she'd forgive my lapse of mental stability."

"You let her think you were crazy?"

"It was far better to think it was I who was deranged than herself, which, if she had spoken of my tale to others, she would have been thought ill."

He used the little spoon to dip into the cup of hot water, which was now brown as coffee.

"What is that?" I asked as he spooned the liquid over my fresh stitches. He held up the round pouch, now open.

"Healing herbs, a mixture from Master Gomfrey. I've used some on the wound prior to closure, it will fight the green vile, what do you call it? Infection?"

I nodded. "It smells awful."

He smiled. "Good. It is doing what it ought."

He placed a bandage over the stitched area and

wrapped my arm in gauze.

"Thanks. And look, I'm sorry about earlier, with Ziggy. I was being stupid."

He gathered his equipment and went to the sink, using as much care for these instruments of healing as he did for his instrument of death. "I fear I've caused some animosity between two friends."

"Did you tell her? Who you really are that is?"

He turned to me, retying the leather strap on his kit. "Mistress Jane is a competent female, but I could not burden her with this truth. There are few I trust with such knowledge, my life and theirs may depend upon discretion."

"You told me right away."

"Indeed, I did." His eyes took on a warmer aspect— still beautiful, but the sadness was gone.

Less than an hour later, we were both quiet during our travel to the Platte Street sewer entrance. I had thought of him as a reveler. Someone with a serious thrill addiction, loving the hunt, living on the edge, adapting well to any surrounding or circumstance. With his story about Mary, I realized that Marlowe had embraced this life of a monster hunter, but it wasn't what he wanted. I could relate.

I couldn't help but think that if he had stayed back in 1863 with Mary, his life may have been longer, even in a time and country ravaged by war.

"What year is it again? Where you come from?"

He looked out the car window. It was still pouring outside. "The year of our Lord, 1587, why do you ask?"

"No reason, just curious."

Soon after Marlowe's arrival—and his subsequent insistence about not knowing anything about his history, or for him, his future—I investigated on my own. If Christopher Marlowe returned to his own time, he'd be dead in less than six years. I watched this man, as skilled with a scalpel as he was with a sword, who was currently playing with the automatic windows in my car. I knew that it was not a matter of *if* he returns, but when, and more than likely, he had less than seventy-two hours left in this time. And on to certain death in a few short years. Everyone dies, it's the circle of life and all that. But to die suddenly, violently, and so young was awful— for everyone. When that person had such potential to impact the world like Marlowe did, it was tragic.

"What vexes thee, Tamberlyn? Are you in pain?" He stopped playing with the windows and reached for my injured arm, his warm fingers clasping around my wrist and sliding down to close around my hand. I didn't move away.

"No, the arm is fine." I drove with my left hand, reluctant to have him let go of me. "I was thinking that I'm going to miss you, dude. When you return home." At his look, I felt suddenly exposed and heat rushed to my face. I pulled my hand away, focused on the road. "I mean, it's cool having someone to do this stuff with, you know? I have Ziggy, who gets it, but she's not in the field. It's nice when someone has your six."

He hesitated for a moment. Out of the corner of my eyes, I could see his perfect smile. "I will miss you as well. Except not thy confounding manner of speech. Pray tell, what is a dude? And why would I want your six? It seems a sexual metaphor."

I laughed. "No, it's not. Dude is a euphemism, a casual terminology for male friends—very casual and used usually by young people. Six is a military term." I paused to parallel park on the street, which takes a certain amount of concentration during peak traffic hours. Putting the gear shift into park, I continued. "When at war, soldiers use the face of a clock to determine position." I indicated with my hands. "You face twelve o'clock, three, six, nine, etcetera. When someone has your six, it means they are your backup and keep the enemy from approaching from behind. Get it?"

We were out of the car and he grabbed the bag from the trunk. A few moments of silence went by and we'd reached the entrance to the sewer before he responded.

"Yes," he said, and together we lifted the grate. "But I think it's much better suited to a sexual metaphor." He grinned at me. "Shall we?" Laughing, I eased my way down the ladder. He lowered the bag of equipment to me and then followed. Only Marlowe could make vampire hunting in a sewer a recreational activity I would look forward to. As he dropped beside me and picked up the duffel bag of our equipment, I racked my brain, trying to figure a way to keep him here. Alive. And with me.

9

Time could not move fast enough for me. Einstein was right, it was all relative. When I was with Marlowe, I wanted to stop time, to slow things down, and have him stay longer. Elsewhere, without him, time crawled like a stakeout in the desert.

I'd left Marlowe underground at the corner of Rat-infested and Grime, armed with a sword, a hunter's knife, and an extra set of batteries. I kept telling myself he'd be fine. After all, he'd faced worse many times and came through them alive and kicking. But then the devil's advocate lounging on my other shoulder said that a *Strigoi Mort* was a super strong vampire with lightning reflexes and a penchant for blood. And did I mention, impervious to bullets? Not that Marlowe had a gun, but I made a mental note to take him to the shooting range. He'd get a kick out of that.

We'd set up the two large floodlights at the nearest exit points to Platt Street hoping to keep the strigoi contained and underground. The other way out was our entryway, which is where Marlowe set up a watch post.

Meanwhile, I sat in a car outside a nightclub where Balfour was hosting a party. Of course. What else would a sleazebag do after three of his men were gruesomely murdered? Not to mention the loss of his girlfriend only weeks before.

Normally, X and I would do this together, but because of the recent murders, Munson had instructed us to arrive in separate cars—X at the rear entrance of the Balfour's club, and me at the front. My stakeout partner was the newbie, Danny Parker, who was rather delighted at the opportunity to pick my brain to death about pretty much everything.

"What made you become a cop?" he asked during his second round of questions.

I shrugged and thought for a moment. There were many reasons I chose this profession—family tradition, my need to be the good guy in the world, rebelling against my anti-establishment grandmother. Perhaps my notion of saving people had started with keeping the entire student body of Benjamin Franklin High from being eaten as a penalty for overdue library books. But I also liked the chase, the thrill of figuring out the whodunit, and the element of danger—and it wasn't a bad cover for my involuntary occupation. Of course, I couldn't tell Parker any of this.

"Oh yeah, your dad was a cop, wasn't he? I think I heard that somewhere."

He probably had. Most of the precinct knew about my sordid family history. I had worked hard to create a new image and wasn't about to dredge up old stuff for the new guy.

"Not something I talk about much, Parker."

"Okay." He fidgeted with the sticker on the dashboard of my car. The edges were frayed and peeling back from the words of my mantra. *Illegitimi non carborundum.* Roughly translated it meant, "Don't let the bastards get you down." As I translated it for Parker, I remembered all the times my dad used to say this very thing to me. Not in Latin, of course, but I'd always thought Latin was an elegant language, dead or otherwise, and buying the sticker was the one homage to my father I allowed myself. I left this history out of my translation and Danny Parker was none the wiser.

I remembered Marlowe's quirk of a smile when he first saw the sticker in my car. Of course, he didn't require me to translate it. I did explain its origins to him—opening up about my father and his death two years before. Marlowe was a surprisingly good listener. During the last two days he had demonstrated honor and bravery, equal skill with sword and scalpel, and was fluent in three languages that I knew of. He was interesting, smart, and quirky.

My current love interest, Rick, had become a whiter shade of pale in comparison to the vividness that was Marlowe. In fact, every relationship I'd ever had seemed two-dimensional and not quite as real. I was deep into this internal monologue when Parker cleared his throat, bringing me back to whatever inane conversation we were having. I changed the subject.

"Balfour should be a little more reserved knowing there's someone out there gunning for him," I said.

Parker went along with my subject change and asked questions about my interview with the crime boss. I answered as best I could, but the truth was I knew very little about what was going to happen, and at that point, I didn't much care. I wanted to bring Balfour to justice, but if the strigoi was after him, I was almost inclined to let the bastard have at it. Cruel and heartless, I know, but the only sure-fire way to kill it was to find its master. For some reason, I couldn't shake the thought that it was Balfour, regardless of what had happened to his men.

"What time is it?" I asked Danny again.

"11:35. Five minutes later than when you asked the last time. You got a hot date or something, Detective?"

"No, not at all. I wish something would happen." This was a lie. I wished for nothing but time to pass so I could get out of there and back to the real job. The radio crackled. X's voice rumbled through.

"Tam. Looks like Balfour's on the move." A few seconds later, another crackle. "Check that, it's Cruz. You guys stay put, we'll go."

My hand hit the steering wheel, startling Parker. I clicked the transmit button.

"Copy. Keep us posted."

"Will do." I recognized the distracted tone X used while driving and talking. A half hour later, X reported Cruz at some house in the Delanco neighborhood. Shortly after that, Munson and Howard arrived to relieve us.

It took me twenty minutes to get to the station, and another six minutes to get Parker out of my car. I didn't drive straight to where Marlowe was trapping the strigoi but hit the corner deli/grocery on the way. I found parking fairly close to the alley and grabbing an extra flashlight and my go-bag, I rushed toward the grate. I hadn't realized how worried I'd been about Marlowe until I got there. My breath caught in my throat as I called out his name and shone my light into the dark manhole. There was an answering light and soon Marlowe's face grinned up at me from the darkness.

"Good eve, Tamberlyn. Was your venture fruitful?"

"Not a bit."

I lowered myself down, feet first, feeling Marlowe's sure hands on one foot and then both. I grabbed for his shoulder in the dark, found it and jumped to the floor.

"Anything here?"

"Perchance, early on. Alas, the beast eluded me. I have seen naught since. I believe the lights are still burning, but I did not want to abandon my post."

I felt a pang of guilt. This was a two-man job and I'd left him to it alone. "You should get some sleep," I said. "I'll keep an eye out."

"I'll check the lights first," he said, and I watched the beam of his flashlight bob as he headed toward one end of the tunnel. I stood at the ladder to the exit, my eyes adjusting to the darkness. My arm at least felt better. Whatever goop Marlowe's apothecary came up with worked like a charm. I was about to go on a search for Marlowe when I saw his light coming toward me.

"No sign of our creature," he looked disappointed. "The lights are still burning. It's quite remarkable. This invention, the battery."

"I brought sandwiches," I found the grocery bag I'd gotten on the way.

Marlowe beamed at me. "You are a true gentlewoman and godsend."

"Yeah, I don't know about that, it's just ham and cheese."

"Still," he said, his mouth full. "The people in your time eat extraordinarily well."

I chewed my own sandwich thoughtfully, washing it down with a bottle of water. Another item, Marlowe had found extraordinary—that we sell water. "Most of us do, eat well, but unfortunately, not all. Even in this country, there are hungry people."

"Strange is it not? That with all your modern technology and invention, you still cannot find a method of curing hunger?"

"Yes," I nodded. "Very strange."

10

After several uneventful hours in the sewer where we had both napped off and on, we packed up the equipment Ziggy had procured for us and headed home. I yawned long and luxuriously in the car before pulling into the lot outside my apartment. Marlowe took my keys from me and set about opening the door, stowing the gear and even making coffee as I plopped down on the couch. I did manage to get my boots off and put my feet up, but I didn't want to sleep. There was a lot to do. We still had a vampire to hunt down and time was short for Marlowe. My desire to keep him here was paramount in my mind.

"Your visits to the future? So, why only a few days? Have you found the reason for that?"

"I've studied it much, but have only a theory— perhaps the moon. My travels seem to occur at the young crescent of the dark of the moon and last until a half moon shows. I've never seen a full moon in any timeline other than my own. I trust it has not changed much?"

I smiled at this. "Nope, pretty much the same, however, you'll be interested to know that man has been there. Walked around, snapped a few pics, planted a flag and left."

He sat beside me, handing me a mug of very strong coffee. He'd mastered my coffee maker almost as adeptly as the remote control. "How is this possible?"

"Massive machines, ingenuity, and lots of money. It was a race between Americans and Russians in 1969. Americans won."

"God's blood, such fantasy as I'd never dreamed."

"Marlowe, you travel through time. You somehow traverse the impossible to experience a completely different life and then go safely back again. That is the most extraordinary thing I've ever heard of, far more so than a trip to the moon."

Since Marlowe and I shared the ability to see hostiles in the world, an ability I'd thought was only mine, I wondered if, at some point, I might also be sparked through time to somewhere five hundred years from now. The thought was daunting. Acclimating to a different time while defending myself from a mystical creature. I'd been hunting hostiles for almost thirteen years, but I'd rarely traveled out of Pennsylvania. Yet his experience was far greater than my own because he'd traveled so far and so often.

He leaned forward, his elbows resting on his knees, his hands clasped around his coffee mug. "Would that our experiences be so uncommon that we'd have no communion with each other, yet, that is not so. We are both defenders, fighting against a common foe. But as far as my stay in your timeline, I fear it is quite finite. By experience, there is no remedy for it. Shall I demonstrate?" he set his mug on the table and looked around, finding the USB cord for my phone. "Heretofore, a mentor and friend used his niece's hair ribbon to illustrate, but since these do not exist in your time, I will make do with this object."

He set the cord on the coffee table in front of me, winding it into a circle. I wanted to tell him that hair ribbons did exist, but in the context of time travel, it seemed a trivial point.

"Originally, I'd thought time may be similar to this configuration. The beginning at one end and continuing outward in a spiral to an unknown end. But after much discussion and thought regarding my travels, we happened upon this theory."

He rearranged the cord into a zigzag along the table. It did resemble a ribbon folded back and forth upon itself or the hard ribbon candy I used to get at Christmas. Marlowe pinched the middle, so the cord intersected at several points. "Time still has its origin, but instead of spiraling, it weaves back and forth, I cross the ribbon from point to point where it touches. Time is also fluid, waning and waxing like the moon, so that the intersection—" He moved the cord again, putting it back into its accordion fold, "is always changing."

"So, there's no way to tell what timeline you will get to when you travel?"

He was silent for a moment and the finality of our friendship hit me. When he left, I would more than likely never see him again.

After only a few measly hours I'd become used to his presence. It was a new experience having someone who truly understood the realm I lived in. But if I was honest with myself, it was more than that. The desire for more than companionship had notched itself up to a nagging pull on my insides. I was hyper-aware of everything he did. The way his hands moved when he talked, the lilt of his voice, his quirk of a smile when he tried to understand modern slang. I told myself I was taken with him because he was so offbeat, and that it would pass. Quite frankly, living in a fantasy world was much easier.

He stood and stretched. Again, my gaze was riveted to his torso, to those fabulous abdominal muscles that peeked out from under the clean T-shirt he'd donned. A dark line of hair under his navel leading to—I startled as he spoke again.

"Soon after my first journey, I began documenting my experiences, hoping it would prove to be a solution, if not to my travel, then at least to my predicament." He went to his cape where it hung on a peg beside my door. Retrieving a small leather-bound book from another hidden pocket, he brought it to me. It was a soft brown and embossed with some Latin words. "'*Ab initio. Ab aeterno.*' From the beginning, from eternity." He shrugged. "I thought it fitting."

I thumbed through the handwritten text. Perhaps somewhere in an archive, maybe a library in Cambridge— if someone had thought to preserve it—this book would be reverently handled, or in a glass case, its fragile pages too delicate to touch. But here the journal was fairly new, only six years old.

Of course, most of it was indecipherable to me, being in the calligraphy of Elizabethan English. But as I read, the words became more familiar, and soon I was immersed in his words. The first entry was the story he relayed to me in the tunnels. Traveling on a packet from Dover to Calais a hundred years in his future.

At some point, I heard him mention a bath and he left me to my exploration of his journal. I admired his confidence. I would be hard-pressed to let anyone else read my innermost thoughts. I delved back into his world, learning a new history from Marlowe's unique point of view. The entries were all carefully dated with the month and day, but in place of the year, (the most important part), there were only symbols.

"Hey," I got up, knocked on the bathroom door, and heard him splashing. "Marlowe, I can't read the years."

"I cannot hear thee." The water turned off. "Enter and speak."

Okay. I cracked the door open. He was immersed in mounds of bubbles. The room was fragrant with super-scented shower gel. I'd never expected him to be one for bubble baths. The idea was somehow more erotic than silly.

"This is most relaxing. I found some scented elixirs."

"Help yourself. I can't decipher your code. Here." I held out his journal. He sat up, the suds falling away to reveal muscles that modern men slave away in gyms for. My eyes traveled down that slippery slope of their own accord.

I envisioned myself naked in the tub with him, our legs entwined, his hands soaping my body. I stood there, caught in my own fantasy of him inviting me to join him.

Have I spoken unduly? The tub is fair large enough for two, and—his voice had a gorgeous timbre to it. I was sure he would be a passable singer. His eyes would flick over me. *Are you ashamed of thy nakedness? I find thee quite pleasing to my eyes.* He would hesitate only a second. *Beauty is the female form, in all states of undress, but none so fair as that of God's cloak.*

Are you trying to seduce me, Marlowe?

Would thou be seduced, if attempt is truly engaged?

His wet hair was dark and the ends of it curled against the nape of his neck, which tapered nicely into well-formed shoulders, leanly muscled and strong. He had chest hair midline and across his pectorals but no more than that.

"Was there a question regarding my journal? Tamberlyn? Detective?"

Detective?

I blinked. His journal lay open on the floor where I had dropped it.

"Was there a question? Regarding the journal?" His look was curious, maybe confused at my blankness.

I shook myself out of it and picked up the book, flipping the pages. "Is there a key? To your coded dates?"

"The key is in my head, but I can explain. It's quite simple really." He started to get up.

"No, it's fine." I held my hand up to keep him from rising out of the water like some Greek god. "We can wait till you're done."

I hastily closed the door, trying to ignore my wayward imagination.

11

The key in Marlowe's journal was simple and ingenious. Elizabethans wrote the year in lowercase Roman numerals. The year 1588 would be depicted as mdlxxxviii. The letter *i* was interchangeable with the letter *j*. This alone would have been enough to mask the year to anyone in the twenty-first century, but Marlowe would have no way of knowing that, so he devised a system for the year, inserting a corresponding symbol for every number. A dot for one, a T for two, a triangle for three and so on. It also made for a more compact date reference.

I skipped around the journal, as some entries were easier to read than others. The initial ones mostly listed facts and were tersely documented. But the latter ones were more fluid, less confused, and had far more detail. People he'd met, some customs he'd found odd, the particular demon he'd been hunting and how it was killed. Other than his first journey, where he was unaware of his purpose, he'd been successful in vanquishing his prey every time, save one. His batting average was far better than my own.

Still, I couldn't seem to recognize a pattern. The journal only documented the dates he was sent to, not the dates of his year. He told me that he didn't travel every crescent moon. So far, there were twenty-seven entries in the journal, so he'd traveled to the future at least that many times over the course of six years. His abilities had emerged much like mine had, with the onset of puberty. Yet, there was so much we didn't know. Like what caused his time travel to begin with? Was it connected to his ability to see hostiles? The travels seemed to follow no pattern that I could discern and without knowing a cause, there was no way we could stop it. Or even control when and where he went.

"So why Philadelphia?" I asked. We'd both slept a few hours and it was afternoon before Marlowe had lobbied for "breaking fast" as he called it. I'd taken him to that most sophisticated of breaking fast establishments—the International House of Pancakes.

He stuffed a forkful of pancakes into his mouth, chewing thoughtfully and swallowing before speaking. "Albert's theory is that Philadelphia is an anchor point, as my place of birth is. Something or someone keeps drawing me back here. I know not what."

"First time you came here, you met Mary, right? Maybe it's her."

"I should like that. I hoped it would be so. But my first trip here was 1952. Believe me, Tamberlyn, I've thought of contingencies. There is naught to be done about it. Even Albert could not fathom it."

"Albert?"

Marlowe indicated the journal lying on the table beside me. I pushed my plate aside as he repeated the year. I skimmed through the entries to find the symbols. It was near the front, his third journey. A dot, a zero with a line, a pentagram, and a T—1952. I read aloud.

"After landing, I secured some clothes from a laundress's drying rack and made my way to the nearest city center." My eyes flicked up at him. "You were naked?"

He shrugged. "This was prior to my obtaining my cloak. The transition through the lightning is most unpleasant, disintegrating a good portion of one's attire."

I continued reading. "The most unusual motorized carriages flew by me at great speed and with great noise. I entered the largest structure I've seen in my travels to find that I was in the colonies. A city called Philadelphia, in the colony of Pennsylvania. I was enormously surprised to find that I could traverse not only time but oceans. I learned the building I entered was a train station, far more modern than the one I'd seen in London during my last travel. Confounded by the sheer outrageousness of my fortune, I sat on a bench to get my bearings. Soon an elderly man with a great nose and hair the length of mine sat beside me and we conversed. At first, he was concerned I'd suffered injury, so addled was I. But as he talked, I began to recover and glean information about this new and amazing time I was in. He was quick to observe my manner of speech, though I thought to hide it well. After my bare introduction, where I was careful not to mention the timeline of which I came, nor the manner in which I arrived, he enlisted me as a traveling companion to carry his great trunk. The trunk was very heavy and contained mostly books and a change of clothes. He was a teacher at a University and had come to the city for a speech. We boarded the train together, and upon our settling into his private car, he introduced himself as Albert Einstein." I looked up at Marlowe.

"Albert Einstein. You rode a train with Einstein? Wait. This is the mentor you've talked about? Time-ribbon-theory-guy? The one who gave you the cape?"

Marlowe nodded. "Yes. His family must be quite prominent; the hospital I took you to when we first met was named after them."

"Not them. Him. *The* Albert Einstein—the greatest mind of the twentieth century. Everyone knows of him."

Marlowe seemed unimpressed that he'd befriended a renowned genius. "He was quite fond of some peanut substance as I recall, brown and pasty."

"Peanut butter?"

"Yes. He had me retrieve several sandwiches from the dining car. And he snored, quite loudly, in fact. He fell asleep halfway through our journey."

As he talked, I watched the people around us in the restaurant. It's habit mostly, being aware of my surroundings. The place was full of people eating lunch—four men in coveralls, two women in office wear, a grandmother and teen grandson. I closed the book and slid it across the table. Questions about Einstein would have to wait. "Put this away."

"Something's amiss?" he asked.

"Do you remember the military technique I told you about when I had your six?" He nodded. "Check out two o'clock."

He turned slowly to his left and glanced in the direction of the grandmother. Now that I was paying attention, I wasn't at all sure she was the grandmotherly type.

"My go-bag is in the car," I said.

"As is my weapon." His voice was low and harsh.

"You can see it too?"

His lips pressed together in a hard line as he tipped his head. I glanced toward the table again.

The old woman faced in our direction, her charge in profile. She smiled benevolently at the young man in front of her, but her hand had claws for fingernails. The middle finger had sunk into her companion's hand to the depth of a first knuckle. He sat perfectly still. We couldn't hear what she was saying over the din of the restaurant, but it looked like some incantation as she never paused in her speech. I told Marlowe to keep an eye while I retrieved my gear from the car. I had my service weapon, but there were too many bystanders, and I wasn't sure bullets would suffice. Before I could get back inside, I saw them exit, followed closely by Marlowe, calling out to me as he gave chase.

I grabbed my bag from my trunk and followed them. Weaving our way through parked cars around the side of the building, I came to a halt in front of the dumpsters. Both teen and grandma had backed Marlowe up against a parked car, their eyes an oily black. Their mouths opened toward him and I could smell the stench of Sulphur from where I stood. I retrieved the silver flask from the duffel, opened it and flung the contents at the grandmother. She hissed as her skin steamed from the holy water, turning on me, her claws growing longer as she approached.

I heard Marlowe spewing Latin phrases in the background, but it was hard to hear over the roaring sound coming from the old woman. It sounded like I was on the tarmac with 747s taking off overhead. I tossed what was left in my flask at her and tried my own Latin, which by the way was not nearly as good as Marlowe's. She responded with some phrase of her own. An invisible force picked me up and I sailed a few feet through the air until I hit a large trash bin and then landed on my ass. Marlowe had been engaged in holding off the teen, trying to survive while not mortally injuring the kid. I managed to hold onto my knife but was still on the ground when the old woman moved in.

Behind granny, Marlowe rolled away from the teen and slashed at her with his own knife. Blood appeared through her cable knit sweater. I pushed forward through the putrid smell and twisted her to the ground, landing a punch at her shoulder.

She rolled me off of her effortlessly and took off toward the parking lot. My last glimpse was of her in tennis shoes and a paisley print dress leaping over a VW bug before she disappeared around the corner. Marlowe had his knife at the boy's throat.

"Don't kill him," I said, crawling over to them. The teenager writhed wide-eyed and gurgled under the words Marlowe was saying. The cadence was hypnotic, as though he were reciting poetry. Suddenly Marlowe stepped back, releasing the boy. The kid turned on all fours and vomited. The process was long, arduous, and painful to watch—black liquid and chunks forcefully spewed from him. Finally, he stopped and rolled to his side, exhausted, but free of whatever had held him. Marlowe reached for me, his hand curling about my shoulder.

"Are you unharmed?"

"Yes. You?" He pulled me into a fierce but brief embrace. We moved apart and turned to the young man. "Was that your grandmother?"

The boy shook his head. His voice was hoarse and raspy. "No. I was hitting her up for change. She said she'd buy me breakfast. I don't remember much after that. I must have gotten food poisoning." He rose and shakily brushed himself off. "I'll never eat here again."

I pulled out a twenty and gave it to him.

"Here, go buy an Egg McMuffin."

Nodding his thanks, he headed back to the street.

"And call your mother. Let her know you're okay." I called out to him. I looked at Marlowe, watching as he replaced the wicked looking knife into his boot. He pulled his pant leg down over it.

"We've lost the other. We should go after it."

"I've marked it." I pulled a ring off my finger and showed it to him. By moving a small lever on the underside, two setting points around the green stone protruded. They had been filed to sharp points. "Don't touch," I warned him and retracted the prongs. "The points have been covered in ox blood and silver nitrate. It seeps into their system, slowly drawing the demon to the surface. Basically, harmless to humans, but not pleasant." He looked at me with new respect.

"You are quite brilliant, Tamberlyn. I shall not underestimate your abilities again."

"Not really my idea. Well, it is, I guess. I had a little

help from—" I stopped. He looked at me quizzically. I don't know why I hadn't thought of it before. "Let's go pay the bill. There's someone I want you to meet."

The Italian market was crowded. After work, shoppers stopped by on their way home for Italian pastries or homemade pasta, creating a human maze in the center of the big vendor warehouse.

I pulled Marlowe along steadily, though he protested the entire length of the place, exclaiming about colors, and smells, and wanting to peruse the vendors' wares. I had a definite destination in mind.

Angelo Volpi was my very own alchemist. My own personal Master Gomfrey, he was a curator, a shop-keeper, and an arrogant SOB, but he was far more versed on supernatural shenanigans than I would ever be. He was the apothecary/conjurer of my century.

Volpi's stall was located at the far corner of the market, a ratty looking clutter of books, candles, and homemade soaps. The shabby look was intentional as it kept the average window shopper away. Marlowe and I came to a stop in front of a sign held by two dragon figurines made from brass. To most people, the dragons looked like cheap plaster of Paris, with brass-colored paint and paste rubies for eyes. I happened to know they were very old, very powerful objects that held a protective aura over the space.

Just before I entered college, I'd found a business card in the pocket of my jacket with Volpi's name on it. Not knowing how I acquired it, I threw it away. Yet the next day, it appeared again. And again. Finally, I gave in and went to the address on the card, searching the market until coming across the dusty shop of knickknacks and the dragon sign.

A strange feeling had come over me when I looked into the eyes of the dragons. As I checked them out, a man of less than average height with a crappy disposition stepped out from behind a shelf full of wooden crosses and Santa figurines, demanding to know who the hell I was. Angelo Volpi knew right away that I was different.

After I bought him a beer as a good will gesture—he was partial to La Tabachera—we'd spent about an hour inside his little stall looking at books and talking. He knew a great deal about the monsters I hunted, and I, having thought I was the only one who knew of this strange world, clung to that knowledge. It was the first time anyone had listened to my stories about hunting monsters and not been completely weirded out. Over the years we had developed a mutually beneficial though strange relationship. I hadn't seen or spoken to him in a while.

"Volpi? You around?" I called toward the back of the shop.

Marlowe came to a halt next to me and finally took his eyes off all the fruits and vegetables to see what was right in front of him. I smiled as I watched his similar reaction to the dragons. He didn't touch them but bent to look at them closely.

"What strange objects. They seem out of another time."

"They are." Volpi's voice came out of nowhere. "What is strange is that you noticed." He moved lithely out from behind a statue of the hunchback of Notre Dame.

He grimaced at me, which is about the most congenial greeting I get with Volpi. "So, you're not dead. Good for you. What have you brought me?" With a long glance, he took in Marlowe's stance, his cape and sword.

Volpi was a strange mix of sloppy and debonair, handsome and odd-looking. As long as I'd known him, I'd yet to determine his age—somewhere between thirty and sixty, depending on the day. His rare smiles were incongruent with his heavy-lidded eyes, indigo blue and sharp. He could be considered attractive, but not in a superficial way. He exuded energy like a fast rolling fog, captivating yet foreboding.

"Volpi, this is Marlowe. He's—" Volpi's reaction was instantaneous. His eyes widened and his frown changed to one of restrained delight.

"So, you are for real."

12

I hid a smile as Volpi's initial astonishment vanished immediately. He invited us to the interior of his little shop flipping the Closed sign around and led us behind a shabby wall hanging of poker-playing dogs. The back of the stall was much larger than it appeared from an initial glance.

I've never been good at spatial perception. I couldn't look at a room and say it's five-by-five or ten-by-twelve. But Volpi's back room felt spacious, maybe because it was less cluttered than the front.

A large mahogany credenza acted as a shelf for a myriad of books, candle holders, and papers. There was a hot plate in the center with a dented and scratched metal teapot. Volpi gestured to a work table and two chairs, then turning to the credenza, he rustled around in the lower drawers to find an assortment of teacups and plates.

Some time ago, Volpi got some wild-ass notion about my abilities, and we'd had a difference of opinion. He'd wanted my whole family history and when he'd heard I had a sister, he'd immediately thought she would be like me.

My sister, Izzy, is the smart one. A college girl, the nice one who goes to church and talks to the aunts and all of that. She's about as far from monster hunting as little Bo-Peep, and I didn't want to knock her off her tuffet by telling her about it. Volpi disagreed. There were words. Not nice words. And I'd left. That had been two years ago.

I stood at the edge of the back room as Marlowe dropped into a bow, giving his usual Queen's-Man-at your-service intro.

"Please call me Angelo." Volpi reached a hand toward Marlowe. "I'd be honored to be on a first name basis with Christopher Marlowe." Marlowe seemed pleased.

"How did you know?" I spoke up. I moved a bedraggled stuffed owl off a stool and sat down. As Volpi prepared tea, he launched into one of his typical long-winded tales. Some story about backpacking through Europe as a young man and finding a rare book shop.

"I was always a treasure hunter, long before discovering you."

I rolled my eyes. It was me who'd discovered him, but whatever.

As he talked there was a moment where I could see how he was as a young man—quite striking, blond curly hair, blue eyes zeroing in to sweep some unsuspecting young girl off her feet.

"I worked at The Pint and Quill. It was a bookstore and a bar combined. I found something quite extraordinary."

"Guinness?" I smirked at him. He scowled at me. Volpi never got my sense of humor.

"Actually, it wasn't a thing but a woman."

Volpi sat down to relish the telling of his tale. His

eyes took on that faraway look.

"She was a novelist, a collector of books and rare objects—had done quite well for herself as a writer. The owner of the shop, a man named Earl, was more interested in the pints than the books so I took on the book duties. I worked in the shop for several months, learning the trade, talking to the patrons. I learned about rare objects, cursed objects, and collected tales of the dark arts. Whenever she came in, we'd usually get into a conversation about her latest story, a murder mystery. She'd find the most fascinating ways to kill a person, quite gruesome for such a dear lady. We'd have tea and talk of all sorts of mayhem."

"Could you please get to the point?" I said this with a smile. I usually liked Volpi's stories.

Undaunted, he continued. "You really have no appreciation for a good narrative, do you? Mrs. Mallowan brought in a very old document. The pages were small and very fragile, encased in the cheap plastic liners—pages from a journal. She wouldn't sell it but wanted me to see them and get my opinion. She thought them to be from the journal of Christopher Marlowe."

Marlowe glanced at me. "My journal survived. Wise to have coded the dates, then."

I nodded assent, sipping hot tea out of a chipped Dresden cup.

"Indeed." Volpi agreed. "We had no idea of the year they were written. With only a few pages, we could not decipher the code. Yet the few journal entries we saw appeared to be either historical accounts or predictions of the future. The language and time period were that of the sixteenth century, but we couldn't explain the knowledge of events far beyond your time." He glanced at Marlowe. "All we could do was to test the paper and the ink. It appeared authentic, but we were clueless as to the entries."

"Mayhap I can provide illumination." Marlowe reached into the folds of his cape and retrieved the journal. Volpi's eyes widened from under his shaggy brows. He jumped up, rattling the teacups in their saucers.

"Mrs. Mallowan did allow me to take some photographs. They're floating around here somewhere." He rifled around in his files—stacks of milk crates filled with paper—finally he yanked a file out from the bottom of a pile with a flourish. "Ahha."

He opened the faded blue folder on the table before us and we moved dishes aside to get a better look. The photos were small, like those taken from a box camera and developed in a shop. Scalloped edges and black and white, sort of grainy. As a unit, the three of us placed our fingertips along the edges of four or five photos, flattening them. Volpi retrieved a magnifying glass and handed it to Marlowe. After a minute, Marlowe flipped through his journal, bringing up the page depicted in one photo.

"May 23, 1879. I was in London, a section called Whitechapel, following a demon who murdered several women."

"Jack the Ripper?" I asked. This was too much—serial killers and geniuses. I suddenly felt quite ordinary. The most famous person I'd ever met was the guy from that one reality show. And Marlowe, of course, but who would believe me about him?

In answer, Marlowe shrugged. At my mention of Einstein, Volpi looked thoughtful. He didn't say anything, merely held up another photograph, and Marlowe found the corresponding page in his journal.

"I thought this might be possible," Volpi said excitedly. "The entries were so authentic sounding, relating the feel of the era as much as bits of historical facts, not known to the common researcher. You truly have a gift of storytelling, Master Marlowe."

Marlowe seemed very pleased with his words.

Volpi asked all the questions that I had—how do you travel? Is there a machine? And the question of the day—can you control when and where you go?

Marlowe quickly related his story, sticking mostly to the actual traveling part rather than where he landed. He started to describe his duties as a hunter of monsters, but Volpi quickly dismissed that part. He'd heard most of my hunting stories already. With an eye on our time, I interjected the reason for our visit.

"We're hoping you could help figure out what triggers the traveling and what the key is to controlling it."

"There may not be a way to control it." Volpi was looking through the journal and sounded a bit distracted.

"This can't be spontaneous," I said, not quite believing myself. "And it's isolated to one person. And why Philadelphia? He always returns home to his time and place, I get that. But why here? Why not Chicago? Or Singapore?" I needed answers. I didn't want to tell Volpi why I felt so strongly about this, but there must have been a note of desperation in my voice because he stopped his journal reading to look at me.

"Returning to his place of birth is a given. It's an—"

"Anchor point," Marlowe finished. "Yes, but I have no ties here."

"None that you know of," Volpi said. His gaze returned to me and I resisted squirming. "Perhaps you haven't made the connection yet. I'll see what I can dig up." He stood up and put the kettle on again. "Let's have another cuppa. Could I take some notes from your journal, Master Marlowe?"

I knew the look on Volpi's face. He was onto something. Before I could ask, he shuffled me out the door to fetch cannolis from his favorite bakery stall. Feeling somewhat cast aside in light of a newer toy, I left them. It gave me a chance to gather my thoughts and composure. Whatever Volpi was thinking, I hoped it worked.

Time is a funny thing. Six years into Marlowe's future may not be six years into mine. Not that it mattered. When he left, there would be no guarantee he'd ever return. He'd really wanted to come back to 1863 and to his love, Mary, but could not. What made me think that he'd be able to return to me? What made me think he even wanted to? Then again, given my own occupation, I may not even be around when and if he did return.

When I returned with paper bag of goodies in hand, both men were deeply engrossed in several musty old books. Once I tried to get Volpi to search his lore and legend stuff on my laptop. The thing never worked right again, and I'd given up on getting him to modernize his research techniques. For him, the written word was irreplaceable. Even old, barely legible words in extinct languages.

I was also a bit surprised at the swiftness that Volpi

took to Marlowe. Volpi was a collector of artifacts. He was rarely impressed with people—he barely tolerated me, and I was damned likable, so to see his warmth toward Marlowe was strange. As they talked, I put the pastries on a plate in front of them.

Marlowe slipped me a grateful smile as he held a cannoli in one hand.

"Angelo has a theory I hadn't investigated before. His knowledge of history and magic is vast." Marlowe said.

I sat down and looked at Volpi. He was busy eating a pastry that consumed his full attention. Ignoring both of us, he chewed contentedly, eyes closed, a bit of crème filling sitting at the corner of his bowed mouth. I wondered again how he stayed so trim with his obvious penchant for high-calorie food and drink. No wonder he chose to place his business in the middle of a market filled with exotic foodstuffs. The next meal was a only few steps away. The idea had come to me that Volpi indulged in more than a good meal and fine wine—all pleasures. I'd never seen Volpi with a woman, but I got the definite feeling he would be the same way he was with food—he had a voracious appetite.

Having swallowed the last of the cannoli, he opened his eyes, and wiped the bit of pastry from his face, licking it off his thumb. He launched into his theory.

"I thought there may be something when you spoke of the Ripper. Marlowe's visits to various points in history correspond with some event or person. I think there is a pattern to his travels, some definite purpose, as yet, unknown to us."

"Okay," I said this slowly. There would be more to

come. I knew it. Volpi pointed to an entry in Marlowe's journal.

"From his first journal entry, he interacts with the slave of a colonist—an American colonist, prior to the French Revolution. The colonist being one Thomas Jefferson." Volpi was excited and pointed out some more entries, citing lesser-known historical events or persons that Marlowe had encountered—the Einstein meeting was of particular interest, as well as the Civil War era, where Marlowe met Mary Beard.

"Why is meeting Mary significant?" I asked, glancing at Marlowe, who seemed a bit uncomfortable at the mention of her.

"I don't know," Volpi admitted. "But if this is a pattern, then maybe it will lead to a reason for his travels and therefore a way of controlling them."

"I'm most encouraged we shall find a solution." Marlowe rubbed the pastry flakes from his hands. I watched them, knowing firsthand how both gentle and strong they were.

"Good. Then Marlowe can stay," I blurted out. They both looked at me.

"No," Marlowe said. "It would be wrong of me to stay. I have a duty. This is my destiny and I cannot thwart it by staying in one time. We seek something that allows me to control my destiny more readily." He watched me carefully.

"Of course, yes. That's what I meant."

Volpi eyed me, licking powdered sugar from a second cannoli off his fingers. I threw him my most withering glance. He didn't say anything, which was unusual. Volpi was not known for keeping his ego-expounding thoughts to himself.

"How do we control time travel? I gotta say, I never thought I'd be saying stuff like 'How do we control time travel?'"

Marlowe flashed his smile again. Volpi sighed. The idea of how strange this was was lost on them. I lived in a strange world, hunting hostiles, saving people from monsters, but I never really felt a part of it. I felt like an ordinary person doing a job. Granted, it was a weird job, but still, it wasn't who I was.

But Volpi seemed to embrace it. He'd dealt with the supernatural far longer than I had and revelled in the mystery and the magic.

When I first met Marlowe, I'd thought he was like me—just a monster hunter with a day job, a poet caught up in a bizarre world and doing the best he could. Now, I realized he was very much into this. He was committed to it—this warrior-against-the-dark thing. It was a duty he took very seriously. He lived the life—it wasn't just a job. I was stunned at this news. And at how depressed his words made me. I had thought I'd found someone who understood my situation but was duty bound to time travel. Turned out, I'd miscalculated everything.

Volpi got up to search again through his haphazard array of books and documents. I watched him with detached interest.

"Things you travel with Kit, what are they? Any dark objects for instance?"

Marlowe gave me a quick look as if to ask if Volpi could be trusted. I looked at him blankly. He'd spilled all his secrets so far, why not more? Volpi cleared his throat and quirked an eyebrow at me.

"Tam?" he asked. Volpi was a decadent, somewhat sloppy, pleasure seeker, but he was also very perceptive. He knew there was something up with me, just not exactly what. Hell, I didn't know exactly what it was either.

Marlowe stood up and emptied the pockets concealed in the deep folds of his cape. The man's jeans were too tight to accommodate anything but Marlowe. This was entirely my fault—his thighs and ass were more muscular than I'd first thought when buying his clothes. Not that the view was unappreciated. I forced my thoughts from what was under Marlowe's jeans to the items he'd placed on the table. The journal, his leather case of medical tools, which Volpi eagerly examined, as well as the pouch with the magic healing powder.

There was another small pouch which produced a tiny pot of ink and three short quills—reminding me that he was a writer as well as a warrior. He pulled off his signet ring—gold with an M in relief against a dark background and decorative scrolls in relief against black on both sides. The ring was not large, but elegantly made. I wondered out loud if it was a family heirloom.

"Alas, my father has not the wealth to afford such a thing. He does well in Canterbury. He's become a law clerk of sorts, but he has many mouths to feed as none of my sisters are of marriageable age. This was given to me by a friend." I wanted to ask more, but the closed look on his face prevented me. After a moment, he gave a little shrug and pulled the dagger he'd held on the possessed teen from his boot and finally his sword, which he'd placed on the floor at his feet when he sat down. Volpi stared at the weapon for a moment, but he seemed to understand Marlowe's possessive anxiety about it.

"Tell me about this," he indicated the sword almost reverently.

"This was passed onto me by a teacher at Cambridge. I'd won a fencing tournament by besting a noble's son. While it brought my instructor great accolades, it thrust myself further into discord with my fellow students. Lord Ferringan's son was my opponent and quite popular, not because of his charm or wit, moreover because of his father's great wealth." Marlowe's hazel eyes looked at me thoughtfully for a moment before he continued. "All I know of the sword is its origin and metallurgy. That it was forged from Damascus steel by a blacksmith who studied the ancient ways of the men in the North." Marlowe flipped the sword over, pointing to an etching near the hilt. "It's inscribed here. His mark."

I looked over his shoulder to see an arrow pointed toward the sky and the letter R.

"*Teiwaz* and *Raido*," Volpi said. "Viking runes. Loosely translated they means 'Warrior' and 'Journey.'"

"Or it could simply be his signature," I said.

Volpi shook his head. "Most sword makers did not sign their work, not until late into the eighteenth century. The Asians did, but this is not an Asian sword. More than likely, these symbols were thought to give the sword power. As the Vikings believed their weapons could wield a power of their own."

Marlowe smiled. "It has served me well. My master called it *Grim*."

"Pretty good name for a sword. Short and to the point." I laughed at my own pun. Both Volpi and Marlowe looked at me blankly. "To the point? Get it?

Never mind."

As they continued to talk about Marlowe's impending disappearance and what could be done about it, I was beginning to fade. It had been a long day and I again marveled at Marlowe's strength and resistance to his body's need for sleep. He noticed my yawn and told Volpi we should be taking our leave of him. Volpi seemed irritated at my very human need for rest, but he relented.

"Okay, you guys should go, but first—blue lightning, is that a euphemism? Or is it real? Perhaps I've read something—" Volpi was muttering under his breath when my phone rang.

It was X. He thought he'd tracked down Cruz. I didn't tell Marlowe. He may well want to accompany me, and I wanted him to stay and work on the time-travel issue. I didn't want to think about how disappointed I was to know he had no wish to stay in this time.

Still, I found myself reluctant to leave him, thinking it may be the last time I would see him. He may vanish from this time and back to his own before Volpi could clean up his teacup. I was too tired to think about fighting the strigoi on my own, or even Cruz and Balfour. Maybe after the incident at IHOP, I'd begun to think of Marlowe as my partner against crime. At least as much as X was. I looked at him as he stood beside Volpi. His strong hands were gentle around the fragile teacup. They were gentle when dressing my arm as well. He turned, his eyes holding mine, his head tilting to the side as if asking a question. My breath caught in my throat and I coughed.

"Art thou well, Tamberlyn?" he asked. "Mayhaps I

should accompany you."

"No, I'm fine. Just routine police stuff. You stay. Maybe between the two of you, you can find something."

"I shall make every attempt." He took my hand before I realized it and placed his warm lips against my knuckles. His eyes never left my face as he did so. It was the sexiest thing I'd seen in a very long time. He released my hand and I backed into a shelf of old toys, knocking some to the floor. A plastic doll squawked at me when I stepped on it. I picked it up and put it back on a shelf of bobble headed-dogs. They grinned at my clumsiness, their heads jiggling up and down.

I left Marlowe in Volpi's care and drove to the old Philly neighborhood of Delanco, where X was waiting for me.

Delanco was made up of small, mid-century style homes scattered over what was once a huge apple orchard. Only a few apple trees now graced the tiny back yards of the well-kept homes. It was tucked away from the hustle of the strip malls and gas stations, but not too far from the warehouse district.

X climbed out of his truck, and I saw that he'd suited up. I got to my trunk and donned a smaller version of the Kevlar vest he wore.

"You're expecting trouble?"

"This is Cruz's grandmother's place. A neighbor reported hearing a disturbance of some kind. When the call came in for a welfare check, I recognized the address and called you. Uniforms are around back. Come on."

We walked up to the door and knocked, both of us turning to the side of the door frame, in case we got a shotgun blast coming through the door instead of a person. The door opened and a tiny woman looked up at X's huge bulk. She was elderly and her face showed years of living, but her hair was still midnight dark with only a few silver strands highlighting its youthful sheen.

"Come in," she said in softly accented English. Her calm at seeing cops at her door made me edgy. With a hand on the butt of my Glock, I followed X into the house.

13

The furnishings were straight out of the seventies, two recliners facing an old boxy TV. A female voice hawked the latest celebrity-designed jewelry.

Mrs. Renard sat down heavily in her recliner. Avoiding the vacant La-Z-Boy, I chose a side chair and sat gingerly, afraid it would collapse. X stood, his head bent under the low ceiling, looking like Gulliver in a Lilliputian living room.

"Mrs. Renard, we're investigating your grandson, Enrico Cruz. Have you seen him?"

"No." Her answer was straightforward enough, but her lack of concern still bothered me. Maybe the cops showed up at her house all the time. The hairs on my neck started to tingle. I looked at her closely, trying to find signs of possession or some sort of monster within. There was nothing, yet I couldn't shake the feeling.

"There was a police call regarding a noise disturbance coming from your house." X tried to make his voice less authoritative and more church pastor. It didn't work.

"Are you okay? Is there anyone else here?"

At his question, we heard sounds of movement from the back room, and even though Granny Renard said she was alone, we both knew she was lying. Perhaps she was under duress, though I saw no signs of nervousness or fear from her.

X spoke in normal tones as we made our way toward the back of the house. I approached a closed door and heard the distinct sound of a long haunting yowl. X turned back at the sound, prepared to come my way. I shook my head. If it was the strigoi, I couldn't kill it, and certainly didn't want X in its warpath. I didn't have my big knife on me, and bullets would be useless. I pulled the flashlight from my pocket, it's pitifully small beam my one and only defense.

A distressed, violent hacking came from where we'd left the old woman. X and I glanced at each other. With a head tilt, he indicated for me to go and check. I shook my head no. I couldn't leave him to happen upon something he'd have no idea how to deal with. X glared at me. I pointed toward myself and then the hallway, and then heard him groan in frustration as I turned away.

I waited until his footsteps faded into the bigger room before I opened the door. The room was dark, and my hand automatically felt along the wall for a switch. I heard the click, but the room remained shrouded save for a silver gleam through the window. I swept my flashlight beam back and forth across the space. Turning toward a scraping noise, my light caught the bulging red eyes of the strigoi as it hissed at me from the corner.

I kept the light on the beast's head, but in the periphery, I spotted Cruz. He rolled up off the floor toward the window, slamming into the old casement and shattering the glass as he escaped. The beast jumped at me and I ducked to avoid the claws. The stench of it almost overwhelmed me, and I wished for Marlowe's insensitivity to smell as well as his battle sword. I swung the light, bashing it into the blood red of one eye. The strigoi shrieked and backed off, and with a hiss, it leaped out the broken window.

I ran for the opening and saw our backup as their lights swept across the empty yard. It was dark, with only a thin stream of light from the streetlamp sifting through the pine trees.

"Did you see him?" I asked. They both look dumbfounded. "Cruz jumped out the window. He's on foot. Approach with caution." I ducked back into the house. What could I tell them? Look out for the creepy cat monster with him? Heading back to the living room, I called to X that we needed to move. There was no answer.

I rounded the corner to find X in a fierce struggle with the little old lady. Seriously, if it wasn't horrifying, it would have been comical. The woman had him around his neck, chanting intently into his face. They were standing face-to-face, or at least, X was. He held Renard up and away from him as much as possible, her tiny feet dangling in the air. She had an unnatural strength and X appeared to be under some kind of enchantment. I tried to make out her words as I pulled my gun.

"Let go of him now!" I didn't really want to shoot an elderly woman, but she had a death grip on my partner. As big as X was, he couldn't seem to pull her off. I holstered the gun and thought about using my

Taser, but that would zap both of them. I was about to run at them when her chanting stopped abruptly, and she dropped to the floor. With the release of her hold on him, X stumbled backward, pulling me with him. We hit the wall and righted ourselves.

"Are you okay?" I looked into his eyes. They were wide with surprise.

"Yeah, yeah, I'm fine." He turned toward the woman. "She was choking, I went to help her and then..." his words faded as we both watched the woman struggle to sit up. Before either of us got to her, she pulled a letter opener from her lace-covered table.

"*Auzi sângele meu, live sacrificiul meu.*" She intoned the words like a priest saying mass before plunging the opener into her splotchy neck. Blood poured out like water out of a broken faucet. She fell to the floor again and I ran for her, watching the fierce light in her eyes fade. X called for paramedics on the radio. I grabbed a lace doily off a nearby table and pressed it onto the wound. It was soaked through in a matter of seconds. Her eyes were closed. She said nothing else. The only word I recognized in her dying phrase was *sacrifice*.

This did not make me feel better at all, considering her hold over X only moments before. I kept muttering the phrase over and over to myself, committing as much of it to memory as I could. Maybe Marlowe or Volpi could translate it. The old woman looked peaceful, as peaceful as someone could with a stab wound in their jugular.

Suddenly, I missed my own grandmother, Freya. She was still very much alive, but not all that grandmotherly, and I missed how she used to be when my sister and I were kids. I remembered ginger cookies and Caffe Lattes on a front porch filled with the sound of with handmade wind chimes. Cruz's grandmother died before the paramedics got to the house, and I thought briefly of calling Freya. I should. We hadn't spoken much since my father died. I wondered if she would have sacrificed herself for me if the situation were reversed. Hopefully, I would never find out.

After what seemed like hours of forensic techs and incident reports and X reassuring me that he was fine and that no one put a hex on him, I left the station. Too exhausted to drive back across town, I was infinitely glad that Volpi had dropped Marlowe off at my place after the market closed.

Letting myself into the darkened apartment, I found Marlowe, in his now familiar place on the couch, his face illuminated by a single candle flickering on the coffee table beside him. He was asleep. I watched him as I pulled off my boots at the door. He looked like a young gladiator in repose, innocent and wise at the same time. I paused to blow out the candle as I passed by. His eyes opened and he reached for my hand. We said nothing, but he tugged, pulling at me. I resisted at first, but I gradually let myself sink down to the couch. Still fully clothed, I tucked in beside him. His strong arm snaked around me and nestled me closer, his chin tucked into that spot between my neck and shoulder. There was a moment, maybe two, where I felt his heartbeat between my shoulder blades, the whisper of something lower, where my ass curved into him, but he shifted away. His breath deepened and I fell into an exhausted sleep.

$$\phi$$

After a blissful six hours, I woke to find Marlowe attempting to cook breakfast on my stove. He'd been stirring bags of instant oatmeal into a pan of water, having an irrational distrust of my microwave. I watched as he leaned over the pan, smelling the brown sugared aroma. Except for opening my eyes, I hadn't moved, but some otherworldly awareness told him I was awake.

"Good, you've awakened. I've prepared a breaking fast of gruel." He held up the torn packaging. "Quaker Oatmeal, as you name it. Master Volpi was kind enough to purchase some wares at the market for us, and I have fresh fruit to accompany our meal." He carefully ladled the cereal into bowls on my counter. I sat up and yawned.

"Coffee?"

It was freshly ground Italian roast and it was excellent. I complimented him on his ability to brew a decent cup and wondered how much money he persuaded the normally stingy Volpi to spend at the market. Marlowe had pulled a rather large blade from somewhere and sliced a red-skinned apple as he answered.

"I allowed him to take some likenesses of my journal in exchange for these wonderful foodstuffs." He popped an apple slice into his mouth, holding one out for me.

"What about your space-time continuum theory? Doesn't Volpi having pictures of your journal mess with that?"

He shrugged. "Master Volpi was already in possession of photographs, was he not? Mayhaps he was meant to acquire them. He should be offered recompense in exchange for his able assistance."

"Trust me, Volpi manages to make his way in the world just fine."

We finished breakfast as I relayed the events at Cruz's grandmother's the night before. Marlowe listened with his usual inscrutable expression, but his eyes grew dark at my mention of her last words. After having me repeat it several times, he wrote it down and translated the words into Latin and then English.

"She cursed his soul to wander," Marlowe said quietly. "To never rest and sealed it with blood."

"That sounds creepy," I replied.

He glanced at me and frowned. "Creepy. Meaning it creeps along the ground like an insect? It is nefarious to be sure. I'd keep a close watch on your friend. Blood sacrifices are not a triviality."

As we went about our morning, neither of us mentioned our sleeping together on the couch and, except for an occasional glance, there was nothing overtly sexual between us.

Later that afternoon, we were on the street, eating another cheesesteak as Marlowe couldn't seem to get enough of them. Passing the familiar street musicians I saw almost every day, I nodded at them and they smiled in return. I was one of the many who threw a dollar in their basket. There were two of them, their dreadlocks bound in knit hats. They sat on folding chairs with curiously indented shields inverted in their laps, creating music by slapping the shields in random patterns. The sound resembled a steel drum. Marlowe was fascinated and we stopped to watch, enjoying our hot gooey sandwiches.

He swayed slightly to the music. I pulled my usual dollar out and it joined the several other bills in the basket. Most people stopped only a short time, anxious to get on with their busy day. Usually, I am too—too much to do to stop and listen for very long. But with Marlowe, things were different. His life was such that everywhere he went he took in as much as he could. I guess he saw that as part of his education. Not just hunting the bad guys, but helping the good guys, and living the good life, as in stopping for a meal and music in the middle of the day. I mentioned this to him, and he nodded in understanding.

We stood together, leaning into each other slightly, swaying back and forth in time with the syncopated rhythm.

"Our lives are only a moment in time. Compared to the rest of the world and beyond. Given that the world goes on for five hundred years without me, I know this for a fact: we should experience everything we possibly can."

"Some experiences I'd rather not have," I said.

"This is true. Alas, there are lessons I wished not to learn as well, but they are behooveful." The song ended. After Marlowe begged another bill off of me to put in the musician's basket, we moved on down the street, both of us quiet in our thoughts. I couldn't seem to keep my mind off the night before, being so close to him.

We walked through Logan Square, dodging kids running around their parents and tourists taking pictures of the Swann Fountain. The water would be turned off soon, as it was every winter, to avoid it freezing.

"You are trembling," he said, speaking in the direction of my handbag. I pulled out my phone. X's face flashed across the screen.

"Hey," I pressed speaker and Marlowe jumped slightly at X's voice coming out of the tiny box.

"Hey, what are you and Marlowe doing this evening? Connie wants to meet him."

"What?" I glanced at Marlowe, whose lovely hazel eyes had returned to their normal twinkle. He smiled as his eyebrows raised in question. Great, now Connie wanted to meet him. So much for him keeping a low profile.

"Arroz con pollo, tonight. Six o'clock. Don't kill the messenger."

X hung up without waiting for a reply. He knew that nothing short of death or duty would keep me from Connie's chicken dish. Marlowe's grin was infectious.

"People in your timeline eat very well. I shall become too corpulent to travel soon."

If only that were true. His perfectly proportioned frame moved ahead of me, sitting on the edge of the fountain so he could touch the cool water.

"In the summer, kids come here and splash around to stay cool." I sat next to him. He reached for my hand which was colder than normal, given the November temperatures.

"I should like to see that," he said, and we were both quiet for a moment. Knowing how unlikely it would be that he would ever see Swann Fountain again, let alone in summer. I got up and walked away.

Marlowe caught up with me and tucked my hand into the crook of his arm as we walked. The gesture didn't seem strange to me, and that was strange in itself. We strolled through the center maze of buildings, ignoring the cold, ignoring the looks from some people at Marlowe's giant cape fluttering around him.

"We must find this Cruz and his pet. The matter is

growing ever dire the longer we wait."

"The police have done a search through the warehouses looking for him and there's nothing. We could hit the sewers again, but I think the strigoi has moved on. We're at a dead end. At least I have this." I pulled out the blood-soaked doily shoved into a Ziploc bag from my inside coat pocket. If Granny Renard was the summoner of the strigoi, we'll need her blood to kill it.

He nodded grimly and absently rubbed at his temple.

"Headache?" I asked. He ignored me, but there was something in his look that made me stop. I pulled on his arm to make him face me. "What is it?"

He turned, his hand touching my cheek. "I fear the transition has started. My time here will not be long now," he whispered.

"How long?"

He shook his head. His eyes were slate gray, luminous against the dark clouds gathering.

"'Tis difficult to ascertain. Mayhaps a day, possibly more."

"And Volpi has nothing?" My voice sounded a bit desperate. "No insight into how you do this? Or more importantly, how not to do it?"

"Alas, no, dear Tamberlyn. Last eve, you mentioned a desire that I stay. Any solution offered by Angelo could allow me to do that, and yet, I declined, saying that I must travel. It is my fate, and even my calling, if you will."

"Of course, I know that you can't stay here." I paused and then murmured, "Your life lies elsewhere."

"That is rapidly changing. It would seem over the

past two days, in the past hours spent with you, my thoughts are increasingly focused here in Philadelphia." He paused. "This is madness. It does not matter. I fear it is not to be. We must not waste a second, not a moment, for time is our most precious commodity."

I started to move away. "As soon as Cruz is spotted, we can move, but—"

"That is not of which I speak."

His arms encircled my waist and I couldn't move, nor did I want to, caught in his gaze. I watched as his mouth came closer, his lips opening. Heedless of our public display, I opened my mouth under his. He still tasted of peppers and onions, but so did I. It felt like a culmination of all I'd been waiting for since he'd arrived. Maybe even before that. As much as I tried to avoid it, there was a frenzied link between us that I couldn't help. I needed this. I needed him, more than I've ever needed anyone, and the thought scared the hell out of me. A passerby muttered at us to get a room and Marlowe pulled away. He looked down at me.

"Excellent thought. A room. Somewhere close, somewhere private in which to—"

"Tam." A voice called out. I ignored it, caught in the moment. "Tam," the call came again, and I turned toward it reluctantly. "Hey, I thought that was you guys." Ziggy, her heavy boots clumping toward us, waved happily, perhaps unaware of her interrupting us.

14

Marlowe greeted Ziggy with a warmth that surprised me. His hand squeezing my arm was the only indicator that he was at all disappointed at the interruption. I, however, was not so good at covering my feelings and my voice was sharp as I spoke to her.

"Hey Zig. What's up?"

She looked at me curiously. "You okay?"

"Fine. Just going over the case with Marlowe, trying to sort things out."

"Yeah, I had Mrs. Renard on my table this morning. Suicide by letter opener. You don't see that every day. I'm glad I ran into you guys. I found out something weird I want to show you."

Marlowe indicated she should lead the way. I followed them, trying to re-focus on the case. I could only think of two things. Marlowe wanted me as much as I wanted him, and he would be gone soon.

We followed Ziggy down the stairs and the narrow hallway into her lair, the basement of doom. She flipped on the fluorescent lights.

"The tooth sample I sent to my old professor. Results came back." She headed to a countertop and pulled out a tablet. Marlowe, who had only seen my ancient laptop, was amazed at the device, but he managed to keep his mouth shut. We both stood near Ziggy, looking over her shoulder. Marlowe's hand was a warm pressure at my back. I leaned against him. His hand moved down to clasp my waist. I stifled a sigh of contentment and pent-up desire. Ziggy was apparently oblivious to this tiny connection between us as she brought up an email from her former teacher.

She scrolled down over the personal stuff, and found the pertinent part of the email, reading aloud.

"DNA strands are human, but with certain markers that have only been seen in Homo sapiens of the lower Paleolithic era, namely the Homo floresiensis." The word slipped easily from Ziggy's practiced tongue, but not so easily into my unscientific brain.

"Okay, for the novice—that means?"

"It means that this guy you're chasing is not of any species found on Earth. At least, not yet. He needs another forty or fifty thousand years of evolution. My professor wanted to know where I came across such a sample. I had to make up some story about extruding dried bone matter from some obscure African sample. And I'll probably have to distract him from investigating further."

"Is that a good thing or a bad thing?" I asked.

She shrugged again, a slow smile coming to her lips. "He wasn't bad. There's something to be said for experience."

"Indeed," Marlowe said wisely. His fingers grazed my skin at the edge of my shirt. I jumped, emitting a startled sound. Ziggy looked from me to Marlowe.

"You guys have been holding out on me," she said.

"What do you mean?" My innocent act left much to be desired. Ziggy rolled her eyes.

"I mean that, regardless of what I told my professor, this sample is not anything from this world."

"Well, no, it's not, but you knew that. You've seen what I deal with, Zig. This is not much different."

Marlowe looked at me, a puzzled expression on his face.

"Tam brought me a case two years ago," Ziggy clarified. "That also defied normal explanation. We've found our fair share of weird since then. Solving that case got her into Homicide."

I was grateful for her explanation and the diversion. I pressed my lips together, remembering the feel of Marlowe's mouth. As long as we kept the conversation on the case, I wouldn't have to talk about who Marlowe really was. I struggled to focus on her words.

"But that's not the thing." She put the tablet aside and opened the fridge, pulling a tray of glass slides out of it. "This sample is that of something not quite human. And its genetic development signifies its origin as very old, but the protein markers are that of a body much younger, newer." She looked thoughtful. "It's as though this creature was alive and well and hundreds of years out of its time."

I could see the question forming as she looked not at Marlowe, but at me.

"Ziggy—" I tried to steer her away from this segue. It

didn't work.

"At first, I thought of the possibility of a being that lives, slash that, exists for hundreds of years. But that's not this creature. This thing is young. Judging from the sample, I'd say anywhere from beyond puberty to young adulthood." She looked at me with one eyebrow arched—her pride at figuring it out almost outweighing her irritation at me. "Which means it hasn't been alive for hundreds of years, but its origins are centuries old."

She sat down, turning away from us to pull a slide out of the tray and under the lens of the microscope. The action served to put distance between us. I started toward her, anxious to convince my friend that I wasn't keeping secrets to hurt her. I sensed that she'd already made the connection between the creature and Marlowe showing up in Philadelphia at the same time. The less she knew of Marlowe and his origins the better. Ziggy pulled the slide from the microscope and dropped it into the bag marked evidence and gave it to me. There was a tiredness in her voice I hadn't heard before.

"You haven't lied to me in a long time, Tam. Not since I learned the truth about things, about you. You kill the bad guys, I cover for you. You trust me more than X, more than your old partner, Ava. I don't understand why you won't tell me what's going on now." She turned to Marlowe, who had picked up her tablet to examine the device further. "But since you've shown up, things have changed."

"It's this case, Zig." I tried to reassure her. "It's a bitch of a case, and Marlowe is helping me."

The statement was generally true, it was a bitch of a case, and Marlowe was indeed helping me. And Ziggy knew about the weirdness I dealt with, but it only came into her purview after they were dead. Like X, I really thought too much involvement would put her in danger. It was the same age-old argument Volpi and I'd had about my sister. He thought it was about my lack of trust. Really it was about my fear. My mother was gone, and so was Dad. Both natural causes but gone all the same. I didn't want to lose anyone else. Volpi and Ziggy had no idea of each other, as that would bring them closer into my dangerous world.

"Don't let this case screw us up. Screw you up."

"I'll be fine," I said.

"Maybe, maybe not." Her tiredness was replaced by irritation. And she wasn't wrong about Marlowe—he had changed things.

"Christopher Marlowe, that's such an interesting name—a famous name." Ziggy looked at him with renewed curiosity. His eyebrows raised but he said nothing. He glanced at me for a second. I shrugged. It was his story to tell.

Marlowe's jaw quirked. He spoke in a considerate tone to Ziggy. "Tempting fate is a dangerous thing, Mistress Jane. Is your desire for answers enough to risk yours? Can you not trust your most trusted friend? She is only doing what she ought." He handed her the tablet back.

"Too much knowledge is not always a benefit," I said, taking a quote from him.

He nodded.

She waved her hand as though it didn't matter, but I could tell her feelings were still hurt.

"Just for now, Zig. I will tell you everything at some

point, I promise," I told her.

"It may be too late then."

I glanced at Marlowe. "We should go. I want to get cleaned up before dinner."

We left Ziggy's lab and headed back to the apartment. The afternoon's heat between Marlowe and I was lost as Ziggy's obvious pain weighed on both of us. I'd felt this before. It did occur to me that I used people—Ziggy, X, Volpi, some in the know more than others, to help me in my task as a hunter. I told myself that it was necessary, I couldn't keep this stuff under wraps and my city safe if I didn't.

Ziggy had come into my world uninvited. Her scientific mind had too many questions to go unanswered for long, and I couldn't keep coming up with excuses about the strange things she found on her autopsy table.

Aside from Ava, my former partner, Ziggy had been my first friend at District 21. On the case she mentioned to Marlowe, she'd put her job and reputation in jeopardy by omitting some things from her report. Things that could not be explained. When I'd asked her why she'd risked her job, she'd said that even a scientist could take some things on faith.

I had a certain skill set to deal with the fanged and dangerous, so did Volpi. But Ziggy and X did not. As a way of protecting them, I told them only what was necessary.

I'd learned to keep things to myself from experience. First with my high school friend who'd used my confession as fodder to make herself more popular. We were kids. Shit like that happens in high school all the time, and I'd moved on.

The second time was after graduation. Naïve and over-confident in a way that only a teenager can be, I fell in love for the first time. My first love affair had ended badly. So badly that I'd blocked most of the details out. Still, there was a dull ache every time I recalled that summer.

Dad used to call me bullheaded. It takes a while for an idea to get through my thick skull, especially an idea I don't like. But I finally learned that my life as a hunter should be a solitary one.

I've played it close to the vest ever since. Not even Volpi, who could ascertain most of my secrets, knew everything about that part of my life. Eventually, it was like it happened to someone else. Someone I used to be. Except in the past two days that someone was re-emerging, and I wasn't sure I liked her. I certainly didn't trust her, that other self. But since Marlowe's arrival, I couldn't deny that I'd felt things that hadn't surfaced since I was seventeen. I felt less alone, in a constant state of both hyper-awareness and relaxation. It was heady, and euphoric, and it scared the shit out of me. Mostly because I knew it would end.

15

Marlowe and I arrived at the Hernandez household fortified with a twelve-pack of Pacifico and additional warnings to Marlowe about not revealing his true background. Both of us had gone about getting ready for dinner without talking much. Feeling awkward with a naked Marlowe in my shower, I'd dressed hurriedly and headed to the corner store for beer. It was an excuse to not be in the house with him.

The kiss we'd shared before Ziggy found us was at the forefront of my mind and yet, neither of us made a move to take things further. It was as if the conversation with Ziggy made us all too aware of the precariousness of Marlowe's situation.

"And remember to say, 'back home,' or 'where I'm from,' not 'this timeline' or 'my timeline.'" I pulled into X's driveway and parked behind his truck. Ziggy's third degree about Marlowe had shaken me more than I wanted to admit. I kept telling myself it was for the safety of all—the space-time continuum yada, yada,

yada—or maybe I hadn't wanted to go there. Everyone has secrets, right? So what if I had more than most.

"I've done this before, Tamberlyn." And then in the next breath, "What an astonishingly large monstrosity." He gazed at X's full-size truck. "And space for hauling hay and materials to market. This is truly a marvelous work."

I slammed the car door and looked at him. "See? Things like that. You can't say things like that. It's called a truck."

Marlowe's disdain was evident. "Of course, it is. I believe I invented the word. Though in my—back home, they were only two-wheeled devices with which to carry large burdens."

"Forgive me, Master Marlowe, for underestimating your brilliance." I handed him the twelve-pack and knocked on the door.

"Sarcasm is light upon thy precious tongue, dear Tamberlyn. Well used to such, I imagine."

I had to laugh.

"What's so funny?" X asked as he opened the door.

"I am, dear friend," Marlowe responded before I could say anything. "Miss Paradiso finds my wit most becoming. We've come bearing gifts for the palette." He held the beer out.

X broke out in a grin. "Good man." He showed us inside where his two boys, Julio and Gus, six and four respectively, bounded into the living room. The baby, Valentina, gurgled contentedly in her play yard situated next to the couch.

I gave hugs all around and introduced Marlowe who bowed and shook the boys' hands. They were mesmerized. Same with Connie, who emerged from the kitchen, wiping her hands on a kitchen towel.

Once again, Marlowe had to show off his Spanish and his courtly manners. Connie's eyebrows rose all the way up into her hairline as he kissed her hand. She giggled and let fly an incredibly fast string of Spanish that confounded my show-off companion. He did not let on, but he switched to English and asked her about things a woman of his or anyone's century would take pride in: her children, her household, her food preparation. Connie was a real estate broker by trade and in a good quarter, brought home more than Xavier, but Marlowe hit upon her passion, which was cooking. She soon had him next to her at the counter, chopping jalapeños.

I begged off playing a video game with Julio to sit and have a beer with X, who held a squirming Valentina. I asked about any effects he may have felt from the struggle with Renard.

"Would you relax? I'm fine. Such a worrier. You're worse than my mother."

"Someone's got to look out for your big ass. I found out she was chanting some kind of blood sacrifice."

"So, she's a witch, and I've been cursed, is that it?"

He was joking, but I found it hard to smile back at him. I'd learned the hard way that witches were not to be trifled with. Other than her proximity to the strigoi, I had no reason to believe Cruz's granny was a witch. Though offing oneself with a silver letter opener seconds after intoning a Romanian curse wasn't exactly baking cookies. X looked toward the kitchen where Connie was laughing at something Marlowe said.

"You haven't kicked him out yet, so that's something."

X smiled at me.

"Would you stop? I'm not that inhospitable."

"Have you ever let Rick the Dick stay the night?" The expression on my partner's face was all-knowing.

"I'm not sleeping with Marlowe." I lowered my voice. Connie's laugh rang out again, this time with Marlowe's baritone chuckle added. The sound of it made me smile.

"Not yet," X said, and before I could protest, he stopped me. "I'm not judging. You're a grown-up. You do what you want. But I like this guy much better." He looked down at his darling daughter, who had caught his mustache in her chubby fingers. She gave it a tug. He gently pulled her hand away as she laughed.

"He won't stay." I heard the sadness in my voice as I said it. A pathetic noise.

"He wants to, I can tell. He's waiting on you." X sipped his beer, keeping it away from Valentina in a well-practiced maneuver.

X brought up the home invasion case again, saying he'd found a possible lead as to who was fencing the stolen items. Often, these leads didn't pan out, but he wanted to follow it up. I changed the subject back to the Balfour case and how it could be connected with Cruz's grandmother. Talking to X about the case while leaving parts of it out required some creative thinking, and once again, I was struck by how much of my time was spent trying to keep things secret.

Connie put the finishing touches on dinner, circumnavigating Marlowe's attempts to help her. I half-listened to X, part of my mind on the events of that afternoon. Marlowe and I being interrupted and the fact that his departure could happen at any moment weighed on me heavily.

I took out my phone and texted Volpi. I got a terse reply saying that he was working on Marlowe's problem and not to bother him. The sense of wasting time started to creep up on me. I was about to fake a work call to get out of there, to do something, anything but sit on my goddamn hands and wait. Connie and Marlowe came to join us in the living room, and I put my phone away.

"Your friend has the most interesting life," Connie said as she sat next to me. Marlowe had the good grace to look innocent.

"I was merely relaying tales of history, as that is my vocation. Elizabethan history." He looked at me pointedly as if to say, *See? I know what I'm doing.*

"He makes you feel as though he's lived through it. I bet he's a great teacher." Connie smiled at him.

"I can only imagine," I said.

"I suppose you two have been talking shop?" She looked at her husband and took the baby into her arms. X splayed his hands out in a shrugging motion, but his eyes flickered over to mine. I knew he hadn't told Connie the whole truth about what happened at Renard's house.

"It's a tough case, but there'll be a break soon, I can feel it." I drank the rest of my beer and got up for another. I'd been getting beers out of X's fridge for two years. I motioned for Connie to stay seated. "Anyone else?"

Marlowe stood. "I'll assist you," he said, following me to the kitchen.

Ignoring glances from our hosts, I headed toward the refrigerator, Marlowe at my heels.

"What are you doing?" I pulled out a bottle and handed it to him.

"I'm merely conversing. A teacher of history seemed more plausible than poet. They might ask for a sample of my work, as did your friend, Rick. And, as you know, I am very well versed in that timeline, err, period in history." He blocked my way out of the kitchen. I stopped, watching as he approached me. I glanced away from his eyes. "'Tis not my topic of conversation you are vexed about. Alas, it is Mistress Connie. Thy jealous bone again? Consuela is a married woman, I have no designs on her, nor she, I."

"I am not jealous. Why would you say such a thing?"

He laughed softly into my ear. I turned my head so as not to crane my neck to look at him. He was too close, but I wasn't going to back up.

"The sun is jealous of thy flashing eyes. The moon hides itself in shame at the face of thy beauty."

"Stop with the poetry. You're a history teacher, remember?" I started to move around him.

"I play the hapless scholar with our hosts, but dear lady, you know me truly. Would you also know my heart as well?"

"We're being rude."

"Shall we pursue this discourse at a later time?" The bastard didn't move, and yet, neither did I. In the space of seconds, my mind ran through images of Marlowe: The way his lip curled in concentration as he wrote in pen at my kitchen counter, his hand automatically reaching for the non-existent inkwell every other line. His finely sculpted torso with its smattering of hair and scars, the other parts of him covered in one of my bath towels. The way his hand covered mine at the fountain, not to mention the way he kissed me. If that was any indication, this man knew his way around a woman. And yet, his wistfulness at having to leave and the tenderness with which he spoke of his love from another time made me believe he was not a casual-sex kind of guy. What was he doing? At my partner's house, while they sat in the living room speculating on whatever was going on with us and he declared...what? His love for me? His desire? Did he expect me to fall into his arms like Juliet Capulet?

"I can't do this, Marlowe, not here."

After a moment, he stepped aside. His frustration flashed across his face as I passed. He followed me back into the living room.

Dinner was kept lively, and the topic of conversation was safely curtailed by Julio, who captivated Marlowe by explaining the more complex features of his *Finding Nemo* video game. I relaxed for the first time since arriving.

"He's a keeper, that one," Connie said as I helped her serve the tres leches cake, "quite the way with words."

"You don't know the half of it," I said. Once again, her eyebrows raised. I was beginning to think this was her normal expression.

"He's a good lover too, eh? I knew it." She grinned at my discomfort and moved on before I could deny the assumption. "I'm happy for you, Tam. You deserve someone good. Someone to love you as much as my Avi loves me." Again, with the eyebrows.

She turned away and I followed her out to the table. Strangely enough, the ride home was not filled with tension, but very relaxed. Marlowe's usual intensity was tempered by good food and beer, and he spent the entire trip proclaiming the wonders of Nemo and tres leches cake.

I let us into the apartment and tossed my keys onto the side table under the coat rack. Marlowe's hands reached for my shoulders.

"Allow me." He gently pulled my coat off and hung it up.

"Thank you," I faced him. "Look, about earlier." He stopped me with his finger to my lips. It trailed down and across my cheek, coming to rest under my chin. Again, he tilted my face toward his. Again, like in Logan Square, I was transfixed by the way he looked at me. His mouth opened slightly, and I closed my eyes and melted into him.

"You're trembling again," he said in exasperation. His eyes closed, then opened, dark with frustration. "That infernal device."

My ringtone blasted and I stepped away to answer it, hearing Marlowe's words in the background.

"It's a wonder the world has managed to procreate as much as it has with this constant interruption."

"Hey," I was smiling as I answered.

"Did Munson call you?" X's voice was breathless.

"No."

"We got something on Balfour. Meet me at his club." He hung up as I turned to Marlowe.

"I've got to go."

He said nothing, but he pulled my coat from the hook and held it out for me. I didn't bother arguing with Marlowe to stay put. The guy never stayed put.

16

It was twenty minutes from my house to the club and X was already there. He was pacing back and forth, not exactly patiently waiting. I nodded at him. Munson was still, his scowl etched into his Mount Rushmore of a face. It cracked as he greeted me. "We could have handled this, Paradiso."

"My case too, Jason." I used his first name because it irritated him. I called him Jason whenever I'd bested him on the shooting range at the academy. I'd had a small advantage—my father and I had been regulars at the shooting range twice a month since I was twelve. I realized with a pang that I hadn't been back since Dad passed away.

"Who's this guy?" Munson's frown deepened as he indicated Marlowe getting out of my car.

"A criminal informant," I said quickly. "I was working an angle when X called me."

Munson hesitated for a few seconds. "He stays down here." He turned abruptly and headed for the main door of the club.

"You okay?" I asked X under my breath as we followed Munson. My last beer was two hours earlier and I'd seen X put away a six-pack with hardly any effect on him, but still, it was good to ask. He knew what I meant and nodded, popping a breath mint into his mouth. He offered me one and I took it.

"Where's Balfour?" I raised my voice toward Munson's back. His suit and tie were rumpled and worn like he'd slept in them for days. Maybe he had. He barely managed an answer. "Upstairs. Gregor Krotsky is here."

This was not good news. In fact, it was unbelievable news. Krotsky would never ask for a meet on Balfour's territory. If he chose to meet at all, it would be some place neutral. The guy wasn't stupid.

We'd stopped in front of the bouncer at the door. I glanced at Munson whose scowl deepened before he passed by the frontman with barely a glance. I had to flash a badge to get myself and Marlowe in.

For once, Marlowe's cape didn't seem out of place. The music's techno-pop beat was thumping, the floor vibrated with the beat of a hundred pairs of feet. I glanced at Marlowe's face when he spotted the woman dancing in a cage, her body covered in nothing but neon paint, save for a tiny scrap of cloth at her crotch. Across the room, an identical cage held a similarly unclad young man. We followed Munson to the staircase. I lingered at the bottom of the steps, yelling into Marlowe's ear.

"Stay here." I pressed my phone into his hand. "I'll call you from X's phone if anything happens." This was police business and while Marlowe was clearly good in a fight, he was still a civilian.

"I should be with you," he shouted.

Shaking my head, I pushed my hand against his chest. His own hand was warm and comforting as it came across mine. But I had to go. Munson and X were halfway up the stairs.

"We have really piss poor timing," I said. He didn't hear me. But he looked worried.

I turned to catch up with the guys, still wondering why Gregor would choose to meet here. The door to the office was closed and I hesitated as the hairs stood up on my neck. I didn't bother knocking. Expecting to find a roomful of mobsters and various evil sidekicks, I opened the door and stood gawking at an empty room.

The room was windowless and dark with two shabby wall sconces providing the only light. I raced to the back wall covered in long black curtains. Curtains that were still swaying. I pulled them aside and opened the metal exit door.

A blast of cold air hit me as I stepped out onto a metal landing. The space below was a square lot, about the size of a three-car garage. Opposite me, an alley opened out onto the side street. To the left, a building loomed stories above me, its metal balconies and emergency stairs hanging down like an afterthought. To the side of the stairway, an enormous dumpster loomed below me. Across the space were two more dumpsters next to a broken-down chain-link fence. One streetlight at the far end of the alley shone its wavering fluorescence onto the scene.

"X?" I called out. Gunfire answered me. I recognized X's P9, as well as the whiffle of a silencer and a ping as a bullet hit the door behind me. Ducking, I ran down the stairs. A security light clicked on as I passed, serving only to paint me as a target.

"Tam!" X grabbed my upper arm to haul me off the bottom stair and pull me behind a dumpster. His big bulk squeezed in beside me.

"Where's Munson?" My gun was out, but I hadn't fired. There was nothing to fire at. Until he'd grabbed my arm, I'd had no idea where X was.

"Disappeared as soon as the shooting started." His breathing was heavy. I glanced at him, but he seemed okay. He was focused on his gun, reaching under his jacket for a spare clip.

"And Krotsky?"

"Not here." He peered around the dumpster. Another shot rang out. Flying cement stung my cheek. The bullets were getting closer. X pulled his head back sharply. "Two shooters, eleven and two as near as I can figure. And wherever the hell Munson is."

"You call for backup?" I asked. He frowned at me, pulling out a smartphone. In the beam of the security light, I saw the cracked screen and no signs of life.

"Yours?"

I reached for my back pocket, finding nothing but my ass. "Marlowe has it."

"Damn it, doesn't he have his own phone?"

I rolled my eyes. They didn't even have snail mail where Marlowe was from, let alone cell service. More shots rang out, pinning us down.

"Can you get the light? We're sitting ducks here."

X turned, aiming at the security light. It took him two tries. In the relative safety of the dark, I scooted a few feet along the wall to the other side of our dumpster.

Maybe I could get a better vantage point. "You sure this isn't the Russians?"

"I'm not sure about anything," X answered. "We came out the door and someone started shooting. I got out of the way, pulled my gun, and Munson was gone. He's out there somewhere." He paused and I looked over. I could make out his eyes and the white of his collar. "I think we've been set up."

"By who?"

He turned toward the club and yelled, "Philadelphia PD. Drop your weapon and come out." The only answer was the return of gunfire.

"Munson?" I asked. X didn't answer right away. I squinted at him in the darkness, his head was down, intent on his weapon and I heard the click of a bullet being chambered.

"Balfour? Or the Russians?"

X's teeth flashed in the dimness. "Our luck, Paradiso, probably both." More gunfire hit the pavement around us. Xavier fired a couple of answering shots.

"What the hell is going on?" My mind reeled. The bullets stopped flying for a moment and instinctively, I knew the shooters were moving. Changing positions, I scanned the small lot, trying to detect any movement.

X watched his side, but he was on a roll. "Munson's tied to every home robbery we've been investigating. Lots of—"

Bullets pinged off my side of the dumpster. A bright hot pain seared across the shoulder of my injured arm. Wrapping my hand around the injury, I moved back toward the center and more cover.

"You okay?" X's bulk was warm against my other

side.

"I'll live," I said. It stung like hell and I could feel the blood run down my arm, but it wasn't gushing, so I figured I wasn't lying. At least for now. "How do you know it's Munson? What does the home robbery case have to do with organized crime?"

I felt X's shrug.

"We need to get out of here and find out." He nodded toward the front of the lot. Between our cover and the entrance to the alley was a concrete stoop of four or five stairs jutting out from the building next door. "Can you make to those stairs?"

I nodded. From the cover of the concrete, it was a straight shot down the alley and onto the street.

"Wait, I'm almost out of ammo."

I pulled another clip from my jacket and gave it to him. "I don't want to hear any more shit about me carrying extra clips," I said.

X's smile flashed again. His voice was strained. "We get out of this, I'll *buy* you extra clips. And a new gun."

I made a run for it, diving on the other side of the concrete steps. X was still firing. Turning, I shot toward the other dumpster where the shooters were. X ran toward me. He was a much larger target and I heard the silencer's whoosh and bullets hitting the cement. In the faint light of the streetlight, I saw X clutch his side.

Why hadn't we put on our vests for this? The answer came quickly—because we trusted Munson. X landed beside me with a grunt.

"You're hit. How bad?" I asked my partner.

"I'll live." He grinned at me, but it turned into a grimace of pain. His breathing came out ragged and gurgling. He coughed. The sound brought more gunfire our way. I shot back, but I was firing blind. I needed another tactic.

"Jason, what happened to you?" I shouted, not really expecting an answer. At that point, all I wanted to do is get X to a hospital. I pressed my left hand over X's wound. He grunted again.

"Life happens, Paradiso," Munson's voice bounced off the enclosed walls. I focused on the sound of his voice, trying to pinpoint his location. "It was a closed case until Hernandez kept poking around." The echo sounded closer on his last sentence. "The two of you had dinner, am I right? I figure you guys knocked back a few. You have that reputation, you know."

X looked at me. "Do we have that reputation?" He whispered, his eyes wide with mock horror. I shrugged. His expression faded into pain.

"I think there's only Munson left," I hissed at X, who by this time, had slipped from his crouch to half-sitting on the ground, his hand across his torso under his jacket. He didn't speak, merely nodded and indicated with his gun that I should try for the alley entrance. In a crouching run, I headed across the alley to a bunch of boxes and trash cans. I tripped on a crumbled piece of cinder block and lurched headlong into the building. Instinctively, my arms went up to protect my head and my injured arm scraped along the rough brick wall. I felt stitches rip open like a reluctant zipper.

My left hand was already covered in blood from trying to staunch X's wound and now my gun hand was covered too. I wiped the sticky wetness on my pants. The second shooter lay on the ground in front of me. We hadn't been shooting in this direction, so Munson must have gotten him. I felt for a pulse. Finding none, I pulled his gun loose from his hand and tucked it into the back of my jeans. The action was automatic. My hands came across a cell phone and I fumbled with it for a moment. The blood from my torn stitches ran down my arm, making the device slick in my hand.

Oddly enough the guy's hands were cleaner than mine. Using his thumbprint to unlock his phone, I dialed 911 and gave our location. I texted Marlowe. "Munson, I've got backup on the way." A guy with a cape and a sword wasn't exactly the backup he would be expecting, but at least it was something.

"Good. This will all be over before they get here," Munson taunted.

"You don't have a chance in hell of getting out of this." I focused on X's slow crawl toward me. I was hoping that Munson would be distracted enough not to shoot. X slumped to the ground beside me. I reached down to touch his chest, checking on his breathing. It was ragged but there.

The streetlight was brighter here, so if Munson moved, he'd have a visible shot. But the light also let me see to X's wounds better. A graze had covered his left side in blood. But the second wound was higher, more centered. Probably a lung. I pulled off my jacket to cover his shaking form. His wide face pale in the light.

"The case, there was–" X talked slowly, his breath coming in slow gasps.

"Don't talk," I said, dodging the pings showering around us. I swore Munson carried more ammo than a swat team. With all the metal and brick, a ricochet was as likely to kill us as anything. "I've got to draw him out. You hang on," I said.

I started to move in Munson's direction. X grabbed my hand, holding me back. I tried to pull away but even injured, his strength was more than a match for mine. Munson's dark silhouette darted toward us. From the street I heard running footsteps and turned to see Marlowe, his cape billowing out around him, racing toward us.

Everything happened in a blur. X shoved me aside as Munson's gun went off. Munson looked up and took aim at the charging Marlowe. I shot Munson and he dropped where he stood.

"Marlowe." My voice echoed slightly in the cold space.

"Are you unharmed?" He was at my side. I turned to where X lay. A large patch of blood had appeared on his white shirt, this one was much closer to his heart. I felt Marlowe's hand come across mine where I'd placed it on X's chest.

Sirens blared as emergency vehicles approached.

"Marlowe, go tell them where we are." My voice was harsh and broken with adrenaline and fear.

I reached for X's hand. My other hand pressed tightly against the new wound and I felt the blood seeping from under my fingers. X's lips moved and I leaned down so I could hear him. There was something in Spanish about Connie and the *niños*, and then his dark eyes reached mine.

"Don't let the bastards get you down," he said.

"You're going to be okay, buddy. Just hang in there." My face was wet. I didn't know with what—blood or tears.

The paramedics gently pulled me away from X so they could work. I stood up shakily and approached Munson in a daze. In the headlights, I saw him quite clearly. He'd worn his vest under his white shirt. Blood seeped onto the white from his neck. But the shot that killed him was mine. A neat little hole over his right eye. Both eyes were open, blank, and careless. Turning back to my two partners, one being loaded into an ambulance as the other stood nearby in the shadows, I left Munson's lifeless eyes staring at the moon.

The ambulance roared away, sirens wailing. I hadn't wanted to leave X, but he had to get to the hospital, and someone had to stay. After a paramedic wrapped my arm and tended my shoulder graze, I headed toward Marlowe. My body ached, my brain was numb. Marlowe was wrapping something in cloth. I looked down to see it was a small dagger, the one from his boot.

"It's his blood," Marlowe said quietly. "If it was he who summoned the strigoi, we shall need it."

He placed the knife carefully away in his cloak. I nodded and asked him to wait in the car. Last thing we needed was Marlowe being questioned as a witness. Patrol units had blocked off the alley, so he took the stairs back into the club. I recognized Parker's stature in the flashing lights. He barely looked at me but approached Munson, kneeling to check a pulse. I looked away from his questioning eyes.

It wasn't Ziggy who arrived with the medical examiner's van, but another forensic tech. They zipped up Munson and the second shooter into body bags after another homicide team arrived, followed by forensics.

Even the captain showed up. It's not every day his detectives have an old-fashioned shootout in the back of a drug dealer's club. I was restless during his questions. I wanted to get to the hospital to see about X. The captain didn't seem to care what I wanted.

"If Munson was on Balfour's payroll, why did he shoot Balfour's man?"

I sighed. "Munson needed someone to blame for shooting X. The guy was a patsy. In the wrong place at the wrong time." I said. "Munson was our third man in the home robbery case. This wasn't about Balfour or even the Russians at all. They were convenient. I'd like to get to the hospital if I could." I glanced over at Marlowe, who, reluctant to leave me, was standing outside the perimeter, watching the teamwork. He absently rubbed his temple. "Can I give this report in the morning? My partner—"

The captain gave a curt nod and I headed for Marlowe and my car. We rode to Sacred Heart in silence.

When Connie saw me covered in blood she started to cry. She told me X was rushed into surgery and there was nothing to do but wait. And pray. I told her briefly about Munson, leaving out a lot of details. The circumstances didn't matter. What mattered was whether X would pull through. I kept telling her how strong he was as if reassuring myself of the same thing. She nodded but kept looking at my hands, my blood-stained shirt. I pulled my jacket together as we sat in the waiting room. Marlowe disappeared and was soon back again.

"Here." He handed me a clean T-shirt from my go-bag. "You should refresh thy appearance." I looked at him dumbly. Indicating the blood on my shirt and

Connie, he lowered his voice. "You and I are used to this. She is not."

I got up and walked numbly toward the unisex bathroom in the hallway, followed closely by Marlowe. It was a small restroom, no stall, one toilet, one sink, but big enough to maneuver a wheelchair if need be. I locked the door and turned to the sink, washing Xavier's blood off my hands. Marlowe stood behind me, his hazel eyes searching out mine in the mirror. I looked away.

"I never told X what I do—the monster hunting thing. I never said a word because I wanted to keep him safe. Isn't that ridiculous?" I stepped away from the sink to give him access and he held his equally bloody hands under the running water. "The whole thing is fucking absurd."

"We do our best to protect those we love. This was your way of protecting him. It's not absurd, Tam. It's very human."

I wiped my hands on a paper towel and then unbuttoned my shirt, pulling it carefully away from my body. Some of the blood had dried and stuck to my skin. Dropping the shirt to the floor, I wet a paper towel and wiped the red smears from my stomach and breasts.

"That's the first time you've called me Tam." I watched him behind me in the mirror. He waved wet hands under the automatic dispenser as he'd seen me do moments before. It didn't work and after a moment's frustration, he whacked the machine with considerable force.

I figured his patience was as thin as mine—both of us were worn down to almost nothing. He turned toward me as the towel dropped down from the machine. His scowl at the machine brought a short laugh from me that sounded more like a sob. Marlowe's hands were still damp as he touched me. Our eyes met in the mirror.

Me in a black bra, hanging on to the edge of the sink, light pink smears still across my stomach. His chin level with my eyes, his face in close to mine, fingers wrapped around the curve of my waist. We stared into the mirror. So far apart in life and yet so close together in that one moment.

"I'm glad you're here," I said closing my eyes and sinking back against his warmth. His voice was rich and velvety in my ear.

"I shall always be with thee." His lips grazed my cheek as he handed me my clean shirt. "We must go."

17

When we got back to the waiting room, Parker and a few other guys from the squad were there. I relayed the short version of X's condition to them. Connie was within earshot and I didn't want to be too morbid, but I'd seen how bad his wounds were. It would be a miracle if he made it out of surgery.

We sat in the polyester-covered chairs. Marlowe, me, Connie, Gray, and Rossi from Homicide, Canfield, and his partner from the home robbery case, another guy from the OCU—I couldn't recall his name. Parker, Whitson, and others sat across the room or milled back and forth offering people coffee from the vending machine.

It may have been a few hours, I really wasn't sure, when a doctor in scrubs came out to tell us X had survived surgery. While it was touch and go, he was in recovery.

For some reason, I have always dealt with bad news better than the good stuff. I could barely get through

Connie's hug and the guys' smiles and negotiation of who would stay, and who would check on the kids, etc. Connie's parents had arrived, speaking mile-a-minute Spanish, and I moved from inner circle to outer fringe as people gathered. Everyone seemed to want to celebrate. Yeah, it was good news, but I couldn't shake the nerves— the foreboding in my gut.

"We have work to do, Tamberlyn." Marlowe reminded me. After a quick hug with Connie and my assurances that I would be back in the morning, we headed out of the hospital.

"Did you know I met Connie before I ever met X?" In my car, my voice sounded strange to me as though I were musing out loud. Maybe I was.

It was the early morning hours now, still dark out, and traffic was light. We hit all green lights on our way to nowhere. I didn't want to go home, but I didn't know where else to go. I didn't want to think anymore about anything. "She showed me my apartment. Before she became a broker, she was in charge of property management. I had just broken up with Rhett and was looking for a new place. With long hours at work, I hated the commute." Marlowe looked at me at the mention of my old boyfriend, but he didn't question it. He let me ramble, perhaps sensing my need to talk about the past. "Connie wasn't like other realtors, not prissy with the heels and big hair. She was tough and down-to-earth. When I showed up in uniform, she mentioned her husband was a cop and we talked about what it was like for the families—always worrying, never knowing if their spouse would make it home at the end of a shift. They're high school sweethearts, you know? Got married after X graduated the academy.

"She listened to me bitch about work. My first year was desk duty as a receptionist. The guys didn't want a female partner. Even though we're trained the same, we are different. I get it. Obviously, I'm not as intimidating as an officer X's size."

Marlowe chuckled at this. "Had any of these gentlemen properly made your acquaintance? Because I can envision thee as quite intimidating."

I gave him a grateful smile. "You're not intimidated by me."

"I've seen far more dangerous things in the world. I have also seen firsthand that you can be quite dangerous as well. Your former colleague found that out tonight."

"If only he'd found out earlier, X wouldn't be in the hospital."

"You were telling me about Miss Consuela," he said, easing me back to a safer topic.

"My beat was in the same neighborhood as her real estate office. At that time, I worked traffic." I stopped at this, wondering if I should explain what that meant. I realized over the course of three days how much I assumed Marlowe would understand me and my colloquialisms.

With very little help, he could track a conversation and decide what piece of information was important and worth questioning.

"Connie and I were both trying to make it in a world where merit and job performance matter, but not as much as they should. Connie, being both female and Hispanic, found herself in a situation where her boss didn't think clients would trust her enough to plunk down millions of dollars for a house, so they stuck her in property management."

"Wait. Millions? You said millions of dollars—for a house? How can this be?"

"Four hundred years of inflation. Of course, there are those of us not in that income bracket."

"It's like a cobbler's son going to Cambridge," he said. "Most students are from the nobility, save for a tiny few of us on scholarship. I had a benefactor. Alas, we attended the same classes, the same school, but I would never be the same because I was not the son of an earl or duke."

"Yet you were as good a student as the others."

"Better, at least at first year, possibly second. But they still disdained me because of my station. I would naught be but a cobbler's son." He paused. "You and Miss Consuela would see this as unfair, but this is the world. I soon neglected my studies, found other pursuits."

"Like hunting monsters and time travel?" I was joking, but he nodded.

"I had a talent for copying documents and there was a need to fulfill. It allowed for a pint of ale. I was also adept at getting in and out of our dormitories after curfew, telling a believable tale as to why I was late or absent from classes. All skills that serve me well in this life." He smiled.

"You do have that criminal element about you."

"Being warriors—as we are—is most isolating. Most would not understand." His hand reached across the car and covered mine for a moment.

"X isn't stupid. He knows that I'm into something. I take off at odd times, and bodies tend to pile up on my watch, but he knows I'm a good cop, so he doesn't ask too many questions. But X is cool. He's a rock."

I fervently hoped that were true as X was fighting for his life. I turned onto my street and we sat in the car. I turned off the engine, released my seatbelt and spoke again.

"After we get this thing, I want to go back to Volpi and see if he can help you stay here. I find this—" I smiled up at him. "warrior thing much easier with someone—no, with you—around."

He leaned in until his mouth was inches from mine. "No."

I sat back. "No?"

"That's not the reason. 'Tis a perfect reason, a noble one in fact—to be compatriots against the darkness. Alas, that is not why you wish me to stay. Speak thy truth, Tamberlyn. Why?"

I felt his presence flowing over me and I was powerless against his eyes. Their intensity shining even in the darkness of my car interior. His breath was audible, his stillness unnerving. He waited—for an answer, for me. He didn't touch me physically, yet I felt like I was held—naked, exposed, and allowing him everything. He spoke again. "Pray tell. What do you want, Tamberlyn?"

"You."

His mouth crushed against me and then withdrew into softness as he pulled me against him. My heart beat wildly, my body as compliant as my lips. I clambered from the driver's side to the passenger's, straddling his hips, grinding myself against him as his mouth trailed heat along my neck. We stayed like that for a while, fully clothed, pushing and pulling against each other, pent-up frustrations, and anger, and desire spilling out of me.

Still, I could not turn off my stupid brain. I wanted this man, wanted him desperately and the want was more than a sexual release. My past failures mingled together in my memory. Relationships that hadn't lasted, most of them ending so badly that I'd tucked them away in a secret bunker.

Either the guys left, like Rhett had, or I left, as I knew I would with Rick because none of them could truly understand me. This man was someone out of his time, out of his culture, with only scant hours left in this life, and yet he wanted to know me. He wanted to know all of me. More than as a fellow warrior or even a lover. Whatever this was, it was unlike anything I'd ever experienced before. I pulled out of his embrace to look into his eyes. The dim glow of streetlamps providing the only light. I kissed him lightly, feeling the prickle of his beard against my skin, relishing the feel of it. The taste of him, his warmth, and his soft and open mouth was like complete acceptance. Something inside me unlocked and my words warbled on the edge of tears. "You've called me 'dangerous' before, Kit Marlowe, yet if we continue this, it may prove to be hazardous to both of us. I don't mean physically, we deal with that every day. But on an emotional level, I'm not sure I can handle it. Hell, I'm not sure you can handle it, but something tells me we should try."

He smiled then and leaned back so he could look at me better. "Your words are that of a diplomat, and your courage is that of a knight. In my world, you would be a queen."

We got out of the car in unison. He held out his hand

toward me and I took it as we walked to the door of my apartment building.

"All due respect to your Queen Elizabeth, but even queens have to submit to someone. I'd want to be king."

"Then I shall make you a king." He pulled me down the hall toward my apartment. His hands were on my waist, under my coat, fumbling along my shirt as I fished for my key. I gave up and kissed him in the doorway, snaking my arms around his neck, pulling his head down to mine. When we parted finally, out of breath, I smiled up at him in the darkened hallway.

"So, you have the power to make kings, then?"

His lips ran along my throat, to my ear, back to my mouth. "I'm a writer, I have the power to make anything." His eyes were dark and intense. "Where is your confounded key?"

I found it and we both burst into my apartment, trying to undress each other. His hands were like fire as they roamed over me, pulling off my coat, pushing my T-shirt up. I shrugged out of my shoulder holster, dropping the gun and leather to the floor. I pulled his shirt collar away to plant kisses along his hot neck. His gasp of pleasure was echoed by my own as his fingers tore at the opening of my jeans and found warmth beneath the fabric. He turned us and my back hit the closed door. His mouth was insistent, his tongue relentless, and I reveled in the feel of it against my skin, over my breasts. I pulled his cloak from his shoulders and reached for the button on his jeans.

Marlowe grabbed my hand, holding me still. He put a finger to his lips. We both stopped, listening. At first, all I could hear was the beating of my heart. Then a low hissing sound, like air through a leaking pipe reverberated through my apartment.

I bent down to pull my gun for the second time that night. Marlowe moved away from me, along the wall. At first, I didn't know what he was thinking. I wanted him to stay behind me. I was the one with a gun after all. He practically disappeared into the shadows, but a tiny sliver of moonlight showed me his face for a moment. Motioning toward the kitchen, he moved again. Marlowe wanted to flank it. Whatever it was. I nodded, waiting for my eyes to get used to the darkness. I smelled it before I saw it. A distinct blood and sewer smell. Well, good news. We wouldn't have to go looking for the strigoi, because it had found us.

18

I sensed rather than heard Marlowe's sword as it left its scabbard. If you'd have asked me last week if I'd even heard of the word "scabbard" save for pirate movies I'd have laughed in your face. That night, the simple movement was reassuring. I motioned to Marlowe in the opposite direction as I made my way toward the living room. We made eye contact in the light from the streetlamp across the way. I indicated outside, realizing I needed the blood sample from Cruz's grandmother to kill this thing. I cursed myself for leaving the cloth in my go-bag, and my go-bag in my car.

Score one for romance distractions, damn it. He gave a curt nod at my wild hand motions and held up his hand. In the light, I could see he held the bloody dagger that he'd used on Munson. I smiled. A consummate professional, he'd come prepared, not letting the potential for sex distract him as it had me.

Giving up my idea of going to the car, I fumbled for the light switch. I had only my service weapon.

No knives, no flashlight, nothing, but I couldn't leave Marlowe to face the beast alone. In the darkness, I could feel his quiet movement across the floor. He worked in the shadows, skirting my furniture with ease.

I remembered I kept another light in the end table drawer and made my way to it. I found it and snapped it on, sweeping it across the room. Marlowe had his sword in one hand, the dagger in the other. The strigoi was circling him, snapping and hissing like a crocodile on Animal Planet. Its clawed hands swiped at Marlowe's torso in a blur of motion. Marlowe leaped out of the way, knocking my bookshelf askew. Books and picture frames went flying.

As my light fell across him, I could see fresh blood stains forming on his shoulder. The creature took a flying leap toward him. Marlowe whirled around, thrusting his sword deep into the monster's belly. It snarled louder and kept on coming, holding the sword fast within it.

Marlowe flipped the dagger in his hand for an overhead strike and plunged it deep into the barreled chest. They went down on the floor, Marlowe on top of the creature. I grabbed a letter opener, and my action was like Marlowe's, thrusting the blade into the scaly chest. It didn't have the grandmother's blood on it, but it was made of silver and occasionally that worked. The thing's bulging red eyes went even wider and blinked at the two of us. It struggled wildly for a few moments and then it stilled. The hissing quieted and its eyes closed. Marlowe relaxed his grip and I backed away to turn on a lamp. Marlowe pulled his sword from the creature's body.

"Are you okay?"

He nodded, putting a hand out to me, trying to keep me away from the monster on my floor. I pulled my gun and cleared the bedroom and bathroom. If Cruz had been here, he was gone. Marlowe stood behind me in the bedroom doorway.

"Cruz isn't here if he ever was," I said, taking a moment to catch my breath. "Let me get his grandmother's blood sample from the car."

At Marlowe's nod, I raced for my car, grabbed the go-bag, and returned.

Marlowe was standing at my sink. "He knows who you are, that you're after him. He's sent the strigoi after you and he will not stop, Tamberlyn. He will not stop until you are dead."

I took a deep breath. God, it had been a long day.

"Well, the son of a bitch will have to kill me himself. No more sending creepy crawlies to do his dirty work." I rifled through the go-bag to get the blood-soaked doily. "Let's finish this up."

We both turned toward the dead strigoi on my floor. All we saw was an empty space save for blood smears, an ancient dagger, and an antique letter opener. The dead strigoi was gone and I suspected, not as dead as we'd thought. A draft blew in through the open window, full of city smells and failure.

"Damn that thing is hard to kill." I tossed the plastic bag holding Renard's blood aside in frustration. "Munson's blood doesn't work," I said.

Marlowe picked up his knife and cleaned it off. "I do not think the old woman is in control of this creature. The creature would be freed upon her death, and yet, it is still here."

"Unfinished business, maybe? At least we've narrowed it down."

Just to be safe, we did a quick search of my apartment and sure enough, scaly butt was gone, only the sticky dark blood was proof he'd even been there. Marlowe went outside to scout around. I simply stopped thinking, because thinking brought me to a dark place. Monsters were real, evil was real, and I'd known that fact for a while now.

Over the years, I'd accepted that it was my job—my lot in life—to be the one to handle these things. And that I'd manage the job in secret, and for the most part, alone. I could handle my solitary existence, or at least I could until I didn't have to.

That had changed with Marlowe's arrival. He truly understood the struggle, the need for secrecy, and the abject loneliness it brought. It was like tasting chocolate for the first time—good, rich, dark, creamy, slightly bitter chocolate—and then knowing that after that first tiny morsel, you would never have it again.

Having a sample of what could be was often worse than never having it at all. X was in the hospital and Ziggy was angry with me, or at least, she didn't trust me. Marlowe's blue lightning was going to zap him away to never-never Land. And the creature was back on the loose again. Thinking that things were pretty piss poor in my life, I poured myself a drink and crashed on the couch, my feet on the table. I was too tired to even take my boots off. Behind me, I heard the familiar sound of Marlowe's boots as he reentered my apartment.

"Hey, love." He let the endearment slip as he came to stand in front of me. He unlaced my boots. "It's gone.

Your grounds are clear of creatures and other nefarious ilk. You rest. I'll keep an eye."

I threw him a tired smile at his words.

"I'm fine. Probably can't sleep anyway." I moved over and he settled on the couch next to me.

"Too many thoughts of Xavier? He is being well-cared for."

"Yes, I know. I was just wallowing. How's your shoulder? We should clean that up." I rose and grabbed my first aid kit from my kitchen and returned to the couch. The end table lamp still worked, and I snapped it on. "Things can't get much worse, can they?" I gently patted antiseptic onto the three gouges on his upper arm. The wounds were superficial, and I pinched the skin together and applied butterfly bandages.

His answering chuckle startled me. "In my experience, dear Tamberlyn, things can get far worse and often do."

His wrapped his arm around me and I leaned into him, both of us staring at my blank television set. I thought about getting some sleep. I needed to, but I was reluctant to leave Marlowe's warmth. My skin flushed, thinking of the two of us only moments before. I could still taste him—his earthy spice lingering where his tongue had explored.

He must have read my mind because he leaned down to kiss my temple. "My actions earlier, I do not regret them, but I fear time, as usual, is against us."

"We have time now," I turned my face up to meet his lips. He kissed me softly, heat sparking again between us, but he pulled away sooner than I wanted him to. His next words bothered me more than his reticence.

"Who hurt you, Tamberlyn? You hide it well, but I sense there is much more to you than what you let others see."

I ran my mouth across his jaw as he spoke. I didn't want to talk. I wanted to lose myself in him.

"No mysterious dark past that you don't already know about," I murmured into his skin. My hands traced across his torso, feeling the abdominal muscles I'd eyed for days. He caught my hand before I could slip it under the waistband of his jeans.

"Do not lie. There is nothing you could tell me that would change my opinion of you."

"I'm not lying." I pulled away, my protest dying away as I saw his face. He was more hurt than angry.

"I have told you of my own love, my regret, and shame at not being able to stay with her. Have I not trusted you with my very existence? Can you not afford me that same trust?"

"It's not that I don't trust you, it's just..." I sat back tiredly. "He's not something I talk about. Haven't for a long time."

"Perhaps it is time?"

"Marlowe, can we not? Let's not. I'm tired, my partner's fighting for his life, you're about to zap back into the past, and oh, yeah, an ancient monster is still out and about. Why do you have to know this stuff?"

"Because I desire you. Immensely. I desire you in all ways, not only the physical. As I said earlier. I would know your heart, Tamberlyn."

I sighed. And with it, all my unmentioned secrets were exhaled. "His name was Theo. I made a mistake in trusting him. I was young, and foolish, and in love."

"Tell me." He wasn't going to let me get away with the short version, and threading his fingers through mine, he settled back to listen.

"After my initial run-in with Mrs. Hatcher, vampire librarian, and subsequent outcasting by my one and only friend, I started hunting in earnest. My schedule included a weekly scout into greater Philly and listening to police scanners for weird things that happened. It kept me busy and my mind off my loneliness. I hunted all kinds of things, weres, ghouls, a nasty poltergeist, a few possessed humans. My very survival in these situations gave me the impression I was invincible, invulnerable. I figured I'd never encounter anything as remotely dangerous or evil in its intent. And then I met Theo. I'm not even sure that was his real name." Marlowe's hand clenched around mine, but only for a moment and he nodded for me to go on.

"He was tall and lithe and more beautiful than any man I'd ever seen." I glanced up at him. "At that time, anyway. He reminded me of a California surfer." I stopped, realizing that Marlowe would have no idea what California was, let alone a surfer. "He claimed to be from across the continent, a warm and sunny place with miles of coastline. Just one of his lies, but to be honest, I would have believed anything he told me at the time.

"It was the summer after graduation, and I'd been accepted to Penn State. His college. We were to be there together. My father would not have approved."

"This man was a cur. A beast who preys upon young women of virtue." Marlowe's voice was sharp.

I started at his words but forced my heart to slow its rapid beat and went on. "I was stupid. And young, I'm sure that was part of it. To think he loved me—wanted me to run away with him. It was all lies. And when he cast me aside, I was so devastated, I can't even remember the details. It's blocked like a traumatic childhood memory. Too traumatic to deal with. I was a stupid teenage girl."

He turned to me, placing his warm hands on either side of my face as he gazed into my eyes.

"Tamberlyn, you were young, and this lying cur took advantage of you. Yet you prevailed and did not become a pawn in his games. Am I correct?"

I nodded, closing my eyes.

"Then, you have nothing for which to be ashamed. To think someone could love you is not a foolish act at all, merely human. Do you not think you are worthy of love?"

I sat back, away from his touch.

"Of course, but my life is complicated. And—"

He smiled. "Alas, mine is as well. What can be done?" Rising in a fluid motion, he held out his hand. "Mayhaps, let us savor the moments that come to us."

19

We stood facing each other in the shadows. His eyes—hazel, gleaming, searching in the dim light. I couldn't look away as I reached for him. His lean torso was pale and beautiful under my hands. He pushed them away so he could rid me of the shirt I'd donned in the hospital bathroom. I unhooked my bra and it dropped to the floor as his hand cupped my breasts. His breath sounded harsh and fast in his throat.

"You are more beautiful than moonlight," he said.

I could have said the same about him with his pale skin and the sheer clean lines of his body, but of course, I didn't.

His hands moved to my jeans and I pulled him away, catching the scent of blood as our clothes came off.

"Don't touch me when I'm like this. I need to be clean," I said.

He started to protest but I pulled him toward my tiny bathroom. The overhead light was out. I flicked it on and off, uselessly. Marlowe left for a moment and returned with two lit candles and placed them on the sink.

"The creature seems to have eliminated all your over overhead lights in preparation for his attack. This beast is more than beast, more intelligent than we knew. I shall take that into accord for the future."

"Later," I said as I turned on the shower. I like this better anyway." I indicated the softly lit atmosphere.

"This is what my world is like," he answered, bending to strip off his jeans. I did the same. "Except, I do love your hot running water." We stood looking at each other for a moment in the flickering candlelight. The light and shadows played across his skin like water nymphs. Defined muscles were ridged as if drawn by a master. Dark hair at the midline of his chest spread across his pectorals. I touched them, moving toward the hard nubs at each center and I giggled when he gasped.

"Are you ticklish?" I smiled at him as he caught my hands. I pulled them free and moved down to feel the hard thickness of his erection. It was my turn to gasp.

He quirked an eyebrow at me. "Are you?"

He pulled the curtain back and we stepped into the shower, the water sluicing hot over both of us, and I shivered at the shock of it. His arms went around my back, pulling me to his chest as we stood under the spray. Then he was kissing me, the taste of him mixing with the clean, slightly alkaline essence of the shower. He grabbed the soap first and it was a playful race to get clean, and then the play became serious as we abandoned the soap for each other. A tiny groan escaped from him when I touched him, and I smiled into the pelting water, blinking it out of my eyes so I could see him better. His eyes were closed, head thrown back, and I wished for more than candlelight.

I turned us, pushing him under the spray of water, wanting that sound from him again. I planted kisses on his chest as I attempted a graceful drop to my knees in front of him. Anticipating my intent, he pulled me up, pushing me against the wall, holding my leg captive until I wrapped it around him. His mouth was hotter than the water surrounding us. and as he dropped to his knees in front of me, it was all I could think about.

His tongue was relentless. My fingers slithered through his wet hair as my leg curled around him, both for balance and to bring him closer. Everything went out of my mind except the incredible heat of his mouth. The slow-moving cyclone of sensation.

His chuckle rumbled against my thighs. The bastard knew what he was doing. As the wave of pleasure threatened to overtake me, I was desperate for release, to let it wash over me and make me forget. Make me quit thinking and feel, if only for a moment. I tugged at his hair, pulling him closer, cursing at him until I lost myself in sensation. I forgot to breathe. The room closed around the white-hot center of me until that's all there was.

I lost my balance and he caught me as the shower curtain came loose, pulling rod and all down on us as we collapsed outside the tub. The curtain hit the two lit candles, extinguishing them. We were plunged into darkness. The smell of soap and wax and my own sex flooded the room. The only sound was the now cold shower splashing Marlowe and the panting exhales of my breath.

We lay on the floor, both of us breathless and wet. I

couldn't see his face in the dark and he made no effort to speak. He moved away from me to turn the faucet off. I lay there in the darkness, my back on the bathroom rug, my calves on the edge of the tub, as he fumbled around for matches. Soon, a candle flickered, and he reached for me. I stood on shaking legs as he wrapped me in a towel and led me to my bed.

Marlowe watched me, his head propped on his hand. More candles had been lit in the bedroom, throwing a golden light across his face. He kissed me.

"Hi," he said.

I giggled at the unexpected greeting. He smiled at me, tilting his head, a damp lock of hair falling over his forehead.

"Hi, yourself," I said and pulled him down for another kiss. The slight tang of me was still on his tongue and he groaned as I sucked on it. His body felt somewhat chilled from the cold shower and I moved across him, pushing him back down on the soft sheets. My mouth roamed the landscape of his skin, my fingers exploring the peaks, the valleys until I came to the crux of him. His groan of pleasure as I took him thrilled me with that singular feeling of power one gets from being able to render someone helpless.

Most men think of the act is a favor, doled out sparingly if they behave. And females unite in their perpetuation of the myth, lest the secret get out. But a lot of women, and some men, see it as strength, a man at his most vulnerable, his manhood trapped between both pleasure and pain, tongue and teeth.

I wanted to feel him. I wanted him everywhere, surrounding me with his power, his smell, everything that was him. Hormones gave me visions of future babies with Marlowe's eyes and fat with dimples and curling dark hair.

He read my mind and tugged at me. I slid up toward his mouth, my hand replacing my lips. We kissed long and languorously until I was dizzy from lack of air. He flipped me onto my back and broke away, his lips kissing down my throat. I shivered each time he pulled away.

Opening my legs to make room, I pulled him to me, slotting the long, lean, length of him between my thighs. I panted, still wet, and hot, and sensitive, my insides screaming for more. More of the pleasure, the white noise of oblivion, a new plane of existence where thoughts were nothing and only the body's desire counted.

He withdrew, leaving an empty ache for him and I clutched at him, almost hating my desperation. I searched for words and came up empty. Words no longer existed in me. Both of us exhaled in unison, our breath mingling and mating in the air. My eyes were closed, and I felt his lips on them, first one then the other. I blinked them open to see him smiling.

"I would see thee," he said. "Please, Tamberlyn."

Still looking into my eyes, he came to me again, and I relished the fullness of him, the feel of all his length. We rocked together, smoothly, and then some part of my brain took over and I rolled us, putting me on top. My eyes closed as I rocked.

His hands came around my waist, stilling me, holding me against him. "Wait," his voice was a cracked whisper. "Wait."

I didn't listen, my eyes slammed shut as I writhed

above him. He turned, flipping me onto my back. "I said wait," he growled. I felt him again, sinking slowly into me. I opened my eyes to see him watching me.

We moved like that for a minute or two, me staring at him until the heat began its slow inexorable climb. Radiating out from my center like a furnace, the ignition threatened to burn me alive. I felt myself swell and flush swollen against him. My eyes clamped shut, both in want and fear of losing my composure in front of him. I pushed my cheek into the pillow, away from his view.

"Tamberlyn, don't. Don't go away from me." His hand grasped my chin, turning me. "Please. Be with me. Be here with me." His plea opened my eyes, and I saw his face contorted with concentration and the effort of restraint. Waiting for me to open up.

"I can't," I whispered. I couldn't. Tears stung at the back of my eyes even as my core burned, and the now familiar wave of pleasure tickled at the edges.

Back behind the surface of my emotions, beyond the body's pleasure, a memory reared its head and laughed at me. Memories of my first time with Theo, where I hadn't known how to protect myself, how to close those parts of me away that could be hurt. Those pieces of me that now floated to the surface as Marlowe moved within me. He moved with fierce grace, hitting the thousand sensitive places with each unerring thrust. He panted with the effort, holding back as he waited for me.

"It is only us, here," he whispered. "I am naught but a man loving a woman. See me, Tamberlyn." His words unlocked something inside, filling my doubting nature with something other. I opened slowly, light coming into darkness, a reluctant moon being coaxed from behind clouds. My first spasm contracted around his girth, and he climaxed above me, his head thrown back, the strong muscles of his jaw and throat working. I came with him. Crying out and clutching his neck as we came down slowly, both of us completely spent.

We stayed locked together for a long time, holding each other. His murmuring words were tattoos against my skin, reassuring me that I was okay. That harm would not touch me if he could help it. His fingers gently wiped the moisture from my cheeks.

"Are you well? Did I hurt you?" He asked.

I turned away, shaking my head.

"Tam, look at me."

I turned back, opening my eyes to his in the shadows of the room.

"I'm fine. I'm...God, I—" I turned away as a sob threatened to overtake me. I did not want to cry in front of him. Who cries during sex for chrissake? What an unbelievable sap I turned out to be.

"God, indeed," he said. He moved one leg outside of mine and pulled away, lying on his back and pulling me into his arms. I nestled against his chest, the hair tickling my nose. "I believe God was here with us, for that was more than..." He trailed off, unable to finish.

And at that moment, I realized that I'd fucked the words right out of the great Christopher Marlowe.

"Everything." I finished for him and then we slept.

Sometime later, my phone started ringing from the coffee table and I clambered shakily out of bed to answer it. Marlowe stirred and then snored a soft snuffling sound. It was oddly more reassuring than annoying.

I grabbed the phone, my naked body shivering in the

cold apartment.

"Paradiso," my captain's voice was flat and hoarse as though he'd been screaming. "Get your ass back here. Hernandez has taken a turn." The line clicked off. Bad news often lies in the words unsaid.

20

Marlowe and I rushed to the hospital in the pre-dawn hours, the sky lightening at the edges of the city. A different set of cops than the ones I had left were gathered in the waiting room, as though they were taking shifts. The captain was there, his stoic face revealing nothing as he nodded at me. He gave a cursory glance at Marlowe, but before he could ask any question, a uniformed officer approached him, and he turned away from us.

Connie and her parents were nowhere to be found. I figured they must be in with X. I'm not good at waiting. Never have been. And waiting in the hospital is the worst. I'd done it twice before. First with my mom and then, years later with Dad. Neither had a good outcome.

I could not go and sit in those chairs again and Marlowe somehow sensed this. "Should we purchase more of the vile brew from the confounded machine again? It's undrinkable, yet everyone seems to think it helps." He studied me, his hand still wrapped around my own. I gave him a wan smile and nodded. It was a distraction, at least.

Behind us, past the nurse and into the ICU, a door opened, and I turned to see Connie's parents emerge from a room. The devastation on their faces told me all I needed to know.

Ignoring the nurse's admonition to wait, I approached them. "When?" I asked.

"About twenty minutes ago. They want to take him downstairs." Connie's dad spoke. Her mom dabbed at her eyes with a wadded piece of tissue. "Consuela's in with him."

"I never should have left." My knees wobbled and I leaned to the side, reaching out for the wall. Marlowe's arm came around me, holding me tight to him. I felt his steady breath and matched my own to his.

Down the hall, I could see the guys from our precinct. They stood awkwardly, their hands in their pockets, all of them, to a man, were looking at the floor.

"Connie said to send you in when you got here." Her dad spoke again.

I knocked softly on the door and opened it a crack. I heard Marlowe's accented condolences to her parents as I went in to say goodbye to my partner. Connie gave me a nod and a brief hug before she left me alone with him.

I wished I could say he looked peaceful, but he didn't. He simply looked dead. I took his limp hand. It was huge against my own.

"Dude, this is so not a good look for you." I could almost hear his laugh, even now.

Xavier's eyes were not only the windows to his soul but everybody else's soul as well. He could look at you and make you feel safe or scared, happy or angry without saying much of anything. When his eyes were open, his face was open too and you could read everything there. In that dim and sterile room, his closed eyes looked bruised and dark—like shuttered windows of a former sunny disposition.

"I miss the smile, X. Give me the goofy smile, okay?" I whispered, though there was no one else to hear me. The monitor that had beeped with his heart rate was silent— no squiggles, no lights. "I leave you for a couple of hours on your own and this is what happens? Come on. Who's going to feed me chocolate kisses and convince me I need breakfast at all hours of the day? I need my partner." I put his hand down on the hospital sheet. His color was off, and he was paler than I'd ever seen him. "Remember that day we busted that bookie in Coniver? And we got to drive his car to the impound lot? The Porsche? I know for a fact we hit a hundred on the straightaway coming into Montgomery County. Good times, X. Good times."

I turned from him to glance out the window. Bleary rays of the sunrise threw color onto the glass tower across the street. Inside that tower, people would be going on about their days as though nothing has changed. To them, it was another day—just another goddamned day. Soon, commuters would snake their way into the city, horns blaring, coffee spilling, morning DJs telling off-color jokes on the radio.

I was no stranger to death, of those close to me or those killed by my own hand. Each time, it changed me. I lost more than that person. I lost a sense of hope and gained a sense of my own mortality. But for X's heroics, it could have been me lying on that bed, useless tubes running out of my arms. I turned back to him and promised to look in on Connie and the kids. I was dreading it already, having to face her every time I showed up at the house, wishing I could have done something to save him.

"It should have been me and you know it," I said quietly, wiping my nose on my sleeve. The orderlies were at the door, waiting to take him. I moved past them and into the hall. Connie and her mother stood amid my co-workers. The captain spoke to her gently, his hand on her shoulder. At our end of the hall, Marlowe stood almost at attention, like an honor guard at a king's funeral.

Back at my office, dispatch would relay calls to units, files would be filed, reports written, crimes investigated. My own work was not finished. Though the guy that did this to X was dead, there was another one out there. And another and another.

Life went on normally for everyone. Everyone except Xavier Hernandez, his family, and me.

I stood with Marlowe. His eyes liquid with empathy and warmth, but thankfully he said nothing. When he held out his arms, I went to him, my face into his chest. Tilting his head toward mine as he embraced me, he said something I didn't catch. Some prayer or condolence that was too muffled in Middle English to comprehend. But the sound of his voice and his warmth let loose what little control I had anyway, and I was soon crying.

It took a few minutes, but other thoughts worked their way through my sadness and self-pity. I could properly mourn later, but now there was too much to be done. I had to get on with it—the business of living, of the job, of my duty to protect and serve. A duty that in Xavier's case, I'd failed in the worst possible way.

Looking for a tissue, I thrust my hands into the pockets of my jacket and my fingers closed around a phone. I pulled it out. The cracked screen of X's phone felt dead and broken in my hand. I must have pocketed it during the fight in the alley. I flipped it over, pulling the smart card out to replace it in my own phone. Marlowe handed me a small box of tissues he'd found, and I blew my nose as I scrolled through the phone.

"Your society is greatly dependent upon its fanciful devices," Marlowe remarked as he watched me. "The idea that a tiny box of lights and whistles hath more importance than humanity is most vexing."

"It's information, Marlowe. Besides, my text to you at the club probably saved us." I winced. "Me, anyway." I thumbed through X's messages, ignoring the ones from Connie and myself.

"I should have accompanied you upstairs. A call to arms would not have then been necessary." I ignored the chiding tone of his voice and to avoid his gaze, I turned and stood beside him, leaning against the wall. I was focused on the phone. As we stood there, silent in the hospital hallway, activity all around us, I gravitated toward him like an ocean wave. I moved closer, showing him the phone as I opened the messages. Texts had come in during the night and went unanswered.

"This one with the address, who is this from?" he asked, his slender finger indicating the message.

"The number's blocked, so I can't tell, but the address is in the warehouse district. Near Renard's house as well as a time to meet."

Marlowe's only response was a quirked eyebrow.

I glanced down the hall to where Connie was still

talking with the guys. I should have gone down there to convey my condolences. I'd already fallen apart once; not sure I could handle doing it again. If I'd approached her, we both would have lost it, and that wouldn't do anyone any good. The whole thing felt like a dream to me—a nightmare really. I turned to Marlowe instead.

"Let's go. Maybe we'll get lucky and find something I can kick the crap out of."

It wasn't long before we were navigating through rush hour traffic and my usual cursing at the bane of my urban-living existence.

"Are you in a proper mind to confront an entity such as the strigoi?" Marlowe's voice sounded strained as he rode shotgun in my car. He played with the sticker's message on my dash. I realized this was the last thing X said to me. *Don't let the bastards get you down.*

"I'm fine. Don't worry about me. I hope Cruz is there. Drive, idiot!" I rapped on the horn with the heel of my hand.

Marlowe barely took his eyes off the road. "I believe the light is red, Tamberlyn. Is that not the rule? To stop at the color red?"

"Yes, the light is red now. But when we were moving at all of point-seven miles per hour, it was yellow and if this prick in the Hummer had moved his substantial ass, we would have made the light."

Marlowe smiled at me. "Is it odd that the only words I truly understood of that colorful tirade were prick and ass?"

I glanced at him before honking the horn again,

passing on the left to a clearer lane of traffic. "Do they have terrible drivers in the sixteenth century?"

"No, but a goodly number of pricks and asses."

The sword, safe in its scabbard, skidded from the backseat to the floorboard as I slammed on the brakes to avoid hitting another prick in front of me. Marlowe cursed under his breath.

"It's not my fault," I protested.

"Perhaps your earlier account of thy disposition is in need of remedy."

"God, I wish you'd speak friggin' English."

"My language is far more English than the bastardized drivel you speak most of the time." It was the first hint of irritation at me since he'd arrived. This was somewhat of a record considering how much time we'd spent together. I usually pissed people off much quicker. "Mayhaps you should drive slower," he said through clenched teeth. "Or less...aggressively."

I ignored his comment on my driving. "It has to be Cruz who summoned the strigoi. We've pretty much tried everyone else."

Marlowe, who was normally gung-ho about hostile hunting, didn't comment. We swerved through traffic in silence for the next few minutes. The quiet started to get to me and I was about to apologize for being snappy when he spoke.

"I am truly sorry for the loss of Xavier Hernandez. He was a good man."

"Can we not talk about this?" I wanted him to talk, but not about X. I couldn't think about him at that moment. I had to keep moving forward.

"I have experience with loss. You need time to

mourn."

"Time is the one thing we don't have, remember?"

He ignored me and continued in what I'd come to know as his theatrical voice.

"Mankind relishes a sense of security in the sameness of their lives. Death changes that. The ones who mourn are outside the normalcy of life. They lose that surety of being one with everything, of being the same."

It took me a minute to think about what he'd said. I certainly did not have a normal life. Every day brought strange events, be it ancient vampires trying to kill me or ancient poets trying to seduce me. Yet I understood the concept. I'd become accustomed to my life and expected that each day I would wake up and go to work and X would be there stuffing his face or razzing the other guys about last night's game. That every Tuesday night I would be with the Hernandez household eating beans and rice and holding the baby. That I could text Rick or call up Ziggy to have a glass of wine and that they would always be around. If I lived in constant fear of that not happening, I could never do my job. In fact, I'd be a wreck, kind of like I was now.

I took a deep breath and blew it out slowly, yoga style—in through the mouth, out through the nose. I did it again. My mind finally calmed enough to not want to scream at the wind and I started to focus on the task at hand.

Marlowe had quit talking, somehow sensing that I was struggling for control. I was more than grateful. If he did anything the slightest bit sympathetic, I might lose it entirely. I wished for this to be over. For Cruz to be caught and the strigoi to be dead. For all the dirty cops in my squad to be brought to justice. And most of all, for X to be alive.

I figured the captain and Internal Affairs would give me twenty-four hours before looking for a report on the alley shooting. The captain already told me I was on paid leave until the investigation was over. I was expected to stand down and wait. Someone else could go after Cruz. But none of my fellow officers knew about the mobster's ties with the dark arts, or the creature roaming the sewers. That was my job. Badge or no, I would go after Cruz and his scaly monster. Hopefully, in twenty-four hours it would be over. And of course, by then, the man who sat next to me, keeping me on a semi-even keel, would also be gone. I turned my thoughts back to the safety of police work.

I handed my phone with X's smart card in it to Marlowe. "Go back through the texts. The ones from the blocked number. I remembered reading something about Balfour."

He read through all the texts aloud. Some of them didn't make sense, some of them didn't apply, but he got to the one about Balfour and I had him read it again.

"It says that Balfour left for Miami late yesterday. What's Miami?" He pronounced it Mee-am-I. I explained Miami to him, thinking I'd like to get him on a plane and fly there just so he could experience it. I realized he had no idea of the vastness of the country he was in. In his time, we were a tiny splat of land that Sir Walter Raleigh raved about to the queen.

"So, Balfour's gone. No wonder Munson felt secure in bringing us to the club. He could frame Balfour's men for our deaths and be the hero in taking down a major crime boss. If Cruz is after Balfour for whatever reason, he could be headed to Miami as well and we're pissing up a rope here." Marlowe glanced at me. I shrugged to let him know that he should ignore my side comments. I thought about how Cruz would explain a strigoi to the TSA. *Yes, sir, I realize it looks like a really big cat in my carry-on, but it's an ancient vampire-like beast that drinks human blood. No problem.* My laugh was a bitter sound in my throat.

"Tamberlyn." Marlowe spoke quietly. His hand reached for mine. "I would stay if I could." His words were off topic and my breath stilled inside of me. I blew out air in a sigh. I wanted him to stick to the case. Anything that touched on emotions threatened to undo me. But I took another deep yoga breath and interlaced our fingers.

"I know," I said softly as our hands rested on the center console. We were stopped at a light and I sat up straight, unlacing my fingers from his and gripping the wheel. "Marlowe, what if you could come back? I mean not to this timeline, but earlier. You could stop us. Just stop us from going to that club. X would still be alive. You remember everything you've done from every journey. You're the key to this whole thing." My previous ache and exhaustion dissipated, my face flushed with excitement. I stared at him—my own personal miracle. We had all the time in the world. I was sitting next to a freaking time-traveler.

"Tam." His voice was gentle, as though talking to a child. "I have rarely come back to the same timeline."

"That's just it, it's not the same. It would be earlier."

"Do you not think I've tried? I've tried and failed to

get back to Mary. There was no remedy for it. The closest I've been to the same time is short of a decade." He opened his journal to the appropriate pages. "I traveled to Leicester in 1924 and then to Bristol in the year 1933. Never the same time."

"So, why do you think those two journeys were so close together?"

"They were not. In my time, there was a span of several months and other travels before Bristol."

"And each time you were chasing a hostile?"

"Each time I encountered a hostile. Chasing is not an accurate term. They don't normally walk the ribbons of time."

I focused on the road ahead of me, chewing on my lip. My hands gripped and re-gripped the steering wheel as his words sunk in. Of course, it wouldn't be as easy as all that. The power to change things was one thing, the skill and know-how to control that power was something else entirely.

"So, the travel thing is unique to you." I spoke without thought, my focus hell-bent on saving X.

"I believe perhaps the strigoi simply got caught in the blue lightning along with me and that is why it is here. I believe traveling is unique to my person. Or at least, I did. Until now."

"What does that mean?" I turned to see his profile, and the muscle in his jaw as it twitched. He was quiet for a moment and I squeezed his hand.

"Just as you did, I thought that I alone could see the darkness surrounding us. But, there are two of us now. The idea pervades that we might be alike in other respects as well."

"Meaning I may be a traveler too."

He nodded. "You haven't though, and so this curse may not be upon you. I sincerely hope it is not. I don't bemoan my calling, for it brought me to you. But I would not wish it upon thee."

"If I were, I'd come back and change things."

He sighed. "You cannot. Even if it were possible, there is the dilemma of ethics."

"What?" Here then, was the crux of it.

"If I happened to travel back here, back to your past, and encountered you or our dear friend, Xavier, there's no guarantee that my intervention would save him. Consequently, it may create even more dire circumstances."

"Circumstances are pretty goddamned dire now. My partner is dead. Five or six people have been killed by your monster from the past. And we're not any closer to killing it than we were on day one."

"I am sorry I've brought such strife into your timeline."

"It's not you," I said wearily. "I know it's not you. The thing with Munson and X has nothing to do with you or the hostile. But you would help, if you could."

The interior of my car was eerily silent.

"But you won't, will you? Even in the far-off chance that you do come back in time to do something, you will do nothing." I spat out the last words. I focused on driving and peered through the windshield to avoid looking at him.

"Knowing too much of one's fate—If I warned you, you may alter your course. Mayhaps to thine own demise. I cannot bear the thought. The thought of this world or any other without thee inhabiting it."

"Now you know how I feel. This is me, bearing the thought of X's demise, as you call it." I pulled into a wide empty lot in front of a warehouse, two buildings over from where we found the bodies of Balfour's men. Marlowe reached back to get his weapon from the floorboards.

"'Tis not the same, Tamberlyn. You love Xavier. He is like a brother to you. But you are not in love with him." He got out of my car, slamming the passenger door, his words stung me in the stark, cold morning. Despite all that had happened, my breath caught in my throat and I reveled in the very thought of Marlowe being in love with me.

I didn't have much time to contemplate the revelation because as we exited the car, a black sedan pulled up. I told Marlowe to stay close, and I turned sideways to the approaching car, my gun hand facing away from them.

One of the same Russian henchmen we questioned the other day exited from the driver's side and opened the passenger door. Gregor emerged, dressed in a dark suit and overcoat. Now that he wasn't reclining in a dialysis chair, he totally looked the part of a high-end crime boss. He stood beside his car in a similar stance to my own. Both of us were less of a target that way. It looked odd, but it was effective.

"I see your father taught you well, Paradiso." He chuckled after his statement and then turned to face me.

"Gregor, what are you doing here?" I'd expected Cruz to be meeting X, not Gregor. I gave a little nod to Marlowe and he relaxed, though I had no idea what he'd do if they'd started shooting. I was pretty sure that cape wasn't bulletproof.

Gregor stared at Marlowe, pointedly ignoring my question. I introduced the two men. Marlowe, having been indoctrinated to our customs, immediately put out his hand. Gregor stared at him with suspicion, but eventually, he smiled at the gesture and after a moment, he approached us and shook Marlowe's hand.

After another quick perusal of Marlowe, Gregor turned to me. "I hear what happened. Your partner, yes? The big guy. This new partner? He's too small."

Marlowe frowned. By his timeline standards, he was quite large—close to six feet tall, with a lean build. I supposed that compared to X he would be considered small, most people were.

I shrugged off Gregor's statements. He always was a small-talk kind of guy. "Is there a point, here?"

He sighed and spoke again. "How do you know to come here?"

"Surprised?" I asked.

He nodded. At least he was honest about that. "Balfour had cops on his payroll. I know this."

"You knew about Munson?"

"Not his name. I knew Balfour had police in, how you say? Pocket. I text big guy to tell him. I did not think you were bad cop."

I grimaced. "Thanks for that. Do you know who it is? On Balfour's payroll."

Gregor simply shrugged. "Ever since my cousin, Ilya's death, I watch. I'm patient man. When I hear of activity here, I text big guy."

"His name is Xavier," I said, and the irritation bled through. "Why not text me? Why not warn me?"

Gregor stepped back, shaking his head. He made a tsking sound in his throat.

"You a stubborn girl, Paradiso. This you get from your father. You are reckless. Your partner is more careful."

"I watched him—damn it. Watched X get shot. He—" I felt a hand on my arm. Marlowe's presence loomed beside me. I took a breath.

"I owe Enzo Paradiso a debt. I promise to look out your way," Gregor said.

I knew that Gregor and my dad had worked together some years before—something of an enemy-of-my-enemy thing. Enzo had pulled Gregor's caviar out of the fire on a grand jury indictment, but I never knew how close their relationship was. Now I had a guardian angel in the form of a gruff, diabetic Russian mobster on dialysis three times a week—sounded about right.

"So, what's going on here?" I indicated the warehouse behind me.

"Ilya died this building. Balfour's crew two buildings that way. I wonder why here. I own building further east, but why here? So, I put Sergei to watch."

"He saw something last night?"

"Da. He see something, he text me. I text big guy partner. Now, I not hear from Sergei."

"Let us to act. We must go now." Marlowe said, a bit impatiently, his quick movement to retrieve his sword alarmed Gregor's henchman who put his hand inside his jacket.

I held my hands out. "Hang on. We're all on the same side here." I cast a reproving glance at Marlowe.

Gregor tilted his head at his driver who gave Marlowe

a stern look, but his hand was empty.

I nodded at him and opened my trunk, pulling the go-bag from it. "I'll take the front. You take the back," I said. "Get a flashlight too," I instructed Gregor's man. "It's gonna be dark in there." Explaining about light-sensitive creatures from another century was more conversation I didn't want to have, but I also didn't need two more victims.

Marlowe stepped beside me. Gregor's comment about his size must have hit a nerve because he towered over me in an over-protective stance. It seemed we'd been here before—about to go into a potentially dangerous situation. This time, I wasn't going to ask Marlowe to stay behind. This was creature hunting, and I needed his skill set. I closed the trunk and followed the elder crime boss and his bodyguard toward the warehouse.

I eyed Gregor's henchman, who now held the 9 mil in his chunky paw. "Don't shoot me," I called after him. "Or him." I jerked my thumb toward Marlowe.

21

As someone who was used to controlling her own destiny, recent events had kicked my ass in the confidence department. I could have handled the vampire demon from the past. I could even handle mobsters battling for territory. But time-travelers and corrupt cops and evil grandmothers all seemed to converge on me at the same time. As always before a confrontation, my stomach jumped, and my armpits itched. It wasn't fear for myself, but Marlowe. I found myself dreading his impending departure, and the thought of his being hurt or killed on my watch made me ill.

Something zinged past my head as I heard the gunshot. Nothing like gunfire to bring you back to the task at hand. I hauled Marlowe's caped-crusader ass down behind a shipping container. The shot had come from above, and I peered into the rafters. A faint movement caught my eye. Someone or something was on the metal catwalk two stories in the air. I figured it was Cruz, as the movement was too slow to be the strigoi. The morning sun streamed through the windows, casting light into the upper rafters of the warehouse. Too much light for our vampire to be out in. The beast would be underground or deeper in the shadows of the building.

"The bugger is shooting at us." Marlowe hissed the obvious.

"Yes, well, that's what they do in my timeline."

"Give me a weapon," Marlowe demanded. "I know you have another."

I frowned, reluctant. He looked at me pointedly and held out his hand. His rate of adaptation was astonishing.

I pulled out a spare gun from my leg holster. My force of habit in arming up every time I walked out the door had not been lost on Marlowe. I showed him where the safety was. "Just point and shoot, it has five rounds. Don't shoot the good guys." He nodded and crouch-walked around some smaller freight containers.

Another shot zipped past us and I returned fire across the warehouse, knowing Gregor and his man should be at the back of the building and would try to flank the shooter. "Did you see where the shot came from?" I asked.

Marlowe had a better vantage point. The scene was eerily similar to the one I'd been through in an alley the previous night.

"Twenty feet up, about half nine," he responded. "I shall go."

I smiled at his quirky use of military terminology. My hand clutched onto his cape.

"No, I'll go. You back me up. Gregor should be coming in the back anytime now."

"We need Cruz's blood to defeat the strigoi and I

don't—"

I stopped him with my hand. I swore to God if I heard how he didn't have time again, I was going to shoot him right there. "I'll get it. Just don't let him get away."

I headed off in a crouch with Marlowe's warning to be careful. The figure on the catwalk crossed to the far side of the building, passing through ambient light as he went. I glanced up in time to see Enrico Cruz holding a gun. Near the stairway, he fired, missed, and Marlowe jumped up from his position and shot in Cruz's direction. Marlowe's aim wasn't bad for a first-time gun user. The bullets pinged on the stair railing and Cruz dropped into the shadows. I shouldn't have been surprised the poet would make an excellent marksman.

I moved across the building to the stairway where I'd last seen Cruz. Sensing him above me, I ducked behind the support beams of the building. The place must have been a manufacturing plant back in the day. Hoists and framework for holding large equipment or machinery now hung lax and useless. The steps were rusted, unsteady, and creaked like a haunted house as I climbed them.

Slinking back against the wall and into the shadows, I reached into my go-bag. I found the last string of firecrackers I'd saved from the Fourth of July. I smiled to myself, thinking that Marlowe would appreciate our struggle for independence, even from his own home country, not to mention fireworks and apple pie. I flicked the small lighter I carried and tossed the string as far as I could across the room. As they went off, I ran up the stairs. When you worked alone most of the time, it was always good to bring your own diversion. In the background, I heard Marlowe's footsteps as he climbed toward the catwalk on the opposite side of the building. Hopefully, we'd catch Cruz in the middle.

Gregor hadn't shown at all, and I wondered where he and his man had gotten to. I fervently hoped his whole promise to my father thing hadn't been a ruse. There could have been others in the warehouse, but I hadn't heard any gunfire except in our direction. The strigoi may have been inside after all, surprising them, and leaving them eviscerated on the warehouse floor. Or maybe this was another setup. I tried not to let my natural distrust in people get the better of me.

A scraping noise from above sped my steps up to the top of the warehouse. A web of catwalks stretched across the ceiling—a system of ancient pulleys and chains, rusted clasps that creaked as I brushed by them. With the sun filtering in through narrow dirty windows, the place resembled a medieval torture chamber. The stair landing narrowed to a catwalk across the expanse of the building. Rungs of an attached ladder led to a higher, narrower catwalk at the topmost space of the building. I took a breath and climbed.

In the darker recesses of the place, the air was stale and unmoving. At the top, I stayed near the ladder, not venturing out onto the metal grate of the bridge. I crouched and made myself a smaller target as I peered into the shadows for Cruz, preparing to move as soon as I spotted him.

"Philadelphia police! Surrender your weapon and come out."

There was no answer, but I heard a movement rather than saw one. He was already on the other side of the warehouse. I scuttled across as quietly as possible on the creaking rusted metal, crouching behind a metal gate at the other end. The narrow walkway swayed back and forth under my weight, and I grabbed onto a railing to steady myself. A gunshot rang out and sparked the metal not three inches from my hand. I moved it quickly and climbed over the gate onto a more stable metal landing. The shot had come from the catwalk thirty feet away and below mine.

"Put the gun down, Cruz. We know that you've summoned the vampire. Where's your pet monster?"

He stopped moving, the catwalk swaying with his weight. "How did you know?"

"We've been tracking it for days."

"You killed my grandmother," he accused me.

"She killed herself Cruz, not our fault. Drop the damn gun."

"She sacrificed herself for me. She wouldn't have had to if it weren't for you." His voice sounded morose and sad. It was a bit like I felt. My cop partner was gone. My hostile-hunting partner would soon be gone and for the most part, it was this yahoo's fault. The vision of Cruz's grandmother whispering some sort of curse into X's face popped into my head.

"What did she do to my partner? What was that chanting all about?"

He ignored the question and moved again. I climbed down the ladder and across the suspended walkway. Below us, there was a noise from the steps on the other side of the building. I hoped it was either Marlowe or the Krotsky team and not a scaly creature with teeth.

The metal catwalk creaked under my feet and Cruz

turned at the sound, firing at me. I returned the favor and heard a grunt, but he was still moving. The sun had risen enough over a neighboring building to shine more light into the space. Dust particles filled the sunlit air. The beam of light hit me, and I heard the click of a firing pin in an empty clip. Cruz's gun clattered to the ground. Judging from the sound we were about twenty feet apart on the catwalk. He moved away from me into the shadows.

"Cruz! Stop. I don't want to shoot you."

He stopped and I closed the distance between us, my weapon in my outstretched hands. He raised his hands with his back to me, only turning his head slightly as he talked.

"He killed her, you know. Cynthia. She and I were in love, and he had one of his goons kill her."

"Balfour? I know, but I can't prove it without your help. Come, testify against him. We can protect you."

His laugh was like four-day-old coffee. "You can't protect me. For all I know, you're on his payroll too." He turned toward me slowly. "There's nowhere I can go."

Hands still in the air, fingertips in the shadows, he stretched higher, as though working at something suspended in the shadows. Behind me, a curious clanking sound rattled, and I started, turning away to see the enormous pulley he'd released whizzing toward me. It was the size of a small safe, heavy, rusted, and moving faster than I'd thought possible on an ancient cable. I flung myself to the wobbly floor of the catwalk and the pulley slid by harmlessly.

The catwalk pitched heavily to one side, tilting the narrow grating I crouched on. I let go of my weapon to hold on and it fell in a clatter, skidding along the grate and over the edge to the distant floor below. Force of habit had me reaching for my spare when I remembered I'd given it to Marlowe.

The catwalk swung precariously, creaking and moaning with a suspicious rusted sound. It jerked and veered as I rose slowly to my knees, the platform rocking beneath me. Cruz was still standing, his feet wide apart, his hands out to the side of him. I pulled myself up on the left side, gripping the rail. He jerked suddenly, throwing his weight to the weaker side—my side—of the railing and it came loose from its mooring, peeling away from the catwalk like a zipper. I let go, throwing myself flat onto the walkway as the metal railing dropped at least a foot.

Cruz pounced toward me, more agile on the precarious footing than I would have thought for a big man. The catwalk rocked back and forth like a trapeze swing as I struggled to stand. His ham-like fist knocked me to the grate, and I stayed down, one arm wrapped around the edge of the structure, my jaw numb from the blow. Suddenly, there was a shudder and an ominous screech of tearing metal, of rusted bolts shearing off. It reverberated through the warehouse with a hollow haunting cry.

"Tam!"

Squinting into the darkness, I could barely make out Marlowe's figure. On the other side of the warehouse, he hurried toward his end of the walkway. I yelled for him to stop. Cruz whirled and ran after Marlowe and the stress was too much for the ancient metal. The catwalk tilted and dropped about six feet before shuddering to a stop. I jumped up and ran back toward my side of the building, stopping as I felt the shudder of stressed metal beneath my feet. Across the way, Marlowe stood helplessly on the stairs as the catwalk broke loose from his side of the platform.

Between us, the rusted metal bent and then crumbled, allowing a section of the catwalk to fall to the floor below. Cruz was closer to the edge of the destroyed bridge, and both of us waited as it swayed and creaked dangerously.

I clung to my section of the structure, calling to Cruz to come my way before the whole thing came loose. I was too late. Cables suspending the middle part snapped, whipping up to hit the ceiling. Without the cables, our weight on the remaining section was too great and the metal brackets at the side of the building screeched as they crumpled. Cruz's side of the walk dropped, its descent and trajectory careening toward my side of the building. I hung on like a squirrel on a metal tree branch. Cruz jumped away from the falling metal, away from me. If he'd waited until the walkway had gotten closer to the ground, he might have made it.

I couldn't see him, but I heard a devastating thump as his body hit the ground. The catwalk hung limply from the platform. What had been horizontal was now vertical, including me. I gripped the sides of the walkway, the metal edge cutting into my palms. The remaining handrail had sheared off. No cross beams or footholds in sight and my feet dangled helplessly. I looked up. Ten feet of walkway loomed above me. I could maybe hand-over-hand it to the top. I turned and looked down. The metal ended at my feet, leaving a twenty-odd-foot drop to the ground. It might not kill me, but I wasn't anxious to risk a broken ankle. Above me, Marlowe's voice called out for me to hold on. Across the warehouse, he rushed down the stairs and crossed to my side of the building.

"Not much else I can do," I muttered. I adjusted one handhold on the slippery metal. My injured arm ached. I heard Marlowe behind me, climbing stairs along the far side of the wall. Ten feet away, he stopped, even with the bottom edge of the walkway I clung to.

"Can you climb down this far?" He asked.

"If this whole thing doesn't come crashing down with me." I braced my legs on either side of the metal walkway. My foot found a large bolt protruding from the side and I used it, inching down to the edge of the grated metal until I reached the bolt where my foot had been.

Marlowe reeled out a length of heavy metal chain he'd found. My palms were sweating, fingers cramping with the death grip I held. I pressed myself closer to the metal in an effort to remain still. I smelled blood and realized I'd cut my hands on the sharp edges of metal. Marlowe moved again and I turned, searching for him. The walkway creaked as it swung with my body 's movement. The sound of distressed metal clanged in my ears. The catwalk was not long for this altitude. I looked up to see Marlowe securing the chain around the scaffold above him. A length of it hung free.

"I'm swinging this out to you, can you catch it?"

I nodded and he swung the chain out carefully. I reached and missed it. The walkway jerked once and leaned crazily to the right.

"Come on, come on." I indicated for him to throw it again. The chain swung my way again. With a screech of tearing metal, the walkway peeled away from its anchor and folded like a giant metal accordion above me. I jumped, both hands grabbing for the chain, swinging Tarzan style toward the stairs and Marlowe's outstretched arms. The catwalk crashed to the warehouse floor, clearing my head by a few feet. My hands slipped on the chain as I swung toward the side of the building. Marlowe grabbed me around the waist and pulled me onto the stairway with him.

I took a breath, happy to feel solid ground under my feet and solid arms around me.

"Thanks."

"Are you intact?" He looked at my injured hands.

"Fine." We both looked at the pile of metal, which by some miracle had completely missed Cruz. Marlowe and I made our way down the stairs to him. His head was bent at an awkward angle. The fall hadn't been that far, and he could have survived if he'd hit the ground correctly, but the impact had likely broken his neck. Cruz's testimony was what I needed to put Balfour away. Now all I had was another body to explain.

He'd been in love with his boss's girl and after she died, he'd snapped. Grandma's old ways provided a spectacular way to become a killer out for revenge. Now that I was positive Cruz was our summoner, I looked around for his pet monster.

Marlowe stood watch over me as I pulled a plastic vial from my pack and gathered a few drops of blood from Cruz's wounds. There was a scant amount on the surface of his skin. I hoped it would be enough.

"Did you see Gregor?" I asked.

Marlowe walked some distance away to retrieve my

lost weapon. I reached out to Cruz's body and gently closed his wide-open eyes. There was a scuffling sound and Marlowe whirled, holding the snub-nosed revolver in front of him like a shield.

"Wait." I peered into the sudden brightness of an open door. A familiar bulk listed to one side, hands clutching his belly. "I think it's Gregor."

After assuring himself that the guy in the light was no threat, Marlowe headed for him, calling back that Gregor was hurt. I wiped my bloody hands on my pants as I ran toward my father's old frenemy. I lifted his hand away from his side to see his white shirt shredded and covered in blood. I slung the backpack off my shoulders and grabbed a couple of surgical dressings and tossed them to Marlowe.

"Open these," I said, putting pressure on the long gash across his abdomen. Marlowe handed me the bandages and I pressed them to the deeper part of the wound.

"My driver went after it." He didn't elaborate, but I could tell from the look of disbelief in his eyes that he'd encountered the strigoi.

"Which way?" Marlowe asked and turned in the direction of Gregor's shaking finger.

I tossed Marlowe the vial of Cruz's blood. He caught it one-handed and was gone before I could say anything. What would I say? *Be careful? Wait for me? Don't leave without me?* Yes, to all of those, but I said nothing as I pulled out my phone to call for an ambulance. Gregor held out his phone and I could see he'd dialed 9-1-1. Sirens in the distance indicated help was on the way. I wanted to go after Marlowe, but Gregor was bleeding to death in front of me. He was a tough old bird, but I was pretty sure he was going into shock. I pulled my coat off and draped it over him.

"You have it then," he croaked.

"Shhh, Gregor, don't talk. The ambulance will be here soon."

He shook his head. "It take more than little scratch to kill me."

"Still, you need to conserve your strength."

"Enzo told me. About you. A father's pride." He winced in pain but went on, ignoring my pleas for him to be still and quiet. "You have the sight."

"What?" His words sounded strangely Macbethian. "What did my father tell you?"

"We drink much vodka. He tell big story about great-grandmother, grandfather, hunters of monster—like werewolf, something. I think it big story. He say is true, but not for him. He didn't have the sight."

"And what is the sight?"

Gregor looked at me with impatience. "Paradiso." He grimaced.

The paramedic unit roared up to our parked cars. I ran to the opening of the warehouse and waved them toward us. A man jumped out with his bag and bent toward Gregor. His partner went to check on Cruz. For what happened to Gregor, I had no explanation, but Gregor lied smoothly, saying something about a dog.

I'd wrapped one palm in gauze from my bag and tightened the knot with my teeth and other hand. The unit that followed was from another precinct. I identified myself, telling them briefly about the chase and what happened to Cruz. I turned back to the paramedics with

Gregor and told them about his kidney issues. He was on a gurney being wheeled toward their unit when he reached out to me.

"Give us, one second," I asked them.

"You talk to Freya," Gregor said. I looked at him curiously. I'd had no idea he knew my grandmother. "You ask her about your family legacy." He nodded then and I let them load him into the vehicle.

Freya. Thinking back to my childhood days, there was little that happened that surprised Freya. Now I learn she may well have known about my abilities. I frowned, thinking that I could have used a little heads-up from her prior to encountering vampires disguised as high school librarians. Maybe they thought I'd go through life blissfully ignorant, like my sister. Could Izzy have known? Not possible, I told myself. There wasn't a secret on Earth my sister could keep, especially not one like supernatural creatures roaming the earth. Or having the ability to see them.

Angry thoughts swarmed through my mind like bees. I watched the ambulance drive off, sirens blaring. Backup would arrive soon, including the coroner, to pick up Cruz's body. Shoving my building resentment of family secrets aside, I called someone I could trust.

"Zig, I'm headed into the sewer entrance near Building 23 at the warehouse docks. I need you to come get my car."

This was not the strangest request I've ever made of Ziggy and she simply said okay before the sadness in her voice edged out everything else.

"I'm so sorry about Xavier."

"Yeah, me too." I clicked off the phone and slung the

backpack over my shoulder. I made my way toward the grated tunnel entrance outside the warehouse complex. The grate had been ripped off its hinges and flung several feet away. I stepped into the tunnel.

22

I switched on my flashlight and nothing happened. After whacking it several times, the shaky beam finally came on, lighting my way into the depths of guck. My life had surely taken a turn for the romantic since Marlowe's arrival. I thought—no—I was positive—I'd spent more time in the sewers than I'd ever had. Perhaps next time Marlowe dragged in a hostile, he could find one that hung out in upscale hotels.

Next time. Like that would happen. No time-traveling poets to hunt hostiles, no time-displaced vampires, no gorgeous man to wrap up in at the end of the day.

I stopped to listen in the darkness. Sound would have echoed and bounced off the damp walls. It was impossible to tell what direction a sound might come from if there was a sound to be heard. There wasn't. The thought came to me that I might be lost, wandering forever in this slimy hell.

And Marlowe could already be gone. I rushed forward. I hadn't told him how I felt. Hadn't said it out loud. We'd definitely shared something the night before, but I still hadn't said it. That was before X died, before my case fell apart. The time with Marlowe caused a turmoil in me I hadn't felt in a very long time. I wanted to push it away, to not acknowledge what I'd felt. If I could go on like normal, everything would be fine. I would be fine. He'd said it just before getting out of the car: *I cannot bear the thought of this world or any other without thee inhabiting it. You love Xavier, he is like a brother to you. But you are not in love with him.*

I adopted a fast gait through the tunnels, turning left and right, hoping for a sound or a sign of which way Marlowe had gone. Every turn, I stopped and listened for signs of life. Hopefully human life. I should have been more worried about me than him, given my poor sense of direction and the fact that he'd been in much tougher situations. He'd fought at least as many hostiles as I had and lived to tell about it. And the sixteenth century was a far more dangerous time than my own. I'd probably die from dysentery within a week of being there. Marlowe had faced dangers I'd never considered. The risk of being hanged as a heretic or radical was common, not to mention his clandestine missions for the queen. Like some fan girl of Helen Mirren, I'd asked him continually about Queen Elizabeth I. Marlowe had seen her of course, but most of his assignments came from someone else.

"I report to Walsingham, who has the ear of the queen." His voice had been far off, as though he were hundreds of years away, instead of next to me in my car. Most of our conversations about his time had been while commuting.

"What sort of missions?" I'd asked, hungry for more of his voice.

"Mostly to see what her enemies have afoot. Spain, France, the Vatican. The Pope is not at all pleased at having lost his control over Britain. With the queen's adage that the country be Protestant, his wealth is greatly diminished, and desperate measures are being taken to dethrone her and put someone more favorable to the church in power. My job is to ascertain these measures and report them."

"Does Walsingham know of your abilities?"

Marlowe had been quiet for a moment, readjusting his feet in the cramped space of my car.

"Traveling or hunting?"

"Hunting," I said.

He gave a short laugh. "Nay. To be sure, I'm not positive that Walsingham isn't part of the darkness. He has a sinister nature and I am careful not to cross him. He has not shown any demonic attribute, save for his ruthlessness. If he did, I would surely have to kill him, and that would be no easy task."

"What of the time traveling?"

Marlowe shook his head. "He knows nothing. Save for Master Gomfrey, no one has knowledge of me. To the people of my time, I am a humble playwright of meager talents. Without my benefactor, I'd have no means with which to produce my works. Any success I have achieved is due to the faithfulness of a few good friends." He'd smiled at me then and reached across my car to squeeze my hand. Had that conversation only happened two days ago? Three? It felt like much longer than that. Scrambling through the tunnels searching for him, I realized that in the short space of four days, I'd gotten to know Marlowe better than I'd ever wanted to know Rick, and I'd been sleeping with Rick for several months.

Marlowe was different, and not just because he was a monster hunter or a time traveler. If he were the guy next door, he'd still be different than any other man I'd been with.

The tunnel narrowed and I stopped to stretch the aching muscles in my back, ignoring the nervous pit in my stomach at the closeness of my surroundings. I switched the go-bag from one shoulder to the other and continued my trek, my shoulders almost perpendicular to the ground.

The conversation with Gregor had reminded me that I hadn't seen Freya since my father's funeral. The last time I'd been to her little house in the Italian district, I'd found it rented to a Jamaican dude with a huge tangle of dreadlocks. He'd told me she was touring Europe with friends. This probably meant she'd found another sugar daddy.

My sister, Izzy had been after me to make contact with our grandmother. I'd been content to leave her to her travels and her dalliances. Now, I had a definite reason to track her down. Trips with sugar pops or not, I needed answers. I smiled to myself, thinking of what she'd make of Marlowe if they met. He'd charm the pants off her, or she, him. It would be fun to watch, nevertheless.

First things first. We had to kill the strigoi and then Volpi would find a solution for Marlowe to stay. Or at least to control his travels enough to come back.

Every hundred feet or so, I'd called out Marlowe's

name. Finally, there was a faint answering shout, as though he was in the bowels of hell. I turned down another tunnel even narrower than the last two. My flashlight bobbed and the light became fainter as I raced toward the clear bone chilling yowl of the strigoi. Its vocalizations pierced the dank air, bouncing off the cement walls like rubber balls. Rising in intensity, clearly hostile, and indicating it was circling its prey. Marlowe. The air in this section of tunnel smelled strangely like the ozone of atmosphere, like rain. My hair stood on end and fairly crackled with static.

I came to another grate blocking an entrance. It was still upright, but loose on the hinges and I squeezed past it. I wanted to call out again, but I was afraid of attracting the strigoi, or distracting Marlowe. Suddenly, it was deadly quiet. I stopped, listening intently. There was nothing. This was about as welcome as a coven of menopausal witches. At least sounds of a struggle indicated life. Quiet usually meant everyone was dead and/or something was lying in wait for me.

There was another yowl, this time from pain. I quit trying to be silent and ran toward the noise, hunching over as the tunnel narrowed down smaller and smaller until I was on my hands and knees. The sound of scuffling coupled with grunts of pain kept me on edge. I shouted for Marlowe. At first there was nothing, but finally, I heard a faint and hurried response.

I was crawling so fast that when the tunnel opened out into an intersection my hands failed to touch solid concrete and I fell into an open space rather gracelessly. Fortunately, it was only a few feet down. I lay there for a second, getting my bearings, mentally checking for broken bones. It was no longer quiet. In fact, the sounds around me echoed in the expanse of the room. The growls and hisses of the strigoi reverberated off the walls. Metal jangles and scrapes on stone, punctuated by Marlowe's grunts with the effort of battle. I stood up gingerly, swinging my light around to get my bearings.

I heard a growl as my light moved over the skirmish in the corner. Marlowe was in full-on battle mode, sword slashing through the air, sparking as it hit the cement walls and floor. He advanced on the vampire creature, trying to trap it into a corner.

"Keep the torch on the exits," he huffed at me. "We must confine the beast to this room."

I thought he should get on with it and kill the damn thing, but whatever. I stepped forward and my foot kicked a body on the cement floor, causing a grunt of pain. My light flicked across Gregor's man, alive, but bleeding badly.

"The light!" Marlowe shouted and I moved my torch back into the correct position. One-handed, I shrugged off my bag and rustled through it for something to stop the guy from bleeding out. He was conscious enough to hold a cloth to his leg and sit up. I moved closer to Marlowe and the creature, but not too close. The strigoi was above him, hissing as it clung effortlessly to cracks in the wall. It skittered over a few feet. With both hands on the sword, Marlowe swiped at it to keep it from moving toward the entrance. He was moving constantly, back and forth, the sword in front of him flashed in the occasional beam of my light. His own torch was on the ground and gave only the barest of ambient light. Until my tiny flashlight and I literally fell into this room,

Marlowe had been fighting in almost total darkness.

"Where's the vial?" I asked.

"My cape," he answered through gritted teeth, his breath coming in fast and shallow. He was tiring. Gregor's man croaked at me and I moved back toward him. The cape lay half under him and I handed him the flashlight.

"Can you hold the light?"

He nodded and shone the light upward as I rifled through Marlowe's cape. As my hand closed around the vial, Marlowe let out an unintelligible shout. I turned to see the strigoi jump from its perch onto him. His sword was caught upright between them. They were face to face, the sword the only thing keeping vicious teeth from sinking into Marlowe's flesh. He grunted with the effort of keeping it at bay and I saw the monster's talons, curved, and razor sharp, sinking into his upper arm. I rushed at them.

"My knife," he commanded.

The stench of the vampire nearly overwhelmed me as I got closer to them. I couldn't remember which of Marlowe's boots held the knife, but I guessed correctly on the first try. Pulling it out, I popped the top off the vial one-handed and poured its contents over the blade.

Gregor's man kept the light on us, but it was shaking and sporadic. I could barely see what I was doing as I tried to cover the blade in blood. The strigoi released one hand from Marlowe and swiped at me. The movement upset their delicate balance and they both fell to the concrete.

They rolled back in my direction and only a quick leap kept me from falling into them. I turned and

scrambled toward the fray, flipping the direction of the
dagger in my hand. Marlowe was under the creature,
his sword between them useless in this close proximity.
I lifted the knife, aiming for the demon's scaly gray
skin. In the shaky beam of the flashlight, I could see
the misshapen knobs of his spine running the length of
his hunched back. They rolled again and this time I fell
across Marlowe's body toward the strigoi. All three of
us became a tangle of human and monster on the wet
slimy floor. I stabbed toward the thing, reaching as far
as I could to avoid stabbing Marlowe. Marlowe turned,
grunting with effort and pinned the creature under him.

"Now, Tamberlyn, now!" I plunged the dagger and
it hit home. The strigoi's pained grunt turned into an
eerie howl. Now that it wasn't a moving target, I could
pull the dagger out and stab it again, this time aiming
for the heart—if it had a heart. I felt the knife hit bone
and I pressed forward, putting my weight against it. I
wanted to retch from the stench of the thing. We were
almost eye to eye and its large, soulless eyes turned
from red to black and finally glazed over as it ceased
its struggle. It gave a last shuddering sigh and fell still.
Marlowe released his hold and fell back onto the cement
floor, heaving with the effort. I sat back on my haunches,
the blood-soaked dagger in my hand. In the beam of
my flashlight, we edged away and watched as the body
shriveled. Its former bone and muscle liquefied into a
puddle of goo. I stood up shakily and Marlowe reached
toward my shoulder.

"Art thou harmed?"

"No. I'm fine. You?" I touched his arm where the
strigoi had sunk its claws. He winced but said he was

unharmed. His arm came around my shoulder as we turned toward the man holding the light. As if signaling the end of everything, the beam flickered weakly and went out. I retrieved Marlowe's torch from where it had rolled out of our reach. I shone the beam over Gregor's man. He was alive. There was a look of astonishment, and horror, and relief on his face. He started cursing madly in Russian.

23

Marlowe's unerring sense of direction had the three of us exiting onto a street in a fairly decent amount of time. I noted the address was several blocks away from the warehouse district. By this time, the coroner would have picked up Cruz's body and cops would be processing the scene at the warehouse. All I could think of was getting Marlowe somewhere safe, even if safety were just an illusion. We walked in the other direction, helping Gregor's man. I dragged out my phone to call a cab or an ambulance, I wasn't sure which. Before the call connected, a black SUV with tinted windows, much like the one Gregor arrived in, showed up on the street. I glanced at the Russian leaning against me, who in the light of day, looked like he'd gone six rounds too many with an MMA fighter.

He grinned back at me and held up his phone. "GPS tracker," he said as he reached for the car door. "Gregor says to take care of you. It is my pleasure for saving my life."

After a quick glance at each other, Marlowe and I got in the back seat. I told the driver we needed to get to the hospital.

"No," Marlowe said. He looked at me. "I fear there is no time. We must go home. I must gather my things."

"We can find Volpi, maybe he'll have—"

"Tam," he used my nickname for the second time. "There is no time." He glanced warily at our friendly Russian henchman in the back seat with us. He lowered his voice. "I believe we have enough to explain already, without further complicating the matter."

I sighed and gave my address to the driver. The car wheeled around, heading back toward downtown. Pulling some more dressings from my backpack, I ripped them open, littering the back seat with first aid wrappers, and pressed the bandage to the Russian's right thigh. I pressed hard and he grunted, but the bleeding seemed to slow.

"You need stitches," I said. "Einstein Medical is the closest. Hold this here." He nodded and grimaced as he pressed down.

I pulled my phone out to call Volpi and almost threw it down in frustration at the sound of his stupid voicemail. "How long?" I turned toward Marlowe, keeping my voice low. His skin almost sizzled when I touched it. I swore I could see tiny blue sparks outlining his hair. He shrugged off my question and laced his fingers in mine. The Russians were watching us warily. I was sure that they had questions about what happened. I'd let Gregor handle those. All I wanted was to keep Marlowe with me.

The car arrived at my doorstep and after the most perfunctory of thanks and a message for Gregor,

Marlowe and I ran up the steps to my apartment.

The last time we were there, in the hallway in front of my door, Marlowe was kissing me, and we were tearing each other's clothes off. I wished for that moment again.

I opened the door and found the apartment much the same as we'd left it that morning before I'd gotten the call about X. Dishes were left untouched in the sink. The books we'd read so avidly not three days ago had fallen onto the floor from the coffee table. My bathroom was a shambles and the bedsheets beckoned.

"Let's look at that arm." I pulled at him and he shrugged me off.

"I need to change. I cannot go back like this." He indicated the slim fitting pants and T-shirt he wore so beautifully. He pulled the shirt off and once again I was struck by the lean sexiness of him.

"All the more reason to clean the wound here, where I have peroxide." I stepped around the downed shower curtain and rod to grab the bottle. I made him sit on the closed toilet seat and hastily dabbed the liquid onto the four gashes etched into his skin. He ignored me pointedly as he pulled off his boots.

"Twice now, the creature tagged you. We don't want this to get infected," I said. "I'm sure it's a common cause of death in your time."

"So is the plague." He smiled wearily. "And I have survived."

I frowned at him and cleaned the wound some more. I didn't mention the early and grisly death he'd face. He wouldn't have listened to me anyway.

"Listen, you have to survive." I wrapped his wound carefully and pulled him closer. "No matter what, you need to be careful. There's got to be some way for you to come back. I'll find it." I looked away as tears came to my eyes. "Though how I will get that information to you, I have no idea."

"Tamberlyn," Marlowe said quietly. "Do not fret so."

"It can't end this way. I don't—"

"I do not wish to leave you. But I must."

"We can find a way to keep you here. Volpi's no Einstein, but he's savvy. We'll find something."

An eerie blue light started to flash from behind him. He left me and moved into the bedroom where his purple velvet costume hung in my closet. When he emerged, he had those ridiculous pants on and was pulling his rough cotton shirt over his head. My phone rang and I let it go to voicemail. I didn't want to waste a moment away from him.

We stood in the center of my living room. He pulled me close against him and I breathed him in. We both smelled like vampire death and sewer, and I didn't care. The air crackled around us. I couldn't seem to let him go.

"Having you here has been so...I don't know, different? Amazing? Yes, all of that and more. I want... damn it, I want more time." I started to pull away, but he stopped me, his hand coming behind my head. He kissed me, long and beautiful. I felt the warmth of his skin at the opening of his shirt. I could sense his heart beat strong and sure. The length of his body was pressed to mine, and I could feel his desire for me. I broke away enough to look at him.

"Are you sure you don't have time? Not even for a quickie? This electric aura you're sporting is kind of turning me on." I nodded toward the blue sparks now randomly filling my apartment.

His seriousness fell away at my words. He knew me too well. My snarky comments were a cover.

"If I infer the meaning of your words correctly, alas, it will take much, much longer in your arms to satisfy this hunger." He pulled away. "Being too close to me during the transition will be harmful to you." He looked amazing, otherworldly, and bathed in blue light, a breeze out of nowhere ruffling his hair. His eyes were hazel and savage looking. "You are a wonder to mine eyes, Tamberlyn. Your beauty is only surpassed by your strength and your wit. Your courage is that of the most fearsome warrior. Do not forget me."

I laughed softly. "Like that's possible." And then as I saw the look on his face, I dropped the comic relief. "I won't forget you."

I leaned in to kiss him again, ignoring his warning about staying away. Ignoring the spark as our lips touched, I opened my mouth under his.

My phone jangled. I ignored it again. I wanted to wrap myself around him and never let him go. "Take me with you."

It was a last-ditch effort to keep him with me. He held me away from him and yet didn't quite let me go. My friggin' phone lit up again, this time with a text, rapidly followed by another.

The room was dark now, as though clouds had moved in on us. The blue sparks that were pretty and harmless a moment before started to grow in strength and the air crackled.

"You know I cannot. 'Tis death for you to come with me."

"You don't know that."

He let me go, almost pushing me away. He nodded at my phone's incessant dinging. I wanted to throw the damn thing across the room, but I finally looked at it enough to see Volpi's name flit across the screen. I hurriedly thumbed open the text messages as Marlowe sheathed his sword and gathered his cape around him. The air in my place moved in a circular motion. The velocity of the air movement was like a dozen fans blowing across us.

I blinked back tears. He reached out to wipe them away.

"Say my name, Tamberlyn. I would hear it upon thy lips as are your tears."

"Metaphors? Now?"

He ignored my comment. "My Christian name. Say it." The electricity caught up my hair, fanning it out like a jagged halo. The wind amped up to hurricane strength. I grabbed his hand, almost shouting.

"Volpi's found something. He says there's a man, a scientist. He thinks he can help."

"There is not time." His fingers pulled away from mine and he seemed to fade away under the whirring onslaught of blue light. "Please Tamberlyn, say it once, for me."

"Christopher," I yelled into the vortex. His smile was almost as blinding as the light was. I could barely see him through the tears in my eyes. "Volpi says to look in 1938, Palermo, Italy. Majorana. 1938. Christopher," I said it again as the lightning struck with a crack. There was a flash and I saw his smile one last time. And then he was gone.

I slumped to the floor, gasping for breath as the air was sucked out of my apartment. My ears rang, and my hands tingled from the static. My heart felt like I'd been struck by lightning. Maybe I had been.

24

After a twelve-and-a-half-hour sleep, I dragged myself to the shower and stayed there until the hot water ran out. Drying off, I dressed in a T-shirt and the last pair of clean jeans I owned. I thought briefly of putting the same shirt on that Marlowe had worn, but it was covered in muck and blood. I threw it in the wash along with my clothes covered in similar mire.

There were things that needed to be done. I put off going into the office, taking a sick day to recover, and giving a slim narration of what happened to Cruz. Incident reports could wait. I called my sister to get in touch with our grandmother. She gave me a new—to me—number, and I left a terse message for Freya to call me back. I checked on Gregor and his driver and was relieved to hear that both men were recovering. Gregor would owe me a favor, and that wasn't a bad thing.

I took an Uber to Ziggy's on the other side of town to retrieve my car. A corner row house of faded red brick she'd inherited from her grandmother. Its dingy white trim outlined a traditional front porch that overlooked what once was a meticulously tended front garden.

Inside, the décor was eclectic, much like Ziggy herself, with a decidedly airy art-gallery atmosphere with its white walls and windows covered in sheer curtains. A brick fireplace squatted in the corner, the bricks painted a glossy white, with a contrasting fire-engine-red mantel. Black and white photos in various frames littered the top of it.

The last time I'd been to Ziggy's was Christmas last year. She'd insisted on having a holiday party because the department's budget cuts had resulted in a listless office party with sheet cake and no booze.

I could almost see X kicking back in her yellow wingback chair, a beer in his hand. Then, the place had been dripping with twinkly lights and mistletoe. Now, it was pristine by comparison. The distinct vocals of Tom Petty emanated from a wireless speaker in the corner.

"I'm making kombucha, come sit down." Ziggy had opened the door and moved quickly into her kitchen. Light from a long window weaved in between the herbs and plants on her shelves. Instead of sitting, I stood in front of her fireplace, looking at the photos. Every picture was of a dog or dogs: puppies tumbling on grass, a dog in a front basket of a bike, another one catching a Frisbee at the park. They were whimsical and captured the motion of the animals perfectly.

"Who are all these dogs?"

"I have no idea," she answered. "I like dogs and photographing them, so I take pictures around town. I was born in the year of the Dog."

"So, kind of like your spirit animal?"

"Chinese Zodiac. Each year is represented by an animal."

"Oh." My life had enough legend and tradition in it that I didn't want yet another thing, so I let it drop. She came back into the small living room and handed me a mug. I was expecting coffee and got some bitter, fizzy drink. "Ugh. What is this?"

"Kombucha. I told you."

I forced myself to take another sip of the nasty stuff. "Yeah, like that explains you trying to kill me."

She ignored my complaint. "Where's Marlowe?" she asked quietly, curling her legs under her as she sat on her overstuffed couch. I had chosen the yellow chair to sit in and picked at a loose thread on the arm.

"Gone." I took a deep breath and looked away from her gaze. "Look, Zig, about before. I was an ass. I'm sorry. I trust you with my life and I never meant—"

She brushed off my apology. "He's like you," she said. "Marlowe."

Her words settled on me. It made sense that Marlowe would be a hunter like myself. Ziggy knew that I wouldn't share the monster element of our world with just anyone.

"Yes," I said slowly. "He really is Christopher Marlowe. From the sixteenth century."

She was quiet as she sipped her hideous concoction. I could see her scientific mind wrapping around theories and facts. "So, he travels through time? Really?"

I laughed. "That's what I said. At first, I really thought he was putting me on, and then maybe he was delusional. I was ready to send him to Belmont. But there were too many things about him that I couldn't explain other than he had traveled through time. It's rather random. He can't control when and where. I was trying to help him."

"You liked him." She smiled. "I don't think I've ever seen you quite like that before."

"Yeah, well. He's gone now, probably for good." My words came out flat like I was reading a crime report.

"I'm sorry, Tam." Her eyes watched me for a split second before moving on. "He'd said something earlier. Like it was his fault the monster was here."

Grateful that I didn't have to elaborate on Marlowe any further, I quickly switched subjects. "Your research was spot-on about the monster. The strigoi followed him to this time. But it's gone now too. A pile of goo in the sewer tunnels."

"I figured. You wouldn't be sitting here complaining over my kombucha if it were still out there. And what happened to X? Was that related to—"

"Not at all. That was the human variety of monster. Munson was dirty and set us up. He was on the take with Balfour."

"Internal Affairs has been interviewing everyone from the Organized Crime Unit. I'm surprised they haven't called you in yet."

"I'm going in tomorrow." My phone rang. "Paradiso." I answered without looking at the caller ID.

"Berly, how many times have I told you to answer with at least a hello first? It's only polite." Freya's voice chided me over a static connection. She used my childhood nickname. She was the only one who called me that, concocting the name from the middle letters of Tamberlyn. She did the same for my sister, Isabelle, who was Izzy to her friends, but Sabel to Freya. Which was much nicer than Berly, but, whatever.

"Hi, Freya. How are you? It's also customary to inquire after someone's health after a year of not hearing from them." We had never called her grandma. She hated the term. Since our mother died and she'd pitched in to help Dad raise us, it had been Freya, or in times of childhood stress, Nana.

I glanced at Ziggy as I heard Freya laugh. I put my hand over the phone and mouthed a sorry to Ziggy, not wanting to end the call. Ziggy nodded and retreated to her kitchen as Freya asked the question I'd wanted to ask of her. "Where have you been?"

She meant this on some metaphysical plane, I was sure. Because I'd been right here—the same number, the same apartment where I'd lived for years. She didn't wait for an answer. "Sabel told me you've been looking for me. I'm in Peru—Machu Picchu to be exact. It's a beautiful place. You should come."

I rolled my eyes. As if I had time for such things.

"Don't look that way, dear. You know what I mean. Of course, you have work, and friends, and things to do there, but at some point, I mean. It's a magical place and everyone should see it." She left off the rest of her sentence, which was "before they die." Mostly because of my profession, but maybe it was said because of something else. The fact that she knew me well enough to know I was making faces over the phone was a throwback from my childhood. As kids, she'd convinced both my sister and I that she had eyes in the back of her head. Izzy had nightmares for weeks.

"Speaking of things to do. I spoke to Gregor Krotsky

the other day. He sends his regards."

There was the tiniest bit of hesitation on the end of the line before she responded. "I haven't heard about Gregor for years. He's still alive? The old goat."

I had to smile at this, as Freya was probably the same age or even older than Gregor, yet she wouldn't see herself that way. Most people wouldn't either. She had the silver hair of a senior, but the gait and energy of someone my age.

"That's all you have to say?"

"The ruins here are completely transformative when the sun hits them in the morning. The air is clear, and it really is very refreshing."

I could tell I wasn't going to get anywhere so I played along. "I thought you were in Europe?"

"One can only stay on the continent so long, it becomes tedious otherwise and Binky had always wanted to come here."

"Binky?"

"Bingham Garfield, my new friend. He's sleeping in, poor dear. I fear I've worn him out." Her words came across as clear as if she were on Ziggy's couch.

"They have a cell tower on Machu Picchu?"

"Well, in certain spots. If I bend thirty degrees and stand on one leg, I can make calls. Those yoga classes have really paid off. Binky thinks so too." She giggled like a young girl.

There was something inherently icky and wrong about knowing too much of your seventy-year-old grandmother's sex life. I changed the subject as quickly as possible.

"Why didn't you tell me about the family trait?

Gregor says you knew. And so did Dad."

There was a slight crackle on the line, but other than that, nothing, and I thought the call had been dropped. "Freya? You there?"

"Yes, yes I'm here. Just what are you on about, child?"

Maybe it was the fact that I'd been listening to Marlowe's accented words for the last four days because it took me a while to realize that she was speaking oddly, almost Brit-like. But I also knew her delay tactics. Freya was the master of avoidance and deflection.

"You know what I mean," I said. "The stories about your grandfather, or grandmother or someone, seeing monsters and demons."

"My older sister Penelope—poor soul, in and out of institutions since she was a teen, which was a shame as she had talent. She was quite the athlete—on the US tennis team back in the day. She died when I was a child."

"I have a feeling she wasn't crazy." Again, there was silence. This was the strangest conversation I'd ever had with Freya and there have been some doozies. Usually, you couldn't shut her up. I vaguely remembered a conversation on her front porch. At the time, I'd been embarrassed, watching Theo laugh at her stories about me. It was a fairly new relationship, and I was madly in love with him—thought he was the perfect man. Of course, Freya didn't, and as usual, she was right.

Now as I thought about it, she'd been keeping a closer eye than usual that summer. "You knew, didn't you? Back when I was with Theo. You told him about the baseball bat I kept under the bed, the supernatural books I read, the whole bit. You made it sound like I was quirky, but you knew."

"I knew that boy wasn't strong enough for you. Very attractive, but not near strong enough. You need a real man, dear. An old-fashioned, knows-who-he-is, man."

A flicker of joy sparked in me as I heard her words. Marlowe knew who he was. And no one did old-fashioned quite like he did.

"Don't change the subject. I need to know this stuff. This is my life now. You know that there are...things in the world. Bad things."

"I've never seen them." Her tone changed—resigned to at least acknowledging my statement. "But your father had a theory. He'd heard enough stories from his grandmother that he investigated. That's what Lorenzo did, investigate. Always curious that boy."

"What did he find?"

"Honestly Berly, we didn't talk about it much. It was something we chose not to talk about."

"But he must have told someone. He told Gregor Krotsky for God's sake. He must have left notes or a journal. I need to know if there's someone else out there like me. Someone who can see hostiles."

Someone who didn't also time travel when the moon was right.

Freya did what she always did when she wanted to avoid a subject. "Oh, the sky is gorgeous. You really ought to see this, dear. I'm afraid my phone is dying. Electricity is splotchy here, so it's hard to keep a phone charged. I'll be back in a month or so, we can talk more then."

"Xavier died." I blurted out the words, to bring her

back to my reality. "Killed by a cop on the take. That was yesterday." As I said the words, I couldn't believe all this had happened the day before. Even a week earlier, my mundane world was predictable and even comfortable. Not anymore.

"Are you okay?"

It was a natural enough question, but I wanted to scream at her. *No, I'm not okay! My partner's dead. Marlowe, the "real" man you've wanted for me is gone and will never come back. I am alone, again, being a cop and a hunter of monsters. And you knew about them, suspected I knew about them, and still chose not to talk about it. My father knew about it and never told me. I've been fighting my way out of this paper bag for years with no help from either of you. So, no, I'm not okay.*

"I'm fine." I sighed. "I'll talk to you when you get home."

She hung up before I could say anything else. I set my phone on the arm of the chair. Ziggy emerged from the kitchen and gave me another mug. This one filled with coffee.

"Thanks," I took a grateful sip.

"So, Freya? That's your grandma, right?"

I nodded and leaned back in the chair, cradling my mug of coffee in my hands and closing my eyes. I loved my grandmother, she took care of us a lot after mom died. But she could be exhausting, and I was still very raw about everything.

Ziggy seemed to get this, and we were both quiet for a few moments. Finally, she spoke.

"I didn't mean to eavesdrop, but it sounded like she

knew. You know, about your undercover work. Your ability."

I drank more coffee. I didn't know if it was great coffee or not, but it was warm, and comforting, and familiar. "Not exactly. I mean she knew about some abilities in the family. Get this, they thought it was schizophrenia or something. Her older sister was committed. So, I think she pushed it under the rug. Out of sight, out of mind."

"So, she knows about you?"

"Well, she does now." I set the half-empty mug on the coffee table. "I should go. Thanks for getting my car."

"Are you okay?" She repeated Freya's question. This time I answered honestly.

"I don't think so. But there's not much I can do about it, is there?" I glanced at her but turned away before her sympathetic eyes discerned more than I wanted them to.

"Well," she began in a brighter tone. "When was the last time you ate?"

"I'm not hungry." Came my automatic reply.

"But I am. You can keep me company while I eat the most fabulous dinner breakfast ever." She stood and grabbed her coat, retrieving my car keys from a hook by her door. "You drive. I'll buy." I managed a grateful smile and studied her dog pictures again.

"What is my Chinese spirit animal, do you think?" I asked as I moved toward her door.

"We'll find out, but if I ventured a guess, it would be year of the Dragon."

25

It was late afternoon the next day before I got myself to the office. The temperature outside had dropped to single digits and the wind rattled our historic windows. Other than the whirring of ancient desktop computers and the sludgy gurgle of the coffee pot, the place was quiet. I may not have been a favorite co-worker—I'm grumpy, solitary, and not always a team player, but X was the opposite. Everyone loved the guy. He was a good cop and a better man. These guys weren't feeling sorry for my loss of a partner, but their own loss of a comrade. At least they weren't blaming me. That was put squarely on Munson's head as details came out.

The Internal Affairs guys were named Charlie and Mike, and they could have been brothers in a Laurel and Hardy sort of way. Both sported super-short haircuts and rat-like eyes. One was tall. One was short. The tall one wore old-fashioned horn-rimmed glasses. The short one's tie was knotted crookedly and drifted to the left side of his overly large Adam's apple. They addressed me only as "Paradiso," skipping the honorific of detective. Mike had known my dad and there was no love lost there.

Mike started. At least, I think the one who talked was named Mike. I hadn't really paid attention during the introduction stage.

"How long was your partner in bed with Balfour?"

"What?" My mouth dropped open despite my usual nonchalance in the face of IA. No way could they think X was dirty.

"You heard me, Paradiso, you had to know. How long?" I fell back to my usual method of keeping calm when the urge to kick someone in the balls hit me. I clenched my fists under the table, my nails driving into my palms until I couldn't feel it anymore. I had known I should have stayed at home, safe and quiet in my dark nest of an apartment. I refused to look at the man questioning me, so I squinted at the tall one, who must be Charlie.

"Hernandez was clean. Munson's the dirty cop. If there's another cop on Balfour's payroll, I don't know who it is. Munson and my partner are both dead. I thought that's what this debrief was about."

The short one spoke next, and I tried not to stare at the jiggling knot at his neck when he talked.

"We're here to get to the bottom of this. Just see how far this corruption goes. This department's reputation has suffered enough, don't you think?"

The inference was that the tarnished reputation existed because of Lorenzo Paradiso—my father. This was all stinky water under an aging bridge as far as I was concerned. I thought I'd lived down my father's reputation and had finally become accepted in the department. I never expected to be liked, but I was a good cop, damn it, and so was my father for that matter.

Enzo Paradiso had simply turned in his corrupt boss and a DA taking kickbacks. No one likes a whistleblower. But this wasn't about my father, the guys were digging up dirt to get me angry. Unfortunately, it worked.

"Look asshole. I'm telling you the truth. Munson was it. Hernandez was clean and so am I. You have no evidence to the contrary. And leave my father out of this." Someone had to have the balls to say what they really meant, even if had to be me.

Crooked Tie looked smug enough to smack. "We have emails on Munson's computer. They indicate a partner, someone on the force who was also on Balfour's payroll."

"Doesn't mean it's Hernandez."

"Doesn't mean it's not." Glasses, whom I'd thought of as less of a dick than Crooked Tie, became my least favorite person. He smiled as he talked—like he already had all the answers.

"If Munson was working with someone, why don't you investigate his partner instead of mine?" I asked.

"His partner didn't shoot him, you did. His partner was nowhere near the only witness that links Balfour and Munson. That was Enrico Cruz, and you shot him too."

"Self-defense in both cases. Cruz died from jumping off a two-story catwalk, not a GSW."

"Maybe it wasn't Hernandez. Maybe good-ol'-boy Hernandez was a patsy or a bystander in the way of your partnership."

I laughed. Maybe it was the whole week of weird that had finally gotten to me. Maybe I was starting to feel the extreme losses I'd had in the past two days and this was my way of dealing. Maybe I was fucking crazy, but I couldn't stop myself. The laughter rang out, hollow and empty in the sparsely appointed room. The session was being recorded and I idly wondered how it would sound on the playback. Would it be used as evidence for my dismissal? Unfit for duty. They'd known it all along. This was too tough a job for little girl Paradiso.

The IA guys glanced at each other, their expressions going from anger to confusion as I struggled to get myself under control. Laughing was better than crying, I guessed. Anger was even better than that. But if I showed anger, it would mean they'd hit a nerve and they'd take that as some sort of confession. I took a deep breath and tried to speak in a normal voice.

"You guys have known Hernandez for a long time. Didn't he stand up for you at your wedding, Charlie?" It was a guess, a mere memory of a long-ago conversation with X, but I ran with it. "And I thought you guys were in a bowling league together? It's a real stretch to think that with his experience as a cop that anyone, even his partner, could put something over on him. Come on, you're grasping here, guys."

Charlie Horn Rims had the decency to look chagrined, but his partner, the bull terrier with beady eyes wiggled his fat neck again. "You guys were close. You probably know his password, right?" He dragged out a folder, opened it to reveal printed emails from Munson. They were addressed to Hernandez. "You could have easily used his account to pass info back and forth."

I had known his password, it was his and Connie's anniversary and their kids' initials, basic and pretty easy to hack for anyone who knew him. He had also known mine, but that was beside the point.

"Anyone in the precinct could have hacked his email. Even Munson, creating a paper trail to misdirect any investigation. Especially Munson," I said.

This was not entirely true. Munson didn't know X that well. We'd only started working with him on the Cynthia Wu murder. I thought it unlikely he'd hacked X's email. Why incriminate him if he intended to kill him? But someone in our department could have. I seethed and spit lightning across the desk from Frick and Frack. "How often do you check your sent mail? You could be hacked too, you know. You seem to be getting info out of nowhere. Maybe pulling theories out of your ass is normal for IA, but it's not the way we do it in homicide."

Mike glared, his face going from pasty to purple. Maybe his tie was cutting off the circulation to his brain. Charlie hastily took over, trying to calm things down. I knew I wasn't helping my case, but damn it, they pissed me off.

After another hour of accusations and denials, I finally got through the entire account of what had happened at Balfour's club. They covered the incident at the warehouse too because of the Balfour connection. I'd left any mention of Marlowe out of my account. Not only would interviewing him be a problem, but it would be one more line of investigation they'd try and follow.

They released me with instructions not to talk to anyone and to make myself available for follow-up questions. I headed back to my desk with the notion that I'd be damned if I let them throw this back onto X's reputation. It had been X's tenacity that brought us closer to revealing Munson as the mole. That investigation was the reason X was killed. That and taking a bullet for me. I still saw it very clearly, Munson's gun barrel glinting in the moonlight, and X's bulk getting in the way.

I looked around at my co-workers. Who could have planted the emails? Whoever it was, they'd probably want to finish what Munson started.

I sat in front of my monitor, my hands shaking as I listened to the murmur of male voices not quite muffled by the cubicle partitions. I typed out my report on the events at the warehouse and Cruz's death. All our unsolved cases had been reassigned to other teams after X was shot.

Looking over at X's empty desk was painful. The techs had taken his computer to ferret out more incriminating evidence. Searching on my computer for the work file, I re-read everything about the home robbery cases. There had to be a detail I was missing. Balfour didn't strike me as an art connoisseur so he wouldn't sanction a series of art thefts. He might like jewelry—I remembered his gold watch and rings from our interview. But the pieces stolen were too recognizable to keep. Fencing them would be the only option.

Besides, he didn't have a girlfriend to give diamonds to anymore. I quit looking at the robbery case and Googled Munson's name. He was a local boy from the South Side and attended Furness High School before getting a basketball scholarship to Rowan University in New Jersey. The rest of his very short bio was unremarkable—a tiny mention of his graduating the police academy and then later being assigned to the Organized Crime Task Force.

We didn't start working with him until after the Cynthia Wu murder. Yet, every time we'd gotten a break in the case, Balfour would slip out of our hands. Of course, now I knew why—Munson was feeding him all the info. I also remembered Munson being in the courtroom for mine and X's testimony in the home invasion case. Trying to make connections, I was writing all this down on a legal pad when my phone rang.

"Paradiso," I answered absently.

"Tam," Ziggy's voice was hollow on the line. "I heard you were coming in today. Thought I'd check on you."

"Thanks. Yep, I'm here, hiding in my cubby. I'm about to get out of here, though. I need to think of something other than Munson for a while."

"Good. You should let the other team work the case."

"Who is the other team anyway?"

"Eric and Canfield."

I nodded. They were good guys. Been on the force a long time, both of them, good solid investigators. "They find anything on Munson? You know IA is trying to pin this shit on X. Like he was the guy working with Munson."

She gasped. "No way!"

"I know. So, anything you got would help. I can't ask because..."

"Sure, sure. I'll see what I can find. You take it easy, okay?"

I hung up and headed out, needing to shut off my brain. Soon I was pulling into the parking lot of the Italian market. At least I didn't have to hide my depression at

Marlowe's absence from Volpi.

He was out in front of his shop when I arrived, speaking with two women as he wrapped one of his candles in brown paper. I didn't approach, just watched the exchange from across the market. He seemed unaware of my presence. Something in how he smiled at the women, his head tilting to the side, the way he leaned down to really pay attention to them. They responded with a coquettish action that was closer to teenagers than middle-aged women.

Most times I'd been at the retail shop, it had been empty of customers and I'd thought for a long time that his income came from less than straightforward sources. As the women left, he turned and looked directly at me, one eyebrow raised up in challenge. He'd seen me all along.

I walked over, dodging shoppers and little kids. We hadn't talked since Marlowe left. Not since Volpi's text message at the eleventh hour. I should have called him, knowing he'd found something—some clue or possibility of Marlowe controlling his travels. I'd been too drained after Marlowe left to do much of anything but fall on my floor in a lump of tearful cursing.

"Why are you lurking around my place?" he asked.

"I wasn't lurking."

"That was definite lurk." He headed into the back room, but at my lack of retort, he stopped, turning back to me. "He's gone, yeah." Volpi made it a statement rather than a question. I nodded. He cocked his head and then turned his sign from Open to Closed. "Come on, I'll let you buy me a beer," he said. We headed to the other end of the market, where a small café sat in the shade of the enormous building.

I wasn't ready to talk about Marlowe yet, so after Volpi ordered his favorite ale—a bitter dark brew that tasted like fermented tires—I told him about Freya. Two years ago, our argument had been that my family was normal. No hostile hunters, no demon killers, nothing. That I was an anomaly. Volpi had disagreed with me, thinking my ability was probably genetic. I'd wanted to keep my family out of it. He thought I should confide in them, at least in my sister. Being an only child, I guess he thought all siblings were close.

"You have a family history of hunters. This is not news." Volpi looked at me pointedly.

"No, it's not news," I said dully.

I thought back to that first year with Volpi. He was difficult, disagreeable, and had no sympathy for a teenage hunter who'd wanted a normal life. We hadn't talked a lot in those early days. I'd been seventeen, hunting on my own for two years and working mostly in the blind. Volpi had been an ally, finding me a weapon or a solution when I'd gone to him for help.

"I think it's time you told me," I said to him.

He stopped in mid-sip and stared hard in my direction. "I disagree."

I tried to meet his eyes with an equal look. "It's been ten years, Volpi. Ten years and still you haven't told me how I found you. Or you, me. You should tell me now. Especially now." I ticked off my fingers as I made my case. "We know I'm not the only hunter. Marlowe is proof of that. My family could be targeted too. I met you right after I broke up with Theo. Does he have anything to do with us?"

His normal scowl darkened at the mention of Theo. "Does it matter how we met? Really?"

"It's one more question I don't have the answer to."

Volpi sighed. And drank. And sighed again. Finally, he finished his beer and talked to me.

"Everything happens for a reason, kid. Maybe your encounter with Theo brought you to me. I don't know." He was being deliberately vague.

"Was it him who gave me the business card? And why can't I remember?"

Volpi's eyes clouded for a brief second as though he felt sorry for me.

"Perhaps it's best forgotten. I believe it was a painful time for you, yes?"

"I hate it when you're cryptic. My last two years of high school was hell. I was consumed with hunting and surviving. Then I met Theo and things felt normal for a while. Freya knew something was up, so did Dad. They knew I was going through something, something I didn't understand, and they did nothing."

Volpi looked at me with an ironic smile. "What did you expect them to do? Hold your hand? Tell you it would all be okay?"

"Yes." I slapped my hand on the table, a little harder than I'd intended. "They could have told me I was okay. I thought I was going crazy, seeing things, remembering things I could not explain. I felt the pain of breaking up with Theo, but I couldn't for the life of me remember why we'd broken up." I frowned into my beer. I had been devastated after the break-up. But I think I missed my dad most of all. We'd been close at one time. At least, until I'd started seeing hostiles, then I was afraid to tell him. I thought he'd send me to a shrink, or worse, a priest. I avoided him, Freya, Izzy—all of them. Dad seemed preoccupied anyway. And Freya, usually so nosy and astute, had said nothing.

We drank in silence for a while and I studied the man across from me. He had a scar shaped like a wide V at the tail end of one ill-kempt eyebrow. It gave him a lopsided look in an otherwise symmetrical face. I had no idea how he got it. In fact, I knew very little about Volpi. Most of our conversations had been one-sided— all about me.

"You never said, did you get my text?" Volpi spoke suddenly.

I blinked at him, a blank look on my face. His left cheek twitched. "Majorana, Palermo. Did you get it in time?"

My voice dropped, thinking of Marlowe. "Yeah, we did. What's Majorana's story?"

"He was a mathematician in Italy. Right up there with Fermi. Brilliant, but his ideas are not significant. What was important was that he disappeared in Palermo in 1938. Got on a boat and was never seen again."

"You think he was like Marlowe?"

"It's a theory. And if he was, then perhaps with his knowledge of physics and mathematics, he might be able to help. Only a few of his mathematical theories survived the last eighty years, but Marlowe has the unique advantage of finding Majorana in his own time. Perhaps his notes would give us a clue to solving Marlowe's dilemma."

"Thank you," I said.

Volpi looked pleased. I was close enough to notice

the fine lines around his eyes. They only happened when he smiled and that was rare. He was in retail so he could charm up a sale when he needed rent money, but I was pretty sure Volpi genuinely disliked everyone. He disliked inane pleasantries even more.

"You hope he shows up again, don't you? Marlowe," I said.

"As do you." He did something out of character. He sympathized. "I'm sorry he couldn't stay. I know he meant something to you."

I turned back toward the café table and faced him. I looked at my mentor with some amazement.

"I think that's the nicest thing you've ever said to me."

He grunted and held up his beer mug like some Viking in a longhouse.

"Don't get used to it."

26

The day before X's funeral I found Marlowe's note. He'd hidden it well, meant for me to find much later. The captain had made it known that I was to take time off—standard protocol after an officer shooting but also because of the death of my partner. The idea that X's reputation was going to be trashed filled me with rage, so being away from the office was a good idea. Suspicion of my co-workers would do nothing to help my already strained office relationships.

X had told me there was something fishy about the two perps in the home invasion and he was sure there was a brain behind the operation. Someone who knew which houses to hit and when. I hadn't disagreed with him, but I'd never thought it would be a cop.

My main question was why Munson was involved. I rolled that around in my head as I cleaned my apartment, the TV providing background noise.

A movie trailer came on—actors in Elizabethan dress in the latest historical drama. The accents and language made me miss him. Our modern way of speaking now seemed harsh and inadequate.

After the beer with Volpi, I'd been reluctant to go back to my empty apartment, so I delayed the inevitable with some retail therapy, buying some little gifts for X's kids and stopping at a local bookstore to buy anything and everything on Christopher Marlowe. Now, I pulled the volumes out of the bag and looked through them. There was a biography with his one and only known likeness on the front. I say likeness because the resemblance to my Marlowe was minuscule, mine being of stronger jaw and deep-set eyes. And sexier, definitely sexier.

Putting the biography down, I turned to the book of works. Included was a play I hadn't heard of before, *Tamberlaine the Great*. I smiled when I saw it. He'd been true to his word and made me a king, though a tragic one.

I sat down in front of my small bookshelf and arranged the books to make room for my purchases. I decided to categorize by genre: horror, fantasy, and graphic novels, then by author, Gaiman, King, etc. I'd turned the TV off and the apartment was quiet, and a draft from nowhere gave me a chill. I turned toward the window, but it was closed. I sat very still, listening, waiting, for what I didn't know, but it felt like I wasn't alone. Strangely enough, it wasn't a scary feeling.

A heavily bound book of Shakespeare's plays thumped over from its hidey-hole against the side of the shelf, startling me. I'd forgotten I had it. I pulled at it, preparing to toss it aside, and remembered Marlowe's words about the bard. My eye caught the tail end of a piece of paper, which served as a bookmark. I opened the book to the designated place. The paper sat along a title page, between plays, namely Richard II. Across the front of the title page, Marlowe's handwriting leaped out at me. He'd scrawled the words *Gong Monger*. While the exact meaning was unclear, I was sure it was an insult.

The paper was folded lengthwise three times. I unfolded it to find more of Marlowe's words. They blurred before me like an ancient document made new.

Beloved Tamberlyn:

i hope thou find this missive in good stead. Mine heart ist laden wit sad longing f'r thy presence. all mine heretofore efforts will be to find mine way back to thy graceful company. n'r shall i lay a mazzard upon mine pillow without thoughts of thy smile and sweet touch upon mine brow. be safe, dear one, f'r i shall return to thee, 'r expire in the attempt, f'r which i shall go to mine rest forev'r content to wot of thy precious love.

As ev'r yours, throughout time
C Marlowe

I brushed the blurriness from my eyes, remembering his words to me at X's, that I knew him truly, but would I know his heart as well. The question was, did he know mine? Did he leave without knowing how much he meant to me because I was too chicken shit to tell him? God, I hoped not. I hope he would know without me saying the words. I made a promise to myself to tell him, should I ever see him again.

Thinking of other promises I'd made, I decided I'd better pay a visit to the Hernandez's. I texted Connie to see if a visit would be possible, knowing—or possibly hoping—that she'd be busy with other friends and family. After my father died, I realized that continually playing hostess to well-meaning folks was often more taxing than being left alone to mourn in peace. Fortunately, for me, both my grandmother Freya and my sister took on those duties so I could avoid the whole thing to go to work.

I knocked on Connie's door empty-handed. No casseroles nor bottle of comfort booze in my hands. It had taken everything I had to even make it this far. Connie seemed to realize this as she pulled me into her arms as soon as she opened the door.

"Thank God you're here," she said. "My sister is driving me crazy." She gave me a watery smile.

"Sisters will do that," I answered.

Connie brought me into the living room where I conveyed polite condolences to her parents again. Connie's older sister, Amaretta, came in from the kitchen, wiping her hands on her apron. We shook hands and made pleasantries. She frowned as soon as Connie told her I worked with X. I glanced over her head at Connie, who shrugged. It seemed the sister disapproved of our chosen calling. I got that. I wasn't all that happy about it myself at the moment.

"Let's go out on the back terrace," Connie said after she asked if I wanted some coffee. Amaretta had made a big pot and handed me a steaming cup. Rather than ask for cream, I thanked her and followed Connie outside.

A cold blast of air hit me in the face, but after a minute or two, I got used to it. We were out from under her sister's disapproving stare and at least it wasn't raining or snowing. Connie closed the glass door with a click, giving us some privacy. We sat at the outdoor table. She pulled a crumpled pack of cigarettes out of a clay pot and lit one, blowing smoke into the cold air. "You want one?" she offered.

I shook my head, a bit surprised. I'd never seen her smoke. But now I knew the reason she'd wanted to go outside. "I thought you had some big secret you were going to reveal out here or something." I joked.

She gave a brief smile. "I was hoping you had one. Something that would explain all this?" Her hand gestured to nothing in particular. I thought of the emails Internal Affairs had traced back to X.

"Sorry. I wish I had something for you. There is no reason at all for this to happen. I can't..." I stopped talking, unable to go on.

Connie took another puff on her cigarette. "You know this is not your fault, right? There was no way you could have known what this cop was going to do. And both of you could have been..." This time it was her turn to fade away.

"At night before I go to sleep, I listen to our answering machine message," she said. "It's nothing special, just 'leave a message,' you know? But it's his voice."

I nodded absently. "I get it. I could not have asked for a better partner." My voice wavered. She had been right, I did feel guilty. I should have told X about my sideline. It hadn't kept him any safer not knowing. "X was right, there was a third man. Someone behind the robberies. We never guessed it was a cop. Well. I didn't, anyway." I thought for a moment and sipped the scalding coffee, compressing my lips afterward to feel the warmth. "Did he talk it over with you? Say anything about the case? He normally runs his theories by me, but I've been a little distracted over the last few days." I realized too late that I'd spoken of X in the present tense.

If she noticed, Connie didn't say anything. "Not really. Our last conversation was about you. And Marlowe. We liked him a lot."

I smiled but it faded quickly. "He's gone back home. Asked me to convey his sincere condolences."

"I hope he comes back soon. I don't think I've ever seen you that happy."

"Really? I thought I was pretty irritated with him when we were here for dinner." I fidgeted. The dinner was the night of X's death. Or rather the events that led to it. Memories of the last meal I'd had with both Marlowe and X flooded me with a dark empty space.

It seemed so far away and yet it was only days ago.

She laughed then and stubbed out the cigarette, tossing the butt in a small Café Bustelo coffee can in the corner. Coming back to the table she sat down and placed her hand over mine for a moment. "You were, but there was a definite spark underneath it."

The kids came to the glass door and I opened it to greet them. All talk of the two absent men in our lives was put aside for conversations about video games and frogs for show-and-tell. After playing a game of *Finding Nemo* with Julio, I said my goodbyes to the family, telling Connie I would see her at the funeral. Before I left, Connie hugged me again and whispered. "He loved working with you, Tam. But if it had been you instead of him? He'd have gone on. I know you will. The world needs you."

I nodded numbly and walked to my car. Opening the

door, I got in and started the engine. I sat there for a long time—on the street in front of X's house. Thinking of all the times I'd been there, right at that spot, picking him up for work. Or him picking me up, armed with coffee and a smile.

Somewhere in all that haze of memory, my brain finally clicked. Connie listened to their outgoing message to hear the sound of his voice. Putting aside the emotional sweetness of that gesture, my cop brain slotted the pieces together. Perhaps X had solved the puzzle. And if he had, there could be more info on his phone. The phone I'd given to IA during my interview. I tapped the steering wheel with my fingers, glancing at my Latin bumper sticker—X's last words to me. He'd known how close I was with my father. How he'd filled up a lot of that void himself. The thought came like a whisper of wind through my car window. The windows were closed but I felt the chill anyway. The memory card from X's phone was still at home, sitting in the dish where I kept my keys.

$$\phi$$

The next morning, I dressed in my blues, as every other cop would. I hadn't worn the uniform since my father's funeral a couple of years ago.

It was a full-honors-law-enforcement funeral, complete with gun salute and pipes and drums. I got out of my car as X's kids saw me and ran into my arms.

The day before, they'd been playing video games while their mother and I talked. Today I could see tracks of tears that had been hastily brushed away. Tears came to my eyes at seeing them, and I blinked. No kid should have to lose their dad this way, at their ages. I had lost my mother when I was a kid, so I knew what it felt like.

We walked into the church and found their mother stoic and tired looking. Their grandmother also had tear tracks and was clutching a squirming baby Valentina. Connie hugged me. "Hey," she said. I smelled the slight aroma of cigarette smoke.

"Careful," I whispered. "Those will become a habit faster than you think."

She nodded at me with a flicker of a smile but said nothing as her sister came into view. I moved away from them to find a seat. During the service, I watched the lines of uniformed cops, searching among the somber faces for a guilty look. The exercise kept me from thinking too much about all I'd lost.

Ziggy found me, and I made room on the bench for her. She'd managed to dress down and looked almost normal—a dark dress and knee-high boots. She even made some remarks about the somber eulogy under her breath that kept me sane. After the service, we walked to the burial site on the far side of the cemetery.

Hernandez was a popular guy and there was a crowd of cops and church-goers along the main drive. Some even drove to the site, but most walked. After the third cop approached me with condolences, I couldn't take anymore, and I pulled Ziggy off the main path. We climbed a small hill and walked among the headstones.

"What's up?" she asked. "You never said much after the IA interview."

"I'm still trying to connect Balfour with the home robbery case. It fits in there somehow but—did Eric and Canfield find anything when they searched Munson's house?" I kept my voice low, but the sound came out harsh and angry.

"Nothing incriminating. Just personal effects, a couple of watches, a high school ring, some old photos. There was one of you there. I didn't know you graduated from the academy together."

"Yeah, me and a hundred other people, but I'm sure IA thinks it somehow incriminates me. Nothing on his computer or phone?"

Ziggy shook her head.

"Someone planted emails on X's computer at work. So there's someone else involved. I've got to prove it. You know how IA is, once they've got someone in their sights, they quit looking for alternatives."

"But you don't," Ziggy said. She stopped, letting a group of mourners walk past us on the path below. "What are you thinking?"

"We know that Munson was on Balfour's payroll, but somehow the home robbery case is part of this. I think Munson was the brains behind that, but why? It wasn't for Balfour. He's into a lot of things, but art theft is not one of them. Too much bother."

"Okay, so..."

"So, why if Munson was on the take, would he jeopardize that with the robbery thing? And how does Cynthia Wu's murder come into this? X had doubts about Balfour being the killer. I mean he's capable, sure, but...And then we thought it was Cruz, but Cruz fingered Balfour for it. X was about to break the whole thing wide open, I'm sure. And Munson thought he got too close."

"And you have a theory."

"X had a theory. I gave IA his phone, but it was

damaged in the alley. I completely forgot that I'd taken his memory card. That's how I found Cruz at the warehouse. IA hasn't even checked it yet or they'd be asking about it."

"Something on it?" Ziggy asked.

"A few notes. Actually, three. Spinelli, NRG Inc., and Furness. Does any of that mean anything to you?"

Ziggy didn't say anything, but we slowed our walk. The burial site was ahead of us, down the hill, and people were starting to gather. Uniforms and black suits dotted the landscape. X's family had settled under the canopy set up. We reached the bottom of the hill, and Ziggy stopped me.

"The name Furness sounds familiar, but I can't place it. Maybe the robberies were a side job and nothing to do with Balfour."

"Balfour doesn't like complications. So, if he found out Munson had a side gig, he wouldn't have been happy." I turned to Ziggy, my breath caught in my throat. "Furness Falcons. Shit. I was so wrong. The imprint on Cynthia Wu's jaw, was made from a ring, right? Like a partial imprint of a bird?"

Ziggy's eyes grew wide. "Yes. We thought it was an owl. Temple University's mascot. Balfour had gone to temple. But it could be a falcon. Hang on." She pulled out her phone. After a second, she looked up. Gianni Balfour graduated from Horace Furness High School in 2004."

"Munson went there too. I remember reading it. That's the connection to Balfour. They were old high school buds, I bet. And then Cynthia Wu found out about Munson's little side project. Cruz thought it was

Balfour who had her killed. Balfour probably thought it was Cruz—"

"When it was Munson all along," Ziggy said. "After this, I'm going back to the lab. And get Munson's effects from evidence. Be careful Tam. If this got the Wu girl killed, it could happen to you."

"Munson is dead."

"But he was working with someone. Someone else. X had more notes than just Furness."

"Spinelli," I said.

"Whoever it is, you need to be careful. X is dead because he got too close."

We joined the mourners in the back of the crowd. I could barely hear the priest as he prayed over the body of my friend. I was too busy thinking. The blood pumping in my ears. Pieces of the puzzle were falling into place with a snap. Munson's OCU task force headed up the murder investigation and despite all the stakeouts and investigations, we couldn't get anything definitive on Balfour. Munson couldn't implicate Balfour because he was on his payroll, and he had to divert any suspicion away from himself. Cruz had been the perfect patsy.

The beginning wheeze of bagpipes sounded as they amped up to a rendition of "Amazing Grace." I jumped at the gun salute. Finally, it was over.

Parker spotted me and gave a brief smile. I nodded back, working to keep my face neutral. I really didn't want to engage in small talk with anyone. Beside me, Ziggy murmured. "You want me to stay?"

I shook my head and with a nod at Parker, she left.

"Paradiso, I'm so sorry. X was a great guy." Parker reached out for a brief hug. He made soothing noises in my ear and I pulled out of his grasp. Turning my head, I took deep breaths to avoid the smell of his cheap cologne. I remembered his omnipresence at my desk, running a finger along the edges of it while he blathered on about how great my last arrest had been, or latest in office gossip. The frantic look on his face when he saw the bodies.

"Yeah," I said, "a great partner. A really smart cop too." I indicated we should walk, and we did, heading toward the parked cars. Up ahead I saw Connie helping the little ones into the car. The line of cars parked at the cemetery extended to the front gates. My car was some distance away and while a part of me wanted to walk the distance alone, I also needed insight into who could be Munson's accomplice. Parker was the office gossip, so if there was something to know, he would know it.

"Could you wait? I need to tell Connie something and then—" I indicated the row of cars. He said sure and stood at the edge of the road while I crossed to poke my head into the backseat of the Hernandez's Suburban. The boys were somber as they settled into their car seats. I reached into the pocket of my uniform and pulled out two tiny figurines. One was a meerkat about two inches high carved from gray-speckled marble. The other was a black onyx whale. Marlowe had found a vendor in the Italian market who sculpted the totems from stone, and he'd admired the artist's work. I handed the meerkat to Gus, the oldest.

"Here, this is a meerkat, who while small is very brave and watchful." I handed the other totem to Julio. "The whale is the king of the sea, strong and yet gentle. They will give you strength." I glanced back to see Connie's mom approaching the car. Nice lady, but very into her religion. She would not approve of protective totems. "Don't tell your *abuela*," I whispered and winked at the boys. Their hands closed around the figurines as I nodded to Connie's mom and gave Connie a quick hug.

Danny Parker and I continued our trek down the road as cars started to peel out of their parking spaces.

"I didn't know you knew his family so well," he said.

"I knew Connie before I met X. She's a realtor and helped me find my apartment. I still think I got into homicide because of Connie talking me up to her husband."

"You got in because you caught the Stickney Strangler. Big case, and you saw what no one else could see."

I stopped and looked at him. His patent leather hat brim glinted in the sun. His eyes were shaded so I couldn't really see them. I tried to remember their color and couldn't. Not that it mattered. I wanted to see his eyes only to see if he was lying. "What do you mean?"

"I mean that everyone thought it was a nutcase from downtown. You figured out the Stickney connection."

Back when I worked vice, I broke a case that basically got me into homicide. I had figured it out, but not without a lot of ups and downs and the eventual death of a fellow officer.

"Not in time to save Johnson," I said.

"Johnson was reckless," he answered. We started walking again.

"Are you reckless, Danny?"

"Me? No. I think I'm very careful." He laughed. The hairs went up on the back of my neck.

"I'm careful too," I said this quietly, letting the words drop. They hung in the air around us, floating in the leaves, settling in the underbrush on either side of the road. A car passed and I waved too cheerfully at the occupants. They waved back, surprised looks on their faces. I didn't know them.

The cemetery was emptying out now, with only a few cars left. "He had a theory you know," I told Parker. "X figured that every criminal he put away would be one less thing his kids would have to deal with as they grew up. It was a whole economic thing. He figured the criminal element cost taxpayers something like thirty-five percent of the gross national product. Less crime, more tax money for schools and roads, and I don't know, art and shit."

"My taxes are going for art?"

"X explained it better." I shrugged. "He knew that having a cop for a dad was tough. That there's always a risk of Dad not coming home at night, or ever." I took a breath, noticing as it shuddered through me. Now was not the time to get all weepy. "But he thought it was worth it. X became a cop to protect his family. That's really all he cared about."

I stopped under the shade of poplar trees and looked into Parker's eyes. I could see them now, clearly, their faded denim color strangely unnerving. In that second, I changed my mind about confiding in him. "Thanks for walking me to my car, Parker. I'll see you at work." I said as brightly as I could manage. His eyes flickered, but he smiled, stepping away to head to his car.

27

I went home and changed out of my uniform. Rick Davenport called, and I didn't answer. He'd been at the funeral, but we hadn't talked. I didn't have the energy to deal with any relationship stuff, and I knew that I would end whatever it was that we had. Sure, Marlowe was gone, but I could no longer pick up where I'd left off. Something had changed and the thought of being with Rick or anyone else left me empty.

The thing about Rick the Dick was that he was persistent, and the third time he called I picked up.

"Paradiso."

"Hey, are you okay?" his baritone was pleasant to the ear, but the words flat, without an interesting lilt or cadence. I wanted to hear an English accent so bad I could taste it.

"As good as can be." I put my feet on the coffee table in front of me, moving the research books and notepads aside. I glanced at the legal pad with all my notes on it, Munson's short bio, his high school. I'd also written the other names from X's phone. Spinelli, and NRG, Inc.

Spinelli was a beat cop in our district. I knew of him but had only spoken to him in passing. The name of the company, NRG, Inc. was a conglomerate out of Chicago. According to wiki, they did everything from investments to insurance.

"Hey Rick," I interrupted his speech about X and the funeral. "Have you ever heard of NRG, Inc?"

He thought for a moment. "No, why?"

"I'm still trying to connect Munson to the manslaughter case. X left some notes on his phone—Spinelli and NRG. So, I wondered if you remembered a connection."

"Not the company, no. But Spinelli. Isn't he from Unit 29? It was one of the units with you and X when you arrested the guys on the Tanner home invasion."

I hadn't thought about the units backing us up. Just that they were there in case something happened. Nothing had.

"Thanks. I'll talk to you later." I hung up before he could say anything else. I dialed the district switchboard and asked her to put me through to Spinelli. I had no idea what I was going to say, but I'd figure out something. As I was waiting to be put through to Spinelli's phone, I tried to remember everything that happened at the arrest. The guy I'd arrested, Rufus Jones, had been talkative, very talkative. The kid would have sung like Beyoncé to save his own skin, but by the time we interviewed him, he'd lawyered up and said nothing. The lawyer was some high-powered shark from downtown. I'd thought at the time that Balfour had hired him. No way could a low-life creep like Jones have afforded him.

Spinelli's voice crackled over the line. "Hey Paradiso, you working? I thought you'd be at the funeral."

"I was. Hey, do you remember when we arrested the home invasion guys? The manslaughter case at the Tanner house?"

"Sure, I remember. Who could forget a bust like that? The perp thought you were part of the S&M scene, Paradiso. He kept saying he was resisting arrest." His chuckle came across the phone. I was happy that dispatch had thought to patch my call to his cell phone and not the radio.

We'd found both guys in a basement. All decked out to look like some sort of dungeon. X had cuffed his guy and hauled him out to the car. Jones was semi-naked and handcuffed to a bed. As I read him his rights, I'd conveniently forgotten all conversation from him. Unless he was confessing, I'd had no interest. "Do you remember who processed him in? Who was around?" I asked.

"We didn't come back to the station with you guys, we got another call. I thought Hernandez processed him into central booking. Sorry to hear about X, by the way. He was a good man."

"Yeah, he was. Thanks Spinelli." I started to hang up the phone when he stopped me.

"Hey, wait. Ricky here reminded me."

His partner came on the line. "We didn't get back to the station till later. I guess it was a slow day as some of the guys were still talking about it in the locker room."

He hesitated and I waited, knowing he was trying to discern what to leave out.

"Just say it, Ricky. I've been around long enough to

not take it personally," I said.

"Well mostly it was stupid remarks about the guy getting a hard-on for the arresting officer, but someone asked if the guy gave up his partners in crime. I think it was Parker who asked. Not sure. Seemed like an odd question because I didn't think he was working the case."

"He wasn't. Okay, thanks guys. Be careful out there." I put my phone away and continued my thoughts. I wrote down more names. There's always lots of people around in central booking. The photo guys, fingerprinters, jailers, etc. Any of them could have had ample time to threaten Jones to keep him from talking.

But the question is, who was around later? And savvy enough to plant emails on someone's computer? The answer was me, of course. X and I both made the arrests, so it was logical that IA would be suspicious of both of us. But there were others. Officer Parker's name kept coming up. I tapped my fingernail on the notepad. Parker had been asking tons of questions while on the stakeout with me, and he came on the scene shortly after X was shot. He'd also been hanging around our section of the office. X and I both thought it was because he had a crush. I couldn't figure a motive, but he had means and opportunity.

It took me a couple of sleepless nights of mulling things over before I called Internal Affairs. I had no proof, only a theory and the lovely tag-team of Crooked Tie and Glasses may not want to hear conjecture. I shouldn't have worried as I only got one of their nasally voices directing me to leave a message. Not wanting to lay out my entire theory on a voicemail, I simply asked for a call back.

Knowing that once they had a suspect in their sights, they weren't likely to deviate without real evidence, I was on my own to prove that Parker had been working with Munson. I called the district office. The desk sergeant said Parker was on duty and out on a call, but he put me through to his voicemail. I'd already planned what I was going to say.

"Hey Parker, sorry I left so abruptly after the funeral. It was a tough time you know? I've had a couple days to think and I need to run something by you. You wanna meet me at the office? Whenever is good. I'm off for the next few days. Just text me." I left him my number.

I really had no desire to meet Parker anywhere, but I couldn't figure out how else to prove my theory. A taped confession or some sort of verbal confirmation was all I could think of. I got a text back saying to meet him the next morning.

I had it all planned. Take Parker to the big breakroom off the lobby. I'd have my phone recording in my lap, and I'd confront him, or maybe just let him talk. Parker loved to talk and if I let him talk long enough, he'd confess or deny or do something stupid and I'd have him.

Driving down the ramp toward the district parking area, I stopped at the underground intersection. Most uniforms parked on the north side close to the motor pool. I glanced in that direction, scouting for Parker's car. He drove a red sedan, nothing spectacular, but I didn't see it. The admin and supervisors' area were more central near the elevators, and I drove past them, the low ceiling and gray painted supports giving the area a claustrophobic feel.

I drove slowly toward my usual space. Last one on

the end of the second row. Today, there were a lot of empty spaces along the wall, most of them designated for detectives. I pulled in to my space close to the wall. I turned off the engine and looked to my right. The space next to me was empty, had been since X was killed. I took a deep breath and blinked several times. No time for nostalgia, I had work to do.

I'd been back and forth a few times since my interview with IA days ago, but I hadn't been cleared for duty yet. I wanted to work—I don't do well with idleness—it makes me think too much. Every time an officer fires a weapon there's a report. When that shooting results in a death, there're more reports. When it's a cop who is killed, everyone gets involved. Captains, supervisors, shrinks, liaisons to the mayor's office. I felt like I had talked to all of them at least twice.

Out of the corner of my eye, I clocked a movement. Parker sauntered around a concrete pillar to come around my car, the buzzing florescent lights throwing his face into shadows. I'd hoped to see him inside, with other cops around, but I was going to do this no matter what. I took a deep breath and turned to him, putting on a smile.

"Hey," I said, getting out of my car. Instead of walking toward him, I stood inside the open car door. About ten feet from me, he didn't move, and I noticed that the security camera's range didn't cover where he stood.

"Hey. I thought we should meet out here so we wouldn't be overheard. Just in case you've found the culprit." He grinned.

The grin had an inkling of falsehood in it. All of a

sudden, every past encounter with Parker was thrown into question. What was his motive? Why was he being so...cagey?

"The culprit? Oh, no." I lied, my self-preservation instinct kicking in. I wanted to hit him in the face. But instead, I forced my lips into a curve, not showing my teeth. But I didn't move toward him either. "Not really. I have a theory, since our talk at the funeral. I thought I'd run it by you."

"Okay, what?" He took a step toward me.

I indicated the elevators. "You wanna get some lousy coffee or something?" I asked, acutely aware of the emptiness of the garage.

"Sorry, I can't. I have somewhere to be. But I want to hear your big theory." Another step.

I took a breath, moving my arms slightly away from my sides, airing out my pits. I should have carried my gun. I did have a knife on me. Always. Safely tucked away in a hidden pocket on the inside of my boot was a three-inch switchblade. Where it was doing absolutely nothing to make me feel more secure.

Parker had made no move or indication to do me harm, but I was on alert anyway. My knife was useless at the moment and my phone was out of reach on the front seat.

"Well, not so much a theory as an observation. And that is that you are really smart. A clever guy—no, really." I assured him as he hedged. "It's a shame Munson didn't figure that out."

His grin faded, but slowly so I shouldn't have noticed. There was no overt reaction to Munson's name. But my senses were all firing now, and I could almost feel the air around us thicken. He stepped forward again and then stopped, ever so briefly, a tiny hitch in his step, a faltering of movement in his hands.

"What do you mean?" He cocked his head with a quick shake—like a curious raven. Watching me watch him. He turned his head in a casual look around before his gaze focused back on me. There was no missing it. This was high stakes poker, and he was bluffing.

I shrugged in the most careless manner possible. "Not that it means anything, because you know, he had us all fooled. Head of the investigation and yet a mole for Balfour's operation. He was a mastermind. And he totally disregarded your abilities." I paused. "I mean, didn't he? Just pretty much ignored you as he did his thing, bringing me and X into the investigation. I'm sure he thought all his bases were covered, but he didn't consider you."

He regarded me steadily, his young face and bashful smile no longer appeared awkward and hesitant. I'd misread the intelligent and devious mind behind his eyes, and I mentally gave myself a kick.

It was time to set the hook. "And you know how IA is. They have X's phone so any notes or phone calls would be there. Except it was damaged in the alley. When we were getting shot at." My voice dripped with barely concealed anger.

"Oh, yeah?" Parker squeaked and then cleared his throat. "What about it?"

"About what? Getting shot at? It's not fun, Parker. People die. Good people."

"No, I mean. Well, yes, of course. And I'm sorry about Hernandez, I really am. But I mean the phone."

I tried my best to calm down. My pulse raced as I focused on controlling my breathing. All my senses tingled like I was hunting a hostile. Only without that physical outlet. This was a battle of intellects, and I needed a clear head.

"Oh, well, I took the memory card out and forgot about it. Maybe there's something on it, you know? Something X figured out. Not that IA will investigate, but I should turn it into them anyway."

"Absolutely," he agreed, his voice hesitant as though calculating numbers. "You have it with you? I'd be happy to turn it in for you."

I looked at him. "I thought you had something to do?" He blinked. So, I rushed on, not wanting to spook him. "But would you? You know I'm really not looking forward to talking to them again." I turned toward my open car door, rummaging in my bag for my phone. "I think I have it here."

Out of his view, I pressed the video record on my phone and left it on the seat. I turned back to Parker, my hand closed into a fist, but held out palm up, as though I held a surprise for him.

He had a surprise for me. I looked down the barrel of his ridiculously massive gun.

"I'll take that, Paradiso." He held out his other hand, his mouth curved into a sneer. It was totally incongruous with everything I thought I knew about him. I felt like I saw the real Danny Parker for the first time.

"You're going to shoot me? Here?" The garage looked empty, but it was a busy place, police units, and people coming and going at all hours. Throughout our conversation, I'd been listening for signs of witnesses. A car engine starting, maybe a door slam, or the elevator doors opening, voices, anything. I knew from the absence of these noises that we were alone at that moment, but he might not. He looked around. Seeing my chance, I stepped in and jabbed my fist into his throat, turning sideways as I pushed his gun hand to the side.

The gun thundered under my wrist as I pushed the barrel away from me. A shot rang out, the sound reverberating throughout the garage. There was the spit of flying cement as the bullet shattered into a concrete post on the other side of my car. The sound of gunfire, the smell of exhaust fumes, and clammy cement, together with the sudden jolt of adrenaline all served to put me right back in the alley where X had died. I flinched, Parker's voice telling me to give up as he hunched over me, trying to gain control of his gun.

I curled into a ball over his gun hand, my own hands clutching at the massive weapon. All I could do was hang on. The sound of my own breath pounded in my ears. The stink of his sweat and discount aftershave blasted my nostrils, and I grit my teeth to keep from gagging. I remembered X's blood all over my hands, the gurgled sounds of his every breath. I heard Munson's gravelly taunts from across the lot as if they were next to me. My heart broke again as I remembered the familiar grin and crinkles around X's eyes as he'd tried to reassure me. The assaulting smell of garbage and nitro—the aftermath of gunfire. I crammed my eyes shut against the memories as everything fell into slow motion.

My hands went numb, my whole body a lead weight as gravity threatened to overtake me. A roar of white noise washing over me, somewhere in the back of my terror-filled brain, I knew that Parker would turn the gun and shoot. I should have died in the alley anyway. This was only delaying the inevitable.

Parker threw himself against me, his body slamming me into the car. The pain of my injured arm seared through me, shocking me out of my paralysis. My eyes opened to see his ugly reflection in the windows. I forced my unfeeling legs into action, trying to keep upright.

X's voice came through in a haze. "Don't let the bastards get you down." It was a memory of course, but so clear I almost heard it. The words pissed me off, and I used that anger for one last-ditch effort to wrench the gun from Parker. I threw my head back, feeling it crash into his nose. He body slammed me again, kicking my feet apart to push me to the ground.

"Bastard," I hissed at him, throwing myself onto the ground beside my car, pulling him with me. I used my body as leverage, his arm caught between me and the cold cement of the garage. My nails dug into his wrist to break his hold.

"Parker, it's over." I croaked out the words. He grunted and punched at my ribs. I curled into a ball and tried to elbow him, but we were too close to gain any leverage. The only weapon I had at hand was the ring I'd used on the demonized old lady in the IHOP lot. I let go of his gun and punched the underside of his forearm, dragging the piercing points down his skin. He was human, not demon but the prongs laced with silver nitrate would sting like alcohol on a wound.

He hissed at the pain, pulling away enough that I got a better grip on his gun hand. I wrenched his little finger out and down, hearing the snap. Parker screamed, and he landed a blow to my temple, knocking me into the concrete. Blackness threatened the edges of my vision, and my ears rang as I lay still—the coldness of the concrete barely noticeable.

"Hey!" A voice and footsteps sounded from behind us. Parker lifted his weight from me for a scant second. I took a deep breath and twisted, elbowing him in the solar plexus as the back of my fist caught him in the nose.

"Let me see your hands," the voice commanded. Parker was suddenly gone from me and his gun fell to the ground. I made no move to grab it. Just got to my wobbly knees and put my hands in the air. They were shaking from pain or adrenaline, maybe both.

"I'm detective Paradiso, homicide. My shield is in the car." My vision blurred as I looked over my shoulder to see a giant of a man, African-American, six-four if he was an inch, with dreadlocks down to his considerable shoulders. The man's stance was professional, and he kicked Parker's gun under my car as he flipped out a shield and ID. I sagged in relief. "Could you put your gun away?" I asked. "I'm really tired of being shot at."

"You want to tell me what's going on here?" his voice rumbled in the hollow space.

Parker groaned, one mangled hand to his bleeding nose, his injured arm tucked in close to him. "You broke my damned finger, bitch. And what the hell did you do to my arm?"

"Can I get up now?" I asked the man with the gun. He nodded and I moved to all fours to get my shaky legs under me. My head reeled from being knocked into the concrete and I closed my hand over my thrice-injured arm. At this rate, it would look like Frankenstein's monster before it healed.

"It's done, Danny," I said. "The memory stick has everything on it. I've got Spinelli's testimony that you had access to the home invasion perps. The insurance company. Everything."

"I still want to know what the hell is going on here." The guy still held the gun on us and looked like he could kick our asses if we gave him any grief.

"You wanna tell me who the hell you are?" I asked.

"Detective Damien Cobb." His voice was deadly casual.

"Detective, this woman—" Parker started.

"Shut up, Parker. For once in your life." I spat the words toward the smaller man. I turned to the detective, whose well-trimmed goatee covered a hastily suppressed smile at my sentiment. By the looks of him, he had to be an undercover cop. "I'm arresting this man for robbery and conspiracy to commit murder. He's a key player in an organized crime mob in town," I said quickly. Cobb didn't move, but he didn't look like he believed me either. "My badge is in my bag." I indicated the car.

"Tam? What's going on?" Ziggy came running up to us from the direction of the elevator. She looked at the over-large man menacing a gun in our direction and her expression grew dark. "Detective? This is my co-worker, Tam Paradiso. Do you mind not shooting her?"

"You know this guy?" I asked her.

"Just introduced. He's transferred from..."

"Pittsburgh," Cobb answered. He glanced at us as though deciding whether to holster his gun or pull the trigger. In the end, he believed Ziggy. "I'm not sure what I walked in on, but I heard a gunshot." Finally, he put his gun back into the shoulder holster under his jacket.

"Yes," I said, casting a vicious look at Parker who had crossed his arms in front of him, holding his injured hand. "Parker tried to shoot me."

Over the last few days, I'd gone head-to-head with ghouls, ancient vampires, crime bosses, crooked cops, and possessed grandmothers. I still had no real proof of his involvement, but I saw it in Parker's eyes—the desperation. He leaned to the side as though exhausted. I remembered to move the lever on my ring to retract the sharp points of the prongs. I really should buy Volpi a six-pack for the handy piece of jewelry. I took a breath.

"It's over," I spoke to Parker again. "Help me understand why you would go in on this with Munson. What was in it for you?"

He laughed through his pain, a short bitter sound. "You think the home robbery thing was his idea? You're not the only one to live with a parent's fall from grace, Tam."

I realized that for all our conversations, I hadn't bothered to learn anything about Parker. He was a co-worker to me, and not one I particularly liked. My brain stopped and started. Running through all our conversations. My dad, his reputation on the force. How that affected me. On the stakeout, Parker had said something about his parents. They hadn't wanted him to be a cop. His mom wanted something safe for him like the insurance business. I had been so preoccupied with Marlowe and hunting the strigoi that I hadn't given it a second thought.

"Insurance," I said, mostly to stall as my brain worked. God, I was so dense sometimes. "Your mom worked for NRG, Inc.—the company that insured the homes." This was a guess on my part, but it was the only thing that made sense.

By this time, a small crowd of bystanders and cops had gathered. Parker said nothing as Charlie Horn-Rims from Internal Affairs approached us with two uniforms in tow. They cuffed Parker on instructions from Charlie.

"Paradiso, you need a doctor or something?" Charlie asked.

"I'll help her," Ziggy said and came to put an arm around my waist. We walked into the station behind Charlie and the others.

After Ziggy cleaned and re-bandaged my arm and flashed her small light into my eyes to check my pupils, we went back up to my cubicle and waited. Charlie's partner Mike arrived and stopped at my desk.

"You look like shit, Paradiso," he said.

"It's been a helluva week, no thanks to you," I answered.

His lips compressed slightly, and he glanced at his scuffed brown shoes. That was as close as an apology as I was going to get.

"You should go home. We're going to be awhile interviewing Parker. He's singing like his life depends on it."

"Good." I handed him my phone and X's memory card. "There's a recording that may help. Notes on the memory card are from X's phone."

Mike took them and pulling out a plastic bag from his pocket, he dropped them into it. "His mom was fired from the insurance company after twenty years. Some sort of accounting infraction. A single lousy mistake. His idea was to make the company pay so he gave Munson the addresses and the info on the home robberies."

"And Munson had the means of fencing the goods." I finally made the connections. "But Cynthia Wu found out and threatened to tell Balfour, and that got her killed."

Ziggy spoke up. "I found trace evidence on Munson's ring. Wu's DNA I'm sure. I've sent it to the lab and a report to the investigating team."

"That should prove Munson killed Wu. X had his doubts about Balfour and the home robbery case, so he started poking around," I said.

Mike shrugged. "Which is motive for the set-up at the nightclub. But we were still looking for his partner. Parker says he wanted to implicate you, not Hernandez. Apparently, you insulted him, Paradiso. But you were too careful, always locked your computer, so he had to go another way." He shuffled his feet again and studied them before speaking again. "Go home, or the hospital, or wherever. We'll call you in when we need you." He walked away.

Still concerned about my head, Ziggy insisted on walking me out. We found Cobb waiting for the elevator.

"Thanks," I said to him. "Your timing is impeccable."

"Don't thank me, I almost shot you. Parker was in uniform. I had no idea who you were and at first glance, it looked like you were trying to kill him."

"I might have. But thanks for not shooting me. This has been an ongoing investigation. My partner was killed by a dirty cop a few days ago. This asshole tried to implicate him as corrupt too."

"Technically, I'm not even supposed to be here yet. I was in HR ironing out my transfer. I'd got off the elevator when I heard the shot."

"You worked vice?" I asked. "You kind of have the look."

He said nothing. His mouth twitched like he wanted to smile but thought better of it. He might even be attractive if he smiled, but that would take away from the whole badass drug-lord image he had going on.

"Well, it's another average day at the office. Cop shoot-out in the parking garage." I gave Cobb a smile. "Welcome to District 21." He grunted as he entered the elevator. Ziggy and I hung back as the doors closed.

"I told you to be careful," she admonished.

"I didn't intend to meet Parker alone. We were supposed to be inside where all the uniforms are. But he was waiting for me."

"You're lucky Cobb came along when he did." She indicated the elevator behind us. "He's interesting."

"I wonder if he'll take Munson's place in OCU. Thanks, by the way, for coming out and vouching for me."

"It's what friends are for, right?"

28

There's something about coming home that always made me feel better. I've always been a solitary soul, a first-class introvert who is happiest alone in my somewhat shabby environment. The apartment had been a haven for me from the time I'd moved out of the ex's classier digs up town. I was particular about who was invited in. X had been at the top of the list, then Ziggy, then Rick and finally Marlowe. Not even Volpi, whom I pretty much trusted with my life, had ever been to my place.

I slid the key into the lock and opened the door. I hesitated for a second in the doorway, making sure the empty sound of the place was exactly that.

The interview with IA had gone considerably better than it had the first time. Parker confessed that he had hacked X's computer and planted the emails to implicate him. His confession to me now had two credible witnesses, the new guy and Ziggy. The connection of the insurance company to Parker and Parker to Munson was clear. Parker had corroborated my theory about Munson killing Cynthia Wu, though he swore he only learned of it after the fact.

I put my keys on the counter, went through my mail, and was going to change my clothes when there was a knock at my door.

I frowned as I let Rick Davenport in. I'd hoped to avoid him a bit longer, my exhaustion overwhelming me with apathy for anything remotely emotional.

"I heard you were attacked in the parking garage." He said it like an accusation. "Why didn't you call me? Last time we talked, you cut me off, and then I don't hear from you."

"Pour us a drink, would you?" I asked, nodding toward the cabinet. I headed to my bedroom and stripped off the sweaty shirt and blazer, pulling on yoga pants and searching for a clean shirt. I found a button-down that Marlowe had worn for a short time. He'd taken it off saying he'd preferred the shirt without fasteners. I pulled it on and buttoned three buttons before walking back into the living room.

Rick was where I'd left him. A suit bearing slight wrinkles from the day's wearing and a loose tie around his neck. He looked tired as he handed me a tumbler of Dewar's. It took a few moments before he cleared his throat enough for me to notice. I poured another glass full on my way to the living room.

The book of Shakespeare's plays that housed Marlowe's letter lay open on my floor. The letter was safely tucked away in my nightstand. I stepped over the book and moved past the couch to sit in my usual space—the rocker, with a drink in hand, and one foot on a stool. Rick poured his angular frame onto my couch and sighed. I sipped the scotch. "It's been a helluva day."

He looked around as if noticing I was alone for the first time. "I haven't been here since...did your cousin go home?"

I didn't answer. Rick had been here more than a few times, and most of those times we'd ended up in my bedroom. Now, I watched his dead-center sprawl over my couch. He looked odd being there, as though he didn't belong. The couch had held Marlowe not that long ago, on an evening when I'd listened to his far-fetched tale. We'd slept on that couch, slotted together like spoons.

"You okay?" he asked.

"Yeah, I'll live." I rolled the glass back and forth in my hand. I studied my ankle, much like Marlowe had. Only Rick's incessant throat clearing brought my attention back around. I thought maybe he had allergies.

"How did you know it was Parker?" he asked.

"I didn't. I had a theory. X had left some notes on his phone. Spinelli, the insurance company, and Furness—the name of the high school that Balfour and Munson attended. I remembered Parker hanging around X and me during the home invasion case."

"Mostly you," Rick said

"I suppose. X thought he had a crush on me. I had no idea he was behind the home robberies. I was so wrong about everything." The rocker creaked as I readjusted my position. My whole body ached. I finished the scotch in my glass.

"You've been through a lot, Tam. Maybe you should lay off a bit." He indicated my glass. My frown deepened, and I realized I hadn't stopped frowning since his intrusion.

"Maybe you should go."

He sat up, preparing to look offended, but at my steady look, he sighed again, cleared his damn throat again and got up.

"Yeah, maybe you're right. It's been a long day. Call me later, okay?"

He was halfway to the door when I spoke. "Rick, wait."

I walked to the door and held it open for him. "Thanks for coming by, and being concerned and all that, but... really, that's not who we are. And I think we've run our course, don't you?"

He reacted like a true lawyer, his puzzlement quickly concealed under a smile and a shrug of shoulders. It wasn't like we'd had something. He'd have someone else to celebrate his courtroom victories with by next week.

"It was that guy, right? Marlowe? Not a cousin at all."

"Not a cousin," I confirmed.

He nodded and gave a genuine smile this time. "Well, good luck, then." He closed the door behind him.

"I'll need it," I said to the empty apartment, sipping the rest of my scotch and remembering the sound of Marlowe's voice.

It had been a month since X's death and Marlowe's disappearance. Finally, I was released to full duty and could go back to investigating crime scenes. Last week, Parker was arraigned and transferred upstate to await trial. I would testify, but it wouldn't be on the docket for months.

I kept my Tuesday-night visits with the Hernandez family. Connie's parents had gone back home, and she had gone back to work. She put on a brave face, but I could see the struggle behind it. I realized even if Parker got life in prison, which he wouldn't, it wouldn't help things. Xavier Hernandez would still be gone. Connie and I both felt fragile and worn.

At work, I was less prone to start fights and push my weight around than I used to be. The loss of both X and Marlowe had left me a shell of my former self. Even hostile hunting was at an all-time low.

After a day of awkwardness and false starts with the large and surly Damien Cobb as my new partner, I returned to my apartment. I found that acting pleasant and affable far more tiring than going three rounds with a werewolf. But Cobb was gruff, experienced, and competent so I couldn't complain. I didn't mind gruff. You could trust it.

Showering off the remnants of the day, I rummaged for leftover pasta in my fridge. A smile worked its way to my lips as I remembered Marlowe opening and closing the door, trying to discern if the light stayed on or not.

The crescent moon had risen on a city filled with activity and teeming with people, and I turned away from its faded light shining in through the window. Its hopeful arc mocked me with the absence of Marlowe. If he was traveling again and made it back to this timeline, I had no doubt he would head straight for my place. I'd waited for the last three days of the moon's phase, hoping he'd show. There was nothing.

I still ached for him. The past month, I'd slept with his letter under my pillow like a silly girl pining for the football captain. He had that effect on me, taking my stubborn hostile hunter self and turning me into something softer. I hated it, but my admission of feeling for him was too little, too late. He was gone, and I would never see him again.

I sat on my couch and flicked the TV on, searching for a mindless reality show to watch. Adjusting my feet on the coffee table, I finished my pasta and sipped at my Molson.

After every successful and sometimes unsuccessful hunt I needed to process the events over a glass or two—or three—of some alcoholic beverage and figure out what went right and what went wrong. Occasionally, I would share this process with Volpi, but not always. I wanted to know how things could go better in the future. How could I not come so close to death next time? This doesn't mean I achieved all the answers. Most of the time, there was little in the way of answers, but the mental process of breaking it down and going through it in my head seemed to help. In the same way that Marlowe kept a journal of his travels.

I got up and looked through the stuff on the built-in shelves—most of my lore books, three volumes of mommy porn received as a gag gift and never read, my collection of graphic novels, a few photographs. Stuck in between dog-eared copies of Neil Gaiman's books was a slim, cheaply made journal I had dallied with long ago—a gift from some well-meaning relative. I felt that chill again, but it passed as I picked up the book and returned to my nest on the couch.

The journal was old, from several years earlier and only sported a couple of entries. They read like a teen girl's diary—the weather, some major whining about some guy or other, or how hard the academy was. I was hostile hunting by that time, but also paranoid about anyone finding out, so there wasn't a mention of anything supernatural in my entries. Things had seemed so much simpler then.

I realized I'd quit writing because I wasn't writing the important stuff. No one cared about the weather or who said what in some bar or at work. The stuff I cared about, the good stuff, were those hours where I'd confront the evil grin of a hostile and fight the monsters, both human and non-human. Marlowe knew that somehow his story would be significant.

Perhaps someday far in the future, if God forbid, I had kids with this same affliction, they should have a clue about what's happening to them. They should know that they weren't alone in this vocation. Not like I was. Or at least, like I'd thought I was. I'd come to realize that I was only alone as I'd wanted to be. I had Ziggy and Volpi, X and Connie, even Rick. If I pushed it, I might even include my sister and Freya in that mix.

The moon had moved from my sightline and this allowed me to breathe easier. I pushed the thought of waiting for his appearance next month to the back of my mind. I resolved to deal with the present, to stay in the present. It was all I had.

After a few tries, I finally found a pen that worked. I fetched another Molson from the fridge and settled down to write. The first line written was about the weather on Friday. I crossed it out. It wasn't on a Friday where the story started. It wasn't back in high school with a librarian either. It was a Tuesday. I'd had dinner at X and Connie's. I drank more of the beer and tapped my pen on the journal pages. Finally, I put pen to paper.

It was another average day at work until suddenly, it wasn't. The story of my life. Lots of waiting around, doing mundane things like data input and research, grocery shopping and dropping off the dry cleaning, until something happens, and I find myself in a ghoul-infested cemetery, covered in tarry blood and a head recently separated from scaly shoulders comes rolling my way. Compliments of a knight in purple velvet, his sword glinting under a crescent moon.

PREVIEW
Battle for Daylight
Crescent Moon Chronicles
Book 2

Kit left the apothecary's shop with his head down. The pressure and throb of his temples was worsening as he stepped over the foul-smelling gutter and hurried toward home. Across the way, he spotted a theater acquaintance. Normally, he would be pleased to converse with Richard, a good fellow, if a bit self-important, but he wasn't sure how much time he had, and he must prepare. He turned to avoid his friend, to no avail.

"Hail, Kit. Good morrow." The stout man with thinning hair had placed himself directly in front of Marlowe, stopping both of them in the middle of pedestrian traffic—peddlers, urchins, harried housewives, a few merchants hawking their wares.

"Richard, how fares thee?"

"I am well. Will you attend tonight's festivities? There's talk of a game later on." Richard knew of Marlowe's propensity for cards.

"Perhaps. If I can garner a benefactor. I am without much coin," Kit replied and patted his woefully thin coin purse under his jacket. Richard looked thoughtfully dramatic. Actors were always on stage, even in a simple discourse. Most likely, he was angling for a part in

Marlowe's next play. Which, Marlowe thought, if he didn't acquire some coin to pay his rent, he'd have no place to pen such work, nor the time to sell it and secure his lodgings. He received a small stipend from Her Majesty's secret service, but it was hardly enough to eat on. And his natural calling—demon hunting—did not pay at all. "Forgive my haste, friend. I have urgent business at hand." Ignoring Richard's prattling, he rushed on into the dark.

As he approached The Hogsbreath, his landlord, Master Swopes, stood outside the tavern's entrance, more than likely waiting to collect his overdue rent.

Marlowe stopped, did a quarter turn and ducked behind a pushcart of mildewed straw. The man owning the pushcart gave him a wary glance, but recognizing him for a scholar, decided he was not a common thief, but a potential buyer.

"Fresh straw for your bedding, sir? Only a two pence."

Too busy avoiding the gaze of the tavern keeper, Kit brushed by the man and circled down a short alley. He came to a small overhang jutting out from the building and pulled himself up, keeping to the solid wood frame so he wouldn't fall through the straw covering. He made his way along the edge of the building, the noise of the street below him. Using protruding stones for hand and footholds, he clambered up to the second floor. Sprawling flat against the wall, he reached toward the window, left half-open for this purpose. Pushing the frame open further, he flopped himself into his room as quietly as possible. He was a fortnight late on rent but had no time to argue with Swopes for yet another day's extension. The move to London a few months ago had been necessary if he were to meet with any success as a serious play-maker, but income was scarce.

Henslowe had agreed to produce his play, *Tamburlaine the Great,* complete with revisions and the new title at the newly opened theater, The Rose on Bankside. As he watched the production, Marlowe wondered if his character's namesake, Tamberlyn Paradiso, would read his work and know that he'd kept his promise to make her a king—though a tragic one.

Once in his room, the air started to burn in a familiar crackle. The hair on his neck stood out and he rubbed it absently. Peering out the window at the rising sliver of a moon, he held his breath. This time, he would concentrate on location and time. Forcing his mind to affect the blue lightning, to change his course across time and space—for her. He had to get back to her as he promised. It had been six months and two journeys, neither to her time nor city.

Faced with the thought he might never see her again, he had thrown himself into his new play, *Dr. Faustus,* inspired by a German work he'd translated. But now another journey loomed, which meant another chance for reuniting with the young woman who'd captured his heart. He changed from his day clothes to the modern pants he'd hidden away after arriving home. He kept his long-tailed, coarsely-woven shirt—it was serviceable in most timelines. His entire head of hair stood on end with ever increasing tingles. Sparks of light flashed, popping through the air like pebbles on a window pane. The eerie flash of blue splashed across his night vision.

The previous throbbing in his head grew stronger,

bringing him to his knees. The faint crackling grew louder, like thunder of an approaching storm. Lurching to his feet, he forced himself to pull on the leather scabbard that held his sword. The contraption was not comfortable nor conventional, but it secured the weapon along the length of his back, between his shoulder blades where it could be hidden from view. He found his cape and tossed the floor-length garment around him, shrouding himself in the heavy material. Pain seared through him, gritting his teeth and locking his jaw. He hunched over and waited. The surge hit him, and his air escaped his lungs, his vision blurred. He heard a *whoosh,* like a great wind was upon him and he was sucked into the blue vortex.

The actual trip was short in duration, only moments, but it felt longer, his body tingling unpleasantly as he was tossed about like a tailless kite. Gradually, he forced his body into a ball—a high diver's somersault, the cloak offering a modicum of protection from the lightning storm. The gale force wind dropped out from under him and he fell onto the hard pavement, rolling into a concrete wall. He lay for a moment, gathering his strength and wits about him. After making sure all limbs and head were intact, only then did he look about. Spying the colorful graffiti and the decaying smell of garbage and exhaust fumes, he smiled. The wonderful scent of urban development. A car drove past the narrow alley. And then another, and yet another. He rushed out toward the traffic. He'd made it.

The day was warm, and he unbuckled his sword and wrapped it in the cape before stepping out onto the sidewalk. As he made his way to a major intersection, he took in all he could.

There were a few pedestrians on the walkway, and he studied their dress and mannerisms with the utmost care—clues to what era he'd fallen into. He searched for familiar street signs, and finally as he made it to the corner and waited for the crossing light, he remembered the license plates on the cars. The one in front of him had large numbers, a flag, and his heart leaped as he read the word *Pennsylvania* in white letters at the top. He truly had made it back.

Perhaps they could go to the fountain again, to watch the children at play, to hear the street musicians, and eat the marvelous sandwiches the vendors sold. His mind was so caught up in these visions he barely noticed where he was going until he'd arrived. The building was the same, large graying marble columns and porticos that once gleamed elegantly. Until this moment, he hadn't been sure he was in in the correct time, only close to it. The building was old, but the sign read *Philadelphia Police Department District 21.* He was here. His efforts and focus on getting back to Tamberlyn Paradiso had worked. After a quick look at himself to assure he was presentable, he entered. The front desk where visitors checked in was front and center, like always, but there was a line and he could not wait. His time here was precious, and he vowed to waste not a second. Edging toward the stairwell, he caught the door as someone exited and he sprinted up to the third floor. Only a moment now and he would see her.

Yanking open the stairwell door he entered the hallway, almost colliding with two men.

"Many pardons," he said. The man he'd brushed

against nodded absently and passed. Marlowe turned to see the man's companion was Xavier Hernandez. In shock at the sight of him, Marlowe hesitated only a second. "Old friend, 'tis so good to see you."

"Do I know you?" The big man stopped, looking at him quizzically. Down the hall, the fellow who had passed Marlowe called back toward them.

"Hernandez, you coming?"

Marlowe stepped back, mumbling an apology and X walked away from him.

Something was wrong. He knew from experience the timeline had changed, but he was still buoyant. If Xavier was here, then so his Tamberlyn. He strode through the frosted glass doors where he'd known her desk to be. He wondered idly if Miss Jane Zigfield were downstairs working away in her white lab coat. He wondered if Tam had waited for him, or if she'd found another in his absence.

"Can I help you?" A young woman at a counter addressed him. He searched beyond her for a glimpse of Tam's dark hair, her familiar crooked smile, and the flashing eyes he often saw in his dreams.

"I am here for Tamberlyn Paradiso," he said, giving the girl a smile he could not contain.

She frowned. His heart stopped for a beat. What had happened since he'd left? The girl consulted her computer. "You have the wrong place. She's on the second floor."

He had no time for wonderment or disappointment, for the doors opened behind him and she was there.

Acknowledgments

I'd like to thank those in on this journey from the beginning. My daughter, Sarah Towne, who is always good for inspirational mantras: "You can do it, and I believe in you." People who read the first paragraphs or excerpts and said, hey you might have something here. My writers group whose insight and comments were so valuable in the formative stages, Jack Lloyd, Jan B. Parker and especially, Nancy Young, whose inspired couplet graces this work. My beta readers, open mic listeners, and those who simply gave me encouragement along the way. My publisher, Literary Wanderlust, for taking a chance on this book, and my editor, Amanda Pecora, who was absolutely right about Ziggy.

Writing is hard. It's solitary confinement with a laptop and a brain. Occasionally we gaze out into the world of monsters and try not to feel so terribly alone. Hopefully, when we do put something down on the blank space before us, it is worth the read, and offers someone else that chance to connect.

Author's Notes

I've always been fascinated with the Tudor period of England and the tragically short but interesting life of Christopher Marlowe. In most time-travel stories, the protagonist goes back to the past. I wanted something different and, quite frankly, easier to write. Bringing Marlowe forward into the present seemed like a solution.

There's a lot of literary license in his creation, and if there are errors or discrepancies regarding Christopher Marlowe or any other famous figure in this story, the mistakes are my own.

Source materials I used were: a great biography by Park Honan titled *Christopher Marlowe: Poet & Spy*, *A Journey Through Tudor England* by Suzannah Lipscomb, and Russell Bintliff's Police Procedural: *A Writer's Guide to the Police and How They Work* (Howdunit). And last but not least, *The Works of Christopher Marlowe* by Christopher Marlowe." 4th para., explain what premise.

Ettore Majorana was a real theoretical physicist who disappeared in 1938 under mysterious circumstances and was perfect for my premise.

The musicians in the park are playing an instrument known as the Hang, or a variation of that instrument known as handpans.

Both Elliot and Mary Beard are fictional characters, but there was a hospital that treated soldiers after the battle of Gettysburg called Satterlee General Hospital in West Philadelphia. It was the largest Union Army hospital in the country.

Thomas Jefferson did travel from Dover to Calais on a packet during his tenure as American Minister to France and the court of Versailles.

Mrs. Mallowan, who visits Volpi in the London Book shop in the sixties, is the renowned mystery writer Agatha Christie. I took the liberty of using her second husband's name.

Tam is purely fictional, but she's a lot like me (the snarky parts) and my daughter Sarah (the brave parts). And she's someone I hope to be best friends with someday.

About the Author

L.E. Towne is a world-traveler and a continual student of the human condition known as real life. Her work has been published in Welter, Legendary, Zouch, and Main Street Rag. In between writing her urban fantasy series, she has written and produced several short plays. She currently resides in Raleigh, North Carolina, with her tuxedo cat, Kat Marlowe. Her aliases on social media are: @LauraEtowne on Twitter, le.townescribe on Instagram, @LETowne on Facebook, and www.letowne.com on the nets.